ONLY THE BRAVE

By Danielle Steel

Only the Brave • Never Too Late • Upside Down • The Ball at Versailles • Second Act
Happiness • Palazzo • The Wedding Planner • Worthy Opponents • Without a Trace
The Whittiers • The High Notes • The Challenge • Suspects • Beautiful • High Stakes
Invisible • Flying Angels • The Butler • Complications • Nine Lives • Finding Ashley
The Affair • Neighbours • All That Glitters • Royal • Daddy's Girls • The Wedding Dress
The Numbers Game • Moral Compass • Spy • Child's Play • The Dark Side • Lost and Found
Blessing in Disguise • Silent Night • Turning Point • Beauchamp Hall • In His Father's Footsteps
The Good Fight • The Cast • Accidental Heroes • Fall from Grace • Past Perfect • Fairytale
The Right Time • The Duchess • Against All Odds • Dangerous Games • The Mistress
The Award • Rushing Waters • Magic • The Apartment • Property of a Noblewoman • Blue
Precious Gifts • Undercover • Country • Prodigal Son • Pegasus • A Perfect Life • Power Play
Winners • First Sight • Until the End of Time • The Sins of the Mother • Friends Forever
Betrayal • Hotel Vendôme • Happy Birthday • 44 Charles Street • Legacy • Family Ties
Big Girl • Southern Lights • Matters of the Heart • One Day at a Time
A Good Woman • Rogue • Honor Thyself • Amazing Grace • Bungalow 2
Sisters • H.R.H. • Coming Out • The House • Toxic Bachelors • Miracle
Impossible • Echoes • Second Chance • Ransom • Safe Harbour • Johnny Angel
Dating Game • Answered Prayers • Sunset in St. Tropez • The Cottage • The Kiss
Leap of Faith • Lone Eagle • Journey • The House on Hope Street
The Wedding • Irresistible Forces • Granny Dan • Bittersweet
Mirror Image • The Klone and I • The Long Road Home • The Ghost
Special Delivery • The Ranch • Silent Honor • Malice • Five Days in Paris
Lightning • Wings • The Gift • Accident • Vanished • Mixed Blessings
Jewels • No Greater Love • Heartbeat • Message from Nam • Daddy • Star
Zoya • Kaleidoscope • Fine Things • Wanderlust • Secrets • Family Album
Full Circle • Changes • Thurston House • Crossings • Once in a Lifetime
A Perfect Stranger • Remembrance • Palomino • Love: *Poems* • The Ring
Loving • To Love Again • Summer's End • Season of Passion • The Promise
Now and Forever • Passion's Promise • Going Home

Nonfiction
Expect a Miracle
Pure Joy: *The Dogs We Love*
A Gift Of Hope: *Helping the Homeless*
His Bright Light: *The Story of Nick Traina*

For Children
Pretty Minnie In Hollywood
Pretty Minnie In Paris

Danielle Steel

ONLY THE BRAVE

MACMILLAN

First published 2024 by Delacorte Press
an imprint of Random House
a division of Penguin Random House LLC, New York

First published in the UK 2024 by Macmillan
an imprint of Pan Macmillan
The Smithson, 6 Briset Street, London EC1M 5NR
EU representative: Macmillan Publishers Ireland Limited, 1st Floor,
The Liffey Trust Centre, 117–126 Sheriff Street Upper,
Dublin 1, D01 YC43
Associated companies throughout the world
www.panmacmillan.com

ISBN 978-1-5290-8578-5 HB
ISBN 978-1-5290-8579-2 TPB

Pan Macmillan does not have any control over, or any responsibility for,
any author or third-party websites referred to in or on this book.

1 3 5 7 9 8 6 4 2

A CIP catalogue record for this book is available from the British Library.

Typeset in Charter ITC by Palimpsest Book Production Ltd, Falkirk, Stirlingshire
Printed and bound by CPI Group (UK) Ltd, Croydon, CR0 4YY

Visit **www.panmacmillan.com** to read more about all our books
and to buy them. You will also find features, author interviews and
news of any author events, and you can sign up for e-newsletters
so that you're always first to hear about our new releases.

To my beloved children,
Beatrix, Trevor, Todd, Nick,
Samantha, Victoria, Vanessa,
Max, and Zara,

May you be as brave as you can be,
May life be good and gentle with you,
May you be safe and loved,
May you be kind to one another, and
May you be compassionate and merciful
to others.

With all my heart and love,

Mom / D.S.

ONLY THE BRAVE

"The only life worth living is a life lived in service to others."

—attributed to ALBERT EINSTEIN

Chapter 1

Even at eighteen, in 1937, Sophia Alexander knew that things in Germany had changed in the past four years since the Nazis had come to power. There had been many changes in her life too, although her family was not Jewish. They were defined now as "Aryan." These days, with even one Jewish grandparent, whether by faith or origin, a person was considered non-Aryan.

Sophia's life in Berlin had altered dramatically ever since her mother fell ill with tuberculosis when she was sixteen, two years earlier. She had been cared for at home for the first year of her illness and was now in a sanatorium for people with tuberculosis. Sophia visited her several times a week. Her younger sister Theresa, sixteen now, went to see her less often, and her father was so busy he hardly had time to visit. Sophia was the family member who went the most frequently. She was a serious student, but always made time to see her mother, as often as she could. Sophia and Theresa went to the same school. Sophia was in the final months of high school, and Theresa had two more years after this one and hated every moment she spent in class. Sophia was a star student.

Their mother, Monika Alexander, was a gentle person, and had always had fragile health. She was a delicate beauty, and adored her daughters. Sophia had long, serious talks with her, and often read to her, as her mother lay in her bed with her eyes closed until she fell asleep, and then Sophia would leave. As soon as her mother was taken to the sanatorium, Sophia had promised her that she would take care of her sister and father, and she had kept her promise and grown up quickly. When she turned eighteen, she had learned to drive. Her father let her use the car, which made Sophia's visits easier, since the sanatorium was outside the city.

Sophia's father, Thomas Alexander, was a famous surgeon, and had his own private hospital. People came to see him for complicated procedures from all over Europe. He practiced general surgery and was highly skilled. It frustrated him that he couldn't cure his wife, but with rest and the medicines available to them, he was hoping she would have a full recovery. Sophia was worried about her. Her mother seemed so frail. She slept a great deal but awoke with delight when her oldest daughter was visiting her, which she did faithfully.

At home, Sophia had taken full charge of her sister, who needed a strong hand to manage her. Theresa took full advantage of how busy their father was and her mother's absence to flirt with every man who crossed her path. Men seemed to fall at her feet like ripe apples, much to her older sister's amazement. Sophia had always been shy, like her mother. She was a dark-haired beauty with huge green eyes, and always looked serious. The men who pursued Theresa didn't notice Sophia, and she wasn't a flirt. If one looked closely, Sophia was in fact more beautiful. She had perfect aristocratic features, a long, graceful neck, and elegant posture. Theresa's looks were showier and caught one's attention faster. She had almost white blonde hair like their mother, translucent porcelain-white skin, which she dusted with powder, full red lips, and brilliant blue eyes the color of a summer sky. She had a wide, instant smile, perfect teeth, and a sensuous figure. She always looked like she was about to laugh. She teased the boys she knew relentlessly. Her long blonde hair fell in thick waves. Sophia's shining dark hair fell straight past her shoulders. She had a slim build like her father, and she kept a stern eye on her sister, as she had promised their mother. She kept her on a short leash and Theresa complained about it constantly.

Theresa meant no harm with her flirting and enticing laughter, and she had little awareness that her natural sexiness was an aphrodisiac to the men who wanted her. Her father assumed it was all harmless and would come to nothing. Sophia wasn't as sure. Their mother thought that Theresa should marry early before she got into more mischief than she could handle. She would need a strong husband to control her. But at sixteen she was still too young to be considered marriage material, and had to finish school. So Sophia played watchdog at the palace gates, waiting for their mother's return, and she hoped it would be soon.

It had been a long year for all of them without Monika, particularly for Sophia. Theresa was enjoying it, although she missed her mother too. She loved to go dancing, and to parties, but her opportunities were limited due to her age. Their parents had stopped entertaining when Monika got sick. Before that, there had been many elegant dinner parties at their home, filled with women in beautiful evening gowns. Theresa crept into her mother's dressing room sometimes and tried on her mother's gowns. When Sophia found her doing it, she scolded her soundly.

"That's Mama's! Take it off immediately! You'll tear it." Several of their mother's most beautiful dresses had been made for her in Paris, others by dressmakers in Berlin. As the wife of the most important surgeon in Berlin, they were invited everywhere, to the most dazzling events. Thomas Alexander was greatly respected. Sophia had loved watching her parents dance with each other, when they gave formal dinner parties at home for important guests.

She knew her father loved his wife very much, but his work kept him from visiting her as often as he wished. Sophia wanted to help him too, and aside from running the house for him now, she worked as a volunteer in his hospital after school and on weekends, after she finished her studies. Her father marveled at how efficient she was, how bright and how dedicated. She had a talent for nursing. Sophia said she would become a nurse one day and work for him in the operating theater. Theresa just wanted to get married and have babies. She hadn't met her future husband yet, but she enjoyed all the attention men lavished on her, as they flew around her like bees approaching a beautiful flower. No one could resist her, and she loved it.

Theresa had no real interest in the boys in school, but flirted with them too. She had an easy way with men, which they found enchanting. Sophia was harder to talk to. She was serious, and spoke to them of important subjects which required them to think rather than just admire her. She spoke of recent medical discoveries, her father's flawless surgical techniques, books she had read on many topics, which usually didn't interest most men, or she spoke of the political unrest in Germany for the past few years. Her father had cautioned her several times not to engage in discussions about politics. It was a sensitive subject in Germany now, with the strengthening of the Nazi party in the last four years. Adolf Hitler had become Führer three years before, in 1934. Privately, Thomas didn't admire his zeal, but he kept his opinions to himself, and was busy with his private clinic. He had operated on several members of the Nazi High Command and had met the Führer himself, but what interested Thomas Alexander was medicine, not politics.

The changes in Germany had troubled Sophia for several years, even before her mother got sick. People with even partial Jewish origins had been singled out and discriminated against. In the beginning, in 1933, when Sophia was fourteen, Jews were suddenly barred from being teachers, professors, judges, or civil servants, and many had lost their jobs. Several of the teachers at her school had quietly disappeared without saying goodbye, which made her suddenly aware of what was going on. Months later, people of Jewish faith or origin were excluded from the arts, then from owning land, and were forbidden from being journalists or newspaper editors. All within a year. And by the end of 1933, homeless and unemployed people were sent to concentration camps that were being opened near Munich. Dachau had opened in 1933, Sachsenhausen, close to Berlin in 1936, and Buchenwald a year later in 1937. No one spoke of it openly, but one heard about it in whispers. A girl in her class had told her. She had heard her journalist uncle talking about it with her father, and they thought the camps were a good idea to get undesirable elements of the population off the streets, which was the Nazis' intention.

By the following year, in 1934, when Sophia was fifteen, she learned that Jews were denied health insurance, and prohibited from becoming lawyers. And the year after Hitler became Führer in 1934, when Sophia was sixteen, Jews were banned from the military. They lost their citizenship and could no longer marry Aryans. A few months before, they had been forbidden to work as accountants or dentists. The list of professions they were not allowed to engage in grew longer every day. Sophia's father had to find the family a new dentist when theirs left Germany, saying that this was only the beginning of worse things to come, which her father thought was an extreme point of view.

Sophia talked to her mother about it at times, and removed from the world, Monika found it shocking. Some of the physicians they knew were Jewish, but Sophia's father said nothing would happen to them, they were respected important men, as he was. In his opinion, doctors would always be exempt from political actions because they were so highly educated, honored, and desperately needed for their skills. Thomas had warned Sophia repeatedly not to talk about such things outside the family, and he scolded her for thinking about it at all. Her mother never scolded her. She shared Sophia's concerns about the ruling party taking such harsh positions.

"How far do you think it will go?" Sophia asked her one day, since they were alone and could talk freely.

"I suppose it's gone as far as it can by now, but I do feel sorry for those people who have lost their jobs and their livelihoods and have families to take care of. The Nazis just want to show people how powerful they are. I'm sure they'll relax the rules in time." Sophia was never as sure, but she didn't want to frighten her mother. She had seen people rounded up in Berlin, and dragged away for deportation, with their children crying and police beating them.

Every year, more people Sophia knew had disappeared, all Jews, and some of her friends' fathers had lost jobs. A dentist, an accountant, a well-known journalist—none of them were dangerous, but all were Jewish. Even some of her classmates said nasty things about the Jews now, when they had been friends before. It seemed so wrong to her, and so hypocritical. How could their friends become their enemies overnight?

"Don't talk to Papa about it," Monika warned Sophia again,

and she promised not to. Her father didn't care about anything but his hospital anyway. Medicine was all that interested him. He lived in a rarefied, isolated world, in his operating theater, saving people's lives with surgery. He didn't care what religion they were. If they were sick, he helped them heal. If they needed surgery, he operated on them. Illness was the great equalizer, just as it was for her mother with TB. Sophia's father was a scientist above all, and cared deeply about his patients. Government policies were of no interest to him.

Sophia had always been profoundly disturbed by all forms of injustice, and had compassion for those less fortunate, almost as though she felt guilty for how well she and her family lived and what they had. Theresa thought it was ridiculous and made fun of her for it. "Why don't you give them your clothes then?" she teased her. "They probably wouldn't want them anyway." Sophia dressed in somber colors and simple clothes not to show off. Theresa longed for her mother's Paris gowns and snuck them into her own closets whenever she could, now that her mother was gone. She planned to put them back when her mother returned. Sophia got angry at her sister whenever she caught her wearing something of their mother's. She recognized the items immediately, beautiful alligator handbags, or exquisite French kid gloves, delicately beaded sweaters, or a well-cut coat, which

Theresa was too young to wear. But she was dying to be fashionable and grown-up. Their father paid no attention to things like that, and often Theresa got away with it, if Sophia was working at the hospital, visiting their mother, or out, when Theresa raided her mother's closets.

They lived in an extremely comfortable, luxurious home, which Monika had decorated beautifully, with art that she and Thomas had inherited from their families, and things they bought. They had built the house when he had built his hospital many years before. It was large and handsome, and suited his respected position in the community. Sophia was embarrassed by how well they lived, which Theresa thought was ridiculous. Sophia thought the trappings of wealth, which were second nature to them, set them apart from others in a negative way. She had always been drawn to religion even as a child, and this too made her different from her family. Her father openly admitted that he did not believe in God. He believed in science and medicine, and a surgeon's skill, not a higher power. Theresa said that church bored her, and avoided it whenever possible, and only since she had been ill had Monika's beliefs grown stronger. She and Sophia talked about it at times. Sophia had a faith which nothing could shake. Her father blamed it on a nanny they had had when Sophia was very young. He had eventually fired her for filling Sophia's head with ideas that he considered nonsense and beliefs he didn't share and thought were dangerous. Sophia had been sad when she left, but her beliefs remained the same. If anything, they grew stronger. She never spoke of them in the presence of her father and kept them to herself, but they were there, a powerful, comforting force in her life. Sometimes she went to church on her own and prayed for her mother. Monika always seemed better to her after she did. But in spite of occasional brief respites, Monika's health had deteriorated in the last year. Sophia was terrified that she would die. Monika was peaceful and philosophical about it, and always reassured her. Sophia wanted to believe that she would come home soon. Her father said so too, and he never lied. He was an honest man, even if he didn't believe in God.

Sometimes when Sophia finished helping at her father's hospital, doing small tasks to help the nurses, or if her mother had seemed weaker that day, she stopped in at a church not far from their home. It was a short walk which always helped her clear her mind of the pain she'd seen. The church was small and peaceful, and she always found solace there. She told no one that she went. There was a convent attached to it, and the nuns who lived there were always warm and welcoming. She was a familiar figure and they would greet her or nod and smile if they were on their way to vespers, their evening prayers, or walking back to the convent after church. She had told a few of them that her mother was ill, and they had promised to pray for her. The convent belonged to the Sisters of Mercy, and Sophia had always been struck by how peaceful the nuns looked and how kind they were. She had lit candles in the church many times. She was well aware that her father would have been horrified if he knew. He insisted that religion was for fools. It was an argument she never embarked on with her father, nor mentioned to her sister. Once in a while, she told her mother about her visits there, but not often. It was her secret place and a source of strength for her.

Some of the nuns had worked in missions in Africa, which Sophia found fascinating, and she knew that they were nurses and teachers, and were devoted to the poor. Sometimes she felt as though she had more in common with them than with her own family, although she couldn't say that to anyone. She had told one or two of them that her father had a hospital, and that she did menial tasks there. More and more, she was thinking about going to nursing school, so she could work in her father's hospital and be more useful to her mother. It felt like her destiny, and her father liked the idea of her working at his hospital.

She hadn't fully made the decision yet, when her mother's condition worsened and she began a steady decline, which came to a tragic conclusion at the end of the summer.

Monika died as Sophia sat next to her and held her hand. Sophia had slept in her mother's room in her final weeks, and Theresa and Thomas were there too when she died. Monika had her loved ones around her. It was as though the bottom had fallen out of their world when she was gone. Theresa had never believed that her mother would die, and Thomas had been so insistent that she would come home again, and had refused to think that she would die. He took it as a personal blow that he couldn't save her. Only Sophia had begun to see it looming, and had prayed for her constantly at the end. But this time her prayers hadn't been answered. After her mother was gone, Sophia had sought out her friends at the convent, and they had comforted her, and assured her that her mother was now at peace, and her spirit would always be with her, which was a very small consolation for having lost the mother she loved so much. She had done everything she could to make Monika comfortable at the end.

Sophia was so young to lose her mother at eighteen. What she had seen and learned made her decision to go to nursing school easier, and her father was pleased when she enrolled. Theresa was still in high school, and Thomas had gone back to his own work as soon as possible, and found comfort there. He worked endless hours and his daughters hardly saw him. In September, Sophia began nursing school, and it provided the distraction and purpose she needed, and seemed to be the right direction. The nuns were pleased when she told them. It was a full life for her.

Theresa was pleased that her ever-vigilant sister was busy. It gave her enough time and leeway to engage in her favorite pastimes and usual flirtations. She never did anything too daring, but by the time Theresa turned seventeen, she had several serious suitors, and Sophia guessed that her sister would be married by the time she turned eighteen. The front-runner was a very respectable young man, Baron Heinrich von Ernst. He was madly in love with Theresa, ten years older than she was, and his family owned an important bank in Berlin. Even their father approved of the match, as he told Sophia repeatedly. She knew she couldn't stop it and didn't try. She was deeply engaged in her nursing studies and doing well at them. She did extra work at her father's hospital, and watched many surgeries, as an addendum to her studies, since she wanted to be a surgical nurse and assist her father.

Heinrich and Theresa got engaged a few days after the first anniversary of her mother's death. She was only seventeen. It softened the blow for Thomas and Sophia too, to have something to celebrate only a few days after the painful anniversary. Sophia was nineteen and had completed a year of nursing school by then, and Heinrich told his future father-in-law that he would wait to marry until Theresa turned eighteen. She was still too young, but already seemed more womanly, as she thought about the house they would live in and she would run. She stopped flirting with other men and acted more grown-up, and Sophia was happy for her. It didn't bother her that her sister was engaged and she wasn't, or that she had no romantic prospects or suitors herself. All she wanted was to become a surgical nurse. It filled her days and her thoughts, and she studied hard for her exams.

Heinrich married Theresa on her eighteenth birthday, in the garden of the Alexander home, since neither Theresa nor her father felt a need for a religious ceremony and didn't want one. Heinrich agreed to being married by a famous judge Thomas had operated on and knew well. The judge credited Thomas with saving his life, and was happy to perform the marriage for them. Heinrich was a very amenable and responsible young man, and was clearly besotted with his beautiful bride. It was a very touching ceremony, and Sophia cried when they exchanged their vows, missing their mother. It was a small wedding with only a hundred guests, mostly Thomas and Monika's friends. Sophia had arranged the whole wedding, with white lilies and lily of the valley everywhere. Only two years after their mother's death, they didn't want a big splashy wedding. Her loss was still sorely felt.

"She would be happy for you," Sophia said to Theresa with tears in her eyes right before the wedding ceremony.

"Do you think so?" Theresa said, equally moved as she dabbed at her eyes. "She wouldn't think I'm too young?"

"You've grown up a lot in the past two years," Sophia said.

"We want to have a baby soon," Theresa whispered, and Sophia wasn't surprised. It had always been Theresa's life plan, to marry as soon as possible and have babies. Sophia was sure she would be pregnant soon, and said a silent prayer for her as Thomas walked her down the aisle. Theresa would be a baroness now, which suited her too. Sophia was her only attendant, wearing a simple pale blue satin dress that she had borrowed from her mother's closet. It was one of the gowns from Paris, by Madame Grès. The wedding breakfast was lavish, and it was an elegant wedding. Several of the Nazi High Command were there. They were friends of Heinrich's or patients of her father's. It made Sophia uncomfortable to have them there, but Thomas had invited them, and had operated on a number of them. They spoke of him with glowing praise.

When Heinrich and Theresa married in the spring of 1939, the news in Germany had not improved in the past two years. Austria had been annexed a year before and was part of Germany now. Jews could no longer own businesses,

Jewish assets had been seized, and all property and real estate owned by Jews had to be registered. Synagogues had been destroyed and burned to the ground. Jews were arrested and sent to concentration camps. Jewish doctors had been forbidden to treat non-Jewish patients, and a month later were forbidden from practicing at all. Jewish doctors could only act as nurses now. Jews were forbidden to attend cultural events. By the end of 1938, six months before Theresa and Heinrich's wedding, all Jewish lawyers were forbidden to practice. They could only "consult" for fellow Jews.

The most shocking event of the previous year had been Kristallnacht in November of 1938. Sophia was profoundly distressed by it, as was most of the civilized world. Hundreds of synagogues were burned, Jewish homes and businesses were vandalized and looted, Jews were singled out for savage attacks, and many were killed. Twenty-five thousand Jewish men were arrested and sent to concentration camps after Kristallnacht. Jewish businesses were destroyed. Afterward, Jews were barred from public transportation, schools, and hospitals, and forced into ghettos or out of Germany and Austria. Jewish students were expelled from non-Jewish schools. And all gold and silver items owned by Jews had to be turned over. There was savagery and mass destruction without remorse. And two months before Theresa's wedding in 1939, the Nazis took over Czechoslovakia, while in Germany Jews could no longer be tenants and had to move into Jewish-owned houses. Some brave, compassionate neighbors and citizens began hiding Jewish friends, at great danger to themselves if they were caught.

Sophia's heart ached with everything she heard and read about it, while Theresa, her new husband, and even her father seemed oblivious to what was going on, as officers of the Nazi High Command danced at their wedding. Sophia couldn't get out of her mind what she knew now, and could barely bring herself to be civil to the officers she met at the wedding. She refused to dance with any of them. She just couldn't, knowing what their policies were, and how many people had suffered at their hands.

Heinrich and Theresa, the Baron and Baroness von Ernst, went to the south of France for their honeymoon, and returned a month later in June. Sophia had finished two years of her nurse's training by then. She had accelerated her studies, gotten credit for her work at her father's hospital, and only had a few months of classes left before she became a nurse.

The house was painfully empty once Theresa was gone. Their father was always working. Sophia started visiting the Sisters of Mercy more frequently, and even had dinner with them sometimes, at their long refectory tables, so she didn't have to eat alone at home. One of the kitchen help at the hospital made dinner for her father now, because he didn't want to go home to the silent house either. Theresa with her exuberance and big personality had left a major void in their lives when she married. Sophia noticed that her father spent longer and longer days and nights at his clinic, and sometimes slept there if he was concerned about a patient post-surgery. She had seen charts, when she worked there occasionally, that led her to believe her father was still treating Jewish patients from time to time and performing surgeries on them. But she didn't dare to ask him. If so, he was violating all the most stringent laws in Germany, and the most dangerous to break. She even recognized one of the patients, an older man she knew her father had operated on previously, who was Jewish. He had been an important art dealer, and he was sent home almost immediately after surgery. His chart was under another name, and it vanished entirely after he left. It gave her new respect for her father when she realized what he'd done. His dedication to his patients was impartial, regardless of race or religion or political convictions.

She went back to finish the last few remaining months of her nurse's training, wondering just how far the Nazis would go to rid the country of all Jews, even though they were German citizens like everyone else—but not anymore.

She never told anyone her suspicions about her father, but she had come to realize he was helping those he could, in the only way he knew how. And he was treating the German High Command and its officers as well. To him, science and the treatments it offered should be available to all, regardless of race or religion, and he practiced accordingly. She only mentioned it to him once.

"It's dangerous for you, Papa," she whispered to him as they left the operating room together. The patient he had just operated on was removed from the surgical theater rapidly, and taken downstairs somewhere in the hospital by two orderlies, moving quickly. She guessed later that he was taken to an unmarked supply room until he left the hospital.

"I don't believe in God, Sophia, and even less so now. But I believe in my fellow man and the oath I swore to care for all those who need my help and to do them no harm." He looked at her intensely and then walked away and disappeared for the rest of the night. She could guess that he was with his patient, hidden somewhere, until he could be transferred to a safe place, as soon as they could move him. She saw her father the next day, and he looked tired. They didn't speak of the incident again, and nothing ever came of it. She assumed the patient had survived and was in hiding somewhere.

It was a frightening time, and on September 3, 1939, Britain, France, Australia, and New Zealand declared war on

Germany, for invading Poland. No one knew what that meant yet, or how their lives would be affected. The Jews had already been fighting a desperate battle for their survival for more than six years by then. Even their food had been restricted, a week before war was declared. They had to survive on two to three hundred calories a day, regulated by ration cards. Many who could had fled the country, others thought things would calm down again. Close to four hundred thousand Jews had left Germany by then in response to the violence and fear of the future.

The night war was declared, Thomas Alexander operated on his emergency patients as usual. Heinrich and Theresa were in the very luxurious Berlin home his parents had provided for them. Sophia went to the convent of the Sisters of Mercy, to attend mass with them and pray for peace in a very cruel, already shattered world. They all knew that nothing would ever be the same again.

Chapter 2

Despite her concerns about the war, Sophia managed to finish her nursing studies by Christmas. With extra classes, and credit for work at her father's hospital, she managed to finish early, with high marks. She was officially hired as a surgical nurse in her father's hospital on a day shift, and worked two or three nights a week with the nuns, visiting poor neighborhoods and tending to the sick and indigent, doing whatever was needed. Her father had no idea that she did that, and never inquired about how she spent her evenings. She had always been studious and retiring, and she was almost twenty-one years old. Her father had no concerns about her, and there were no men in her life. She wasn't Theresa, who would have worried him if she weren't married. Sophia being an adult now, with a respectable job,

23

allowed him to work night and day himself. He had no interest in a home life, once his wife died. Sophia thought he looked tired and worn, and ever since her mother's death there was an intensity about him that worried her. He was only fifty-six years old, but he looked considerably older. Widowhood and hard work had aged him.

Theresa had invited her father and sister to spend Christmas Eve with them, but Thomas was quick to say that he would be working through the holidays. He had nothing to celebrate since Monika's death, and he encouraged Sophia to accept her sister's invitation and spend the holiday with her. Sophia had lunch with Theresa and told her their father was declining her invitation, and Sophia was startled by Theresa's good spirits despite the fact that the country was at war. Theresa was going to parties every night with Heinrich. They had friends among the Nazi High Command and a flood of invitations from old friends and new ones.

"How can you bear to be with them?" Sophia said somberly. Theresa was wearing a striking red dress and a large pair of ruby earrings her parents-in-law had given her early for Christmas, and she had a beautiful fur coat over her shoulders when she walked into the fashionable restaurant. Sophia was wearing an old black dress of her mother's and looked like a schoolteacher going to a funeral. Theresa looked at her with disapproval.

"Can't you find something happier to wear in Mama's closets?" Theresa said, as they sat down.

"I think you took them all," Sophia dished back to her. "Besides, how can you be happy and going to parties, with everything that's happening?"

"Nothing is happening," Theresa said blithely.

"Are you serious?" Sophia was shocked. "They're sending Jews away to labor camps, taking away their property, stealing everything they have, their homes, their jobs, their money. They're *killing* people."

"They're trying to get the undesirables off the streets, to keep us safe," Theresa said firmly.

"Doctors and lawyers and dentists? They're doing it to people we went to school with. *Real* people, Theresa, not just 'criminals and gypsies,' as they claim. And you're dancing with the people who give the orders to kill them."

"That's all propaganda circulated by the Jews to make us feel sorry for them." Sophia couldn't tell her that she had seen many of them on her rounds with the Sisters of Mercy at night. She didn't want Theresa or her father to know she did that. It wasn't dangerous so far, but it was heartbreaking. "You need to meet a man, Sophia, before you turn into a sour old woman. Heinrich has lots of friends we can introduce you to," Theresa said with a bright smile. Her lipstick was the same color as her new earrings.

"And they're all in uniform?" Sophia said with a chilly tone.

"Yes, most of them. It makes them look more handsome. Heinrich isn't in uniform." He had been given a deferral for his "important work" at the bank, according to Theresa, and the fact that his family made substantial monetary contributions to the Reich and the war effort. So, for now, he was remaining a civilian. His father had orchestrated it for him. He didn't want his son being sent to the front or cleaning out the Warsaw ghetto of the rabble that lived there. The city of Warsaw had surrendered to the Germans in September, three weeks after war was declared. "You have to stop listening to all that gossip about the Jews," Theresa said after they ordered lunch. "None of it is true."

"It's *all* true," Sophia insisted. "I've seen it. And so would you, if you weren't at parties or the hairdresser or shopping all the time. I've seen people dragged from their homes with their children screaming in terror." Heinrich had given Theresa a car and driver, and she led a thoroughly protected life, far from the realities that Sophia was more familiar with.

"They were probably criminals who had stolen something or killed someone." There was no getting through to Theresa, and no way to convince her that the Reich was committing atrocities. Sophia had seen evidence of it in the homes she visited with the Sisters of Mercy. In a few instances, they had been called on to help tend to someone that the people who had called them were hiding. In two recent incidents, a neighbor had pressed a child, and once a baby, on them just before the police came and took the parents away. The infant was only two months old, clean and swaddled and wrapped in an expensive blanket, and might be an orphan by now. The nuns had taken them to an orphanage, where they were picked up by "relatives" hours later.

Sophia found lunch with her sister awkward. Theresa greeted countless women who came past them in the restaurant, all expensively dressed and wearing fur coats. She was part of the cream of Berlin society now. The Alexanders were a respected family, and most of Thomas's patients were wealthy and important, but even though the Alexanders had entertained elegantly before Monika fell ill, they had never been part of the really showy, snobbish group that Theresa was part of now and thoroughly enjoying. She was rapidly becoming someone Sophia hardly recognized and didn't want to, though she loved her. All her friends were rabid supporters of the Nazi party and their leader. Theresa spoke of him like their savior who was going to correct all the ills in Germany. Sophia already knew better, and that they were trying to eradicate an entire race of people they treated like animals. Her love for her sister surpassed politics but it upset Sophia to see how blind and superficial Theresa was. She refused to hear the truth.

Right before she graduated from nursing school, Sophia had met several student nurses, and a young medical student who had invited her to a friendly gathering at a bar in a student neighborhood. After they each drank a beer, the medical student led them down a dark staircase to the basement, where Sophia saw a large group of young people milling around in a candlelit subcellar with no windows. The crowd was large and noisy, and some of them were quite rough-looking. A young woman called them to order, and a number of people spoke—mostly men, but not all—and talked of the horrors they had seen in their ordinary lives, and took a strong stand against the Nazis, the police, the SS, and even Hitler, warning the listeners that there was worse to come, and that Germany was rapidly becoming a police state, led by fanatics. The theme of the evening was to not follow along like sheep and to stand up for decency and humanity and the principles the country once stood for in better times.

"It's up to us to defend the honor of Germany," one of them said fervently, "with courage, no matter what it costs us. The country has been taken over by wolves, and no one will defend her but people like us." They were encouraged to start small groups like this one, to form a strong dissident population that would rise and take over one day and restore Germany to sanity. "The country is insane now. We have to stop the madness. If we and people like us don't, no one will." Sophia wasn't clear on how they intended to do it, but they encouraged each other to seize every opportunity for opposition, even if you had to kill someone to do it. When she left the meeting that night with the other student nurses, she had the feeling that she had done something very dangerous. What if someone reported them to the police? Sophia agreed with everything they said, but she had no idea how to put it into action efficiently. And she wasn't prepared to kill someone. What they were suggesting was anarchy. She didn't want to become a murderer or a revolutionary, she just wanted to heal people and live in a country where people were treated fairly and equally and could live safely.

Sophia could only imagine what Theresa would say if she knew about the meeting she'd gone to, or their father, who was a law-abiding man who didn't like Hitler's policies, but whose mission was to save people, not kill them.

Sophia had attended half a dozen of those meetings, and met people there she liked, but she could never figure out how she could be useful to them without getting into serious trouble.

When she and Theresa left the restaurant after lunch, Sophia felt as though she was the little sister and Theresa was the sophisticated older one. She was so sure of herself now, so proud of who she was married to. She loved showing off their house and her elegant clothes and jewelry, and she fully believed that the Nazis were the master race, the messengers from the gods. The sisters kissed on the sidewalk, Theresa got back into her chauffeured car, and Sophia took the bus back to the hospital. Theresa had offered to drop her off, but Sophia was embarrassed to be seen in a fancy car driven by a chauffeur and preferred the bus. She had a lot to think about after she saw her sister, and her mind kept going back to the most recent dissidents' meetings she'd been to.

The population of Berlin was following the rules the Reich had set down for them. Most citizens were too afraid to intervene on behalf of the Jews, no matter how unfair they thought their treatment was. But people had families to protect, jobs they needed to pay the rent and buy food for themselves and their children. They weren't willing to risk everything they had built and were clinging to, in order to save or shelter an entire race of people who had been designated as scapegoats and victims. Sophia felt increasingly helpless the more she thought about the situation. The nuns were sympathetic to the plight of the Jews too, but the Mother Superior had warned them all not to get involved, that it was not their place to take a position against the government. But at times, Sophia found it very tempting to do so.

She said nothing to the nuns or anyone else about it and continued to attend meetings. At least she could listen, which she did, avidly, learning more and more about the shocking treatment of the Jews in a country she had once been proud of and no longer could be. She relayed some of it to the younger nuns when they went out into the neighborhoods together, and they were as upset as she was. But none of them saw a way that they could make a difference. Sophia would have liked to discuss it with her father, but she couldn't. He didn't want to hear about it and didn't want to get involved, and suggested she do the same.

In contrast, Sophia saw high-ranking officers of the SS come to see her father as patients every day and had to maintain a neutral demeanor when he introduced her to them. All Thomas allowed himself to see were the parts of their body which needed surgical attention. He didn't see their heart or their soul or their conscience. He didn't know which of them had committed some unthinkable crime in the name of the Reich. They were just bodies he was going to work on, and he explained their surgeries to them as he would have to anyone else, and operated on them as carefully as he did all his other patients. Sophia was always fascinated by how he managed to cut himself off emotionally from them. And after war was declared, the attacks on the Jews seemed to be even more frequent and more vicious. The Nazis had a free hand now, and too much of public opinion was with them, in a frenzy like no other, whipped up by the Führer and his generals. Some people actually believed that the Jews were a national danger that had to be eliminated. Sophia was astounded that they believed that.

As he had said he would, Thomas worked straight through the holidays, on an emergency appendectomy of the daughter of one of his patients, broken hips, and a delicate heart surgery. Sophia went to Theresa's home alone on Christmas Eve. Several of Heinrich's relatives were there, and Theresa whispered to her sister after dinner that she was pregnant and was elated. Heinrich looked at her as though she was a rare gem of some kind, or the first woman to be carrying a baby. The baby was due in July, two months after their first anniversary.

"Fast work," Sophia commented with a smile and hugged her.

"Heinrich says he wants five more." Theresa grinned shyly. "All boys. He wants to name this one after the Führer." Sophia's stomach turned over when she said it, and she frowned. "I want to name him after Papa."

"It might be a girl," Sophia reminded her. "You could name her after Mama," she said tenderly, and Theresa nodded.

She had thought of it too, and Heinrich had agreed, but he hoped it wouldn't be a girl. He wanted sons and was counting on Theresa to produce them.

The guests all talked after dinner, sitting around the enormous Christmas tree in the living room, with the candles lit, as was their tradition. Everyone kept an eye on the candles to make sure that none of the branches caught fire.

They played cards and games after dinner. The women were all in evening gowns and the men in black tie. It was an elegant evening with a warm cozy feeling to it. They put records on at the end of the evening, and Heinrich danced with his wife. Sophia was relieved that for once there were no uniforms present, no armbands with swastikas on them. One could almost close one's eyes and pretend that there wasn't a war on. It felt like old times except that Monika wasn't with them, nor their father.

Sophia drove herself home in her father's car when she left with the last of the guests. She drove past the convent, and noticed that the lights were on in the chapel. Through the open car window she could hear voices raised, singing Christmas carols. She parked in front of the church and went in. It was after midnight, and the church was full of nuns, and some of the neighbors, for a midnight mass. Sophia slipped into a pew toward the back, and after a few minutes joined in the familiar carols. It was a perfect end to the evening, and she went to wish a merry Christmas to the Mother Superior and some of the nuns before she left.

"You're alone tonight, Sophia?" Mother Regina asked her, and she nodded.

"My father's working and I just left my sister. She's expecting," she said in a whisper, and the Mother Superior smiled.

"That's happy news. We need it these days." They had made their rounds among the families they served earlier that night, and left them little baskets with fruit and nuts, and some sweets for the children. But Sophia had been at her sister's and couldn't join them when they had asked. She stayed for a few more minutes and went home to the empty house. The housekeeper and the young girl they employed as her helper had gone to bed hours before, and Sophia walked slowly up the stairs, and was surprised to see her father outside his bedroom, still fully dressed.

"I thought you'd sleep at the hospital tonight," she said. He had a small functional bedroom next to his office there, to use when he needed to stay close by to be available for a patient in distress.

"It's been quiet for the last two hours, so I thought I'd come home and sleep here." He smiled at his daughter and gave her a warm hug. "How was it? Was half the Reich there tonight?" he inquired, curious, and she shook her head.

"No, just Heinrich's family. Theresa is having a baby, in seven months." He looked surprised and pleased at the news.

"I'm not sure I'm ready to be a grandfather but I'm happy for them. Are they excited?" He couldn't imagine his youngest daughter as a mother at nineteen, but thought it would be good for her.

"Heinrich is over the moon. He's sure it's a boy and wants to name him Adolf." Her father winced.

"It had better be a girl," and the obvious choice of name to all of them would be that of his late wife. "Merry Christmas, Sophia," he said, looking at her proudly, and she hugged him again. She was looking forward to working with him in the operating theater and learning more from him. He was known to be an extraordinary, deft surgeon, with highly skilled, precise fingers, and incredible instincts, and she still had much to learn.

They both went to their rooms then, and she was just falling asleep an hour later, when she heard the phone ring, and five minutes later, heard her father's bedroom door open and close. She got up and hurried to stick her head out of her bedroom.

"Do you want help?" He hesitated for a fraction of a second.

"You don't need to come. Get some sleep. It's Christmas."

"I have nothing to do tomorrow." She knew the hospital was often short-staffed on holiday nights, so most of the medical staff could be with their families. But she was still wide awake.

"If you want," he said hesitantly. "It's not a surgical emergency, it's medical. A child," he said with an odd glance at her, and she didn't question him further.

"I'll dress and meet you there in five minutes," she said, and darted back to her room, as he rushed down the stairs and she heard the front door slam minutes later. She brushed her hair and wound it in a tight bun, washed her face and hands, brushed her teeth, and put on her uniform, not sure what to expect. She put her nurse's cape on after pinning her starched hat in place, her black nurse's shoes completing her uniform, which was the all-white dress of a surgical nurse with a white apron, which she was so proud of. The other nurses wore a blue dress with white collar, cap, and apron. She flew down the stairs and out the front door, closing it more quietly than her father had. She ran down the path that led from their home to the hospital and was there in the five minutes she had promised.

She found two young nurses in an exam room who were picking up an armload of wet towels, and one of them pointed upstairs to a floor of rooms where nonsurgical patients spent the night, sometimes with a bad stomachache, being monitored for appendicitis or some other medical condition. Sophia left her cape and hurried up the stairs, and heard voices coming from behind a closed door of one of the rooms. She knocked and opened it gently, and saw a small boy on the exam table, wrapped in blankets. She could barely see his face, but she could see that he was trembling violently and that his lips were a deep blue, his face so pale it was almost colorless. He was very thin, and he looked terrified, as Thomas spoke to a young woman who Sophia assumed was the boy's mother. She was saying something to Thomas about the house having been searched, and the child had been outside in a shallow pool for an hour. It was freezing outside, and he was suffering from hypothermia. The woman, who was well dressed, was rubbing the child's body and arms through the blanket and Thomas had placed a small heater next to him and turned it up high.

"Hot-water bottles," Thomas said to Sophia softly, and she came back with four of them minutes later and tucked them around the child under the blanket. She spoke soothingly to him and he smiled at her, as the woman explained that she was his aunt, and told a disjointed story about the boy falling into the pool. Thomas understood the situation immediately.

"My sister and her husband were . . . are away . . . and Bertie is staying with me until they get back." What Thomas had understood instantly was that his parents had probably been deported, or fled before they were, and couldn't take the child with them, and she was hiding him. The house had been searched that night. The boy, six years old, had hidden in a pond outside her home that wasn't deep and was partially frozen. He hadn't drowned, but he had nearly frozen to death. It took two hours to warm him, and he was still shaking slightly while they continued to wrap him in warm blankets and surround him with hot-water bottles, but his lips were no longer blue. He was very pale, probably because he hadn't seen daylight since his parents left. There were more and more children like him, and he wasn't the first one Thomas had seen. Eventually many of them got caught, often reported by zealous neighbors who discovered them, and then they were sent away to meet the same fate as their parents.

Thomas handed Bertie a lollipop once his teeth stopped chattering and he was starting to talk.

"You can't go swimming on Christmas, you know," Thomas said, and the boy smiled, enjoying the lollipop, as his aunt sat down on a chair, looking shaken and pale herself.

"I don't know why they came," she said, looking panicked. "He hasn't left the house in five months." She whispered that he was living in the attic and was a very good boy. Clearly one of his parents was non-Aryan, and if the authorities found him, he was doomed. He was out of physical danger now, but she'd have to keep him warm. Thomas could see from the address she'd given that she lived just down the street. And she had come to Thomas's hospital because it was private. No one knew anymore what secrets were hidden in their neighbors' homes, and it was best not to know.

"You should go home soon, before daylight," Thomas told Bertie's aunt, and she nodded.

"I'll take him away tomorrow, to be hidden somewhere else." Sophia wondered if she knew where to go for help or if she had some plan. She didn't look very old herself, in her mid- or late twenties, and she had explained that Bertie was her older sister's child.

Thomas nodded. "You should go. Keep him warm tonight, he'll be fine. And no more swimming," he said to Bertie with a smile. Sophia went to get warm pajamas for him and wrapped him up in another blanket, and Thomas carried him out to the car. The two young nurses on duty in the emergency room were having a tea break with an orderly from the surgical floor and paid no attention to them when they left.

Bertie's aunt had tried to pay Thomas and he refused. "Good luck," he said to her, and waved at Bertie. They didn't have far to go, and Thomas and Sophia walked back to the hospital, upstairs to his office, and closed the door. She sat on the other side of her father's desk. He looked tired and sad, but they had saved the boy. "I wonder how many children there are like him in Germany now, and Austria and Poland, and Czechoslovakia. I wonder how many of them will survive the war."

39

"His aunt seems like a sweet woman," Sophia added, as affected by it as he was.

"It's an enormous responsibility for her, and if they're found, they'll both be killed, she for hiding a non-Aryan child. These are the criminals the Reich wants to punish. A six-year-old child, and his aunt who's barely more than a child herself. She's not much older than you are."

"You were brave to do it, Papa," Sophia said softly. "If they found out, they would punish you too," and maybe kill him.

"We're here to save lives, Sophia. I should have sent you home, I put you at risk too. Thank you for helping me." He smiled at her, and her face broke into a slow smile, as the sun began to rise.

"Merry Christmas, Papa," she said, and they held hands across his desk. They had just had the best Christmas gift of all. They had saved a life, and they both silently wished Bertie well. Sophia had realized that night that there was more to her father than she had ever known. She was proud to be his daughter.

Chapter 3

Thomas kept Sophia busy working in the surgical theater, where he taught her something every day. She continued visiting her friends at the convent at night, which he was unaware of, since he always worked late, checking post-surgical patients himself before he went home, or spending the night if he wasn't satisfied with their condition.

On the nights Sophia wasn't working or visiting the Sisters of Mercy, she continued attending meetings of dissidents, which changed locations occasionally if they thought the police were beginning to suspect their meeting places. She learned at the meetings that some of the participants took more active roles, and they talked about safe houses for children in the countryside, and paths into Switzerland across the mountains, which were extremely dangerous.

There were trails into Alsace in France too, but France wasn't as safe as Switzerland. Getting into Switzerland safely was a Herculean task, which many didn't survive because of border patrols on the German side, and arduous conditions due to the difficult terrain, weather, and other unpredictable elements. Several of the "guides" had been killed escorting people through.

Sophia was fascinated by it the more she heard about it, and she wished she were brave enough to be a guide, but she wasn't sure she was, and she didn't know the mountains well.

One of the friends she made at the meetings had been a guide for nearly a year. He had been a ski instructor before the war, and a mountain climber as well. His name was Claus. None of them knew each other's last names. He was twenty-four years old, and Sophia saw him regularly at meetings. He was tall, blond, and handsome, a perfect Aryan specimen. He had been rejected by the army because he'd had severe asthma as a child, and had used it as a plausible excuse to avoid serving an army he detested and wanted nothing to do with.

He had successfully taken five groups across the mountains in the last six months. Sophia thought he was a hero and enjoyed talking to him at meetings. He was impressed that she showed up so faithfully. They had coffee together afterward a few times, but he never asked her out, and she didn't expect him to. They weren't there for romance. They were there because they believed in a cause.

She had also learned of another hero recently from the Sisters of Mercy, a woman named Edith Stein, a devoted intellectual, born Jewish, who had entered a Carmelite order of nuns in 1934 in Cologne, and was a strong opponent of the Nazis. Her sister had also joined a Carmelite order as an extern sister. Four years later, in 1938, feeling that the risk was too great for Edith Stein in Germany, the convent had transferred her and her sister to a Carmelite convent in the Netherlands, where Edith was writing and teaching as Sister Teresa Benedicta of the Cross. She was a brave woman and an outspoken critic of the Reich, which Sophia admired tremendously. There seemed to be so many heroes in the making, including her friend Claus.

And all the while, Sophia went on working as a nurse at her father's hospital, feeling she wasn't doing enough to counter the evils of the Reich.

Her father never told her but in October, a month after war was declared, one of his military patients, a general of the Reich, had made an appointment with him for a consultation. They chatted at some length about the direction the war was taking. It took the general nearly an hour to get to the point, after closely questioning Thomas's loyalty to the

Reich, and his feelings about the scourge of Jews the Führer wanted eradicated. The general then confided that they had begun a program to speed up the process and euthanize "undesirable German citizens," who were either physically or mentally disabled, or who simply did not belong in German society in the current climate, given the Führer's dedication to the purification of the German race.

At first, Thomas thought he had misheard him, or misunderstood.

"Euthanize them? Kill them?" Thomas asked, wide-eyed.

"Yes, painlessly of course, by injection. We have centers where we send them now. But you have an ideal setup here, to help us speed up the process, to dispose of more controversial cases where discretion is advised." Clearly someone who was well known and was not supportive of the Reich. A quick visit to Dr. Alexander's private hospital, a lethal injection, and problem solved. Thomas was stunned. They were even more evil than he thought, and more efficient.

"Who decides this?" Thomas asked, amazed. "Is there a legal process involved?"

"It's not necessary. We decide who are the enemies of the Reich. We are in the best position to judge. And in some cases, sending them to a euthanasia center would be unwise. You're here in Berlin, a loyal supporter of the Reich, and your center is perfect for us. In your case, only for special situations of course. It wouldn't affect your flow of patients, or the people you see normally. We all need you fully operative." The general smiled at him, and Thomas felt as though he was watching devil's horns grow from the general's head while he spoke. It was the most shocking abuse Thomas had ever heard of for the practice of an honorable physician, seeking to heal not harm. "My brother-in-law's knees have been fully operative since you operated on him, and my right elbow is fully mobile now. The military provides us with wonderful medical care, but there are some geniuses like you who stand out. This would only take minutes of your time occasionally and not impact the efficiency of the center at all."

Thomas was silent for what seemed like a long time as he sought the words to respond, without getting shot at close range across his desk and being accused of treason. But he could not be a traitor to his morals and his code of ethics, to satisfy the bloodlust of the Reich. He could only imagine the high-level people, dissidents, whom he would be told to kill.

"As you know, General," Thomas said cautiously, "I took an oath when I became a physician, the foundation of which is to heal and never to harm. 'Nil nocere.' I take it seriously, and even when faced with the most devastating agony in a patient, I am not able to relieve them from their suffering.

Even if I wanted to, I cannot euthanize a patient. I would be breaking the law and every code of ethics that applies to my profession. I simply cannot. I'm sure you understand," he said to enlist the general's alliance.

The general waved a hand as though he had a magic wand in it. "Oh of course, the Führer would absolve you from all that."

"But my conscience would not. How could I spend hours in surgery, saving someone's life, and then walk to the next room and end another's? What kind of doctor would I be then? You would not want me to operate on your elbow, or your brother-in-law on his knees. It would be a crime, morally and medically, contrary to the oath I have taken."

"I had no idea you were such a purist," the general said, with a look of annoyance. "These are details, you know. And no one would need to be aware of the process. We can provide you with military nurses to assist you, women who understand the importance of this project and would not interfere." The vision it conjured up of SS thugs holding someone down while Thomas administered a lethal injection was horrifying. He would be a simple murderer and no longer a physician.

"I hope the Führer will understand I must respect my oath in order to serve him well, and while I wish to be a good citizen, I must be a good doctor, without blemish on my character." It was a long way to say no, but Thomas would have died before he would have assisted them with their plan. Just knowing that they had set up killing centers to murder "undesirable citizens" was shocking beyond belief.

"He will be very disappointed," the general said, frowning. "We could have benefited from your advice about our centers as well, to speed up their efficiency. We haven't gotten the technique to be as effective as we want yet. You could have helped. I assume you don't want to do that either," he said, and Thomas shook his head, sickened by everything the general had said.

The general left a few minutes later, and for the next week, every day, Thomas expected a squad from the SS to come and remove him and put him in front of a firing squad for treason or shoot him on the spot. But nothing happened, and no one had mentioned it again. It had been several months, and he knew about the killing centers now, and that the Reich was euthanizing dissidents, but no one had renewed his invitation to participate. It had been a chilling conversation, which he knew he would never forget. He never told anyone about it and was amazed that there had been no fallout from it. It seemed like dangerous ground and a very close call to him.

In January of 1940, months after invading Poland, the Reich began building a new concentration camp in Poland, called Auschwitz. In February, the first major deportation of

German Jews to Poland began. And in April, the Nazis invaded Denmark and Norway, adding two more countries to their map. Thomas and Sophia were talking about it quietly over breakfast shortly after it happened when Theresa called them and sounded hysterical. She was six and a half months pregnant, due in July. Sophia wondered if something had happened to the baby, or maybe Heinrich was being inducted into the army, despite all of his father's generous "contributions" to keep him away from the front. Theresa had had an easy pregnancy so far, but it was obvious that something was terribly wrong.

"What happened?" Sophia asked, trying unsuccessfully to calm her.

"Can I come and see you and Papa?" Theresa asked. Sophia checked with her father about his surgical schedule, and he said he would be free until ten, and she told Theresa, who said she would meet them at the hospital in a few minutes.

Sophia and Thomas walked to the hospital quickly, and were in his office when she arrived, her belly enormous now, and her face streaked with tears. She sat down in a chair in his office after Sophia hugged her, and she started to sob again. It took her several minutes to be calm enough to talk.

"It's Heinrich," she said in a single breath. "His father got a call last night from a distant cousin, Heinrich doesn't know him, but his father says he's for real. The cousin said that my father-in-law's mother was Jewish. She died when he was born, and his father was ashamed of her being Jewish, and thought no one would ever know, so he never told him. He's been dead for years too. No one ever told us, and the cousin said he thought we knew, but Father von Ernst is half Jewish and didn't know, which makes Heinrich a quarter Jewish. His cousin works in the records office in Cologne, and he saw some paperwork the other day saying that they're going to arrest my parents-in-law, and they're going to take us too. My parents-in-law are acting as though it's not true. Father von Ernst has a bad heart. Heinrich says we have to go and leave everything behind. His brother Bernhard lives in Zurich. Heinrich is going to try to get an emigration visa, but he thinks it will be denied. He says we have to run. But where and how? My parents-in-law want to stay. They don't believe that the High Command will allow them to be arrested. Heinrich thinks they will."

"Oh my God, Theresa." Sophia looked at her with horror. "That can't be possible. Is the cousin sure about Heinrich's grandmother being Jewish? Or is he just trying to scare you, or wants blackmail money? It sounds crazy." Suddenly one of the most respectable and well-connected families in the city, in Germany, and ardent supporters of the Reich, was at risk, and her sister, brother-in-law, his parents, and the unborn child were in danger too. She thought of the little boy with hypothermia on Christmas Eve. And there was no way to hide an entire family of four adults, and especially with Theresa in the condition she was in. She couldn't give birth in someone's attic, and who would hide them?

Sophia was looking at her father, who was trying to figure out what to do. While they discussed it, Heinrich called Theresa and told her that their visa request to travel to Switzerland had been denied, even for a visit. There was no way they could get out of Germany. And if the paperwork for their arrest had already started, they had to leave very quickly. Thomas canceled his next appointment after the call, to buy some time to advise her.

"I can't believe this," Sophia said to her sister. "You've been entertaining half the SS and the Wehrmacht at your house for the past year, and they're going to arrest you? How is that possible?"

"It's possible," their father said quietly. "As far as the Reich is concerned, if you're one-quarter Jewish you're a Jew, and his father is half, which makes Heinrich a quarter. Theresa isn't Jewish, but it's against the law for Heinrich to be married to an Aryan, and for Theresa to be married to a Jew. It's all part of the Nuremberg Laws of 1935," he said. "And your parents-in-law's situation is even more severe, if he's half Jewish. If they're willing, they should try to leave with you."

"If Heinrich couldn't get us a visa, he won't be able to get them one either. And they don't want to leave. They think the SS won't touch them because of their connections and that Heinrich is panicking unnecessarily. They feel totally secure. Heinrich doesn't agree."

Sophia had been listening intently, with a serious expression, and there was only one solution she could think of, which seemed even more impossible to achieve. With Heinrich's father an older man with a heart condition, and Theresa almost seven months pregnant, she couldn't imagine anyone except Heinrich being able to hike over the mountains into Switzerland, but it was the only way they were going to get out of Germany now, on foot.

She looked at Theresa and asked her, "How soon do you think they would arrest you? Did Heinrich's cousin say?"

"He doesn't know. He said it usually takes two or three days to process the papers, maybe longer, but not much. He said to go, anywhere, as fast as we can. And Heinrich says he's right. He wants us to leave now."

"Can his brother do anything from the Swiss side?" she asked, and Theresa shook her head.

"Heinrich doesn't think so. And we have no safe way to reach him and tell him what's happening."

"What do you have in mind?" their father asked Sophia. He could see that she had an idea.

51

"I have a friend. He's been walking people over the mountains since war was declared. Usually children, and he's taken adults across too. But Theresa is in no condition to do it. She could give birth along the way." But she could wind up dead or in a concentration camp if she stayed.

"She may have to take the risk," Thomas said. He didn't ask how Sophia knew the man who walked people across the mountains. "Can you get in touch with him?"

"I can, tonight." If he went to the meeting. He didn't always come, if he was on a mission. But their only hope was her contacting Claus. She didn't even know his last name or where he lived. The only way she knew how to find him was at the meeting. She'd been planning to go that night anyway.

Theresa stayed until her father had to leave to see patients. He was already late. Sophia took her home and then came back to work. It was an endless day, waiting for that night. She went straight from work, in her uniform, after an emergency. She was one of the first to arrive at the meeting, and Claus was one of the last. She thought he wasn't coming, and then he slipped in just before they closed the door and came to sit next to her. He glanced at her with a smile and saw the tension on her face.

"Are you okay? Is something wrong?" He was instantly alert. She nodded in answer to the second question, and whispered.

"I need your help."

"Do you want to leave?" he whispered back, and she nodded. They left the meeting only minutes after he arrived, and walked slowly down the street, while she explained the situation to him where no one could overhear them. You couldn't trust anyone now. People reported each other regularly. Claus listened to the whole story and then stopped walking and looked at Sophia. "They have to go soon. It's unpredictable. The SS could show up tomorrow to arrest them, and then it's all over. And they can't take his parents with them. He's too old and with a bad heart, he'll never make it. He'd slow them down, and they're more likely to get caught that way."

"They don't want to leave anyway. And one more detail about my sister," she said unhappily.

"What? Does she have a handicap?"

"No, but she's almost six and a half months pregnant."

"Jesus," he said, giving it some thought. He wanted to help Sophia, but it wouldn't be easy. Speed was of the essence. They had no time to plan carefully or let anyone in the network know they were coming. He had enough supplies for the three of them, and the equipment they'd need, but a heavily pregnant woman would be at high risk. Her risk was even greater if they stayed, which Sophia understood too. The SS was merciless when they went after Jews, especially very wealthy ones, who owned banks and spectacular homes filled with valuable things.

"I'd like to go with them," Sophia said quietly, and his eyes opened wide in surprise.

"And stay in Switzerland?"

"No, to help get her there, in case she gives birth on the way. The baby won't survive if that happens. I don't want her to go through that alone, and she could die."

"You can only go as far as the Swiss border, or I probably won't be able to get you out again."

"At least I can go that far," she said with a look of determination.

"Are you sure? It's dangerous," he warned her.

"I'm sure," she said, and he looked at her and knew she was. "Can you do it?" He nodded.

"We have to leave tomorrow night. My guess is they'll come to arrest them the next day. I'll bring everything. They have to wear warm clothes and sturdy boots. I'll bring the rest." He told her where they would meet, at a noisy restaurant on the far side of Berlin, in the early evening. And then he smiled at Sophia. "And I'll get you back here. There's a cabin where I can leave you just before the border. I'll pick you up on the way back. And if I don't show up, you go back on your own. Don't try to make it into Switzerland by yourself. It's a rough road with crevasses and sharp drops." Thinking about it was frightening, but if they weren't caught on the way, she knew that Claus would get her home.

They left each other in the street, and Sophia stopped at Theresa's house on the way home, the house they were about to leave and might never see again. Theresa and Heinrich were in the library talking, and Sophia told them in whispers everything that Claus had said.

"So soon?" Heinrich looked shocked.

"He thinks they might come for you the day after tomorrow, and then it's too late." Heinrich nodded and looked devastated. He had warned Theresa there was no time to waste if the order for their arrest had already been drawn up.

"And what about my parents? If I can convince them to come." They were being stubborn about it, and overly optimistic.

"He doesn't think they could make it." Claus wasn't sure about Theresa either, but she had youth on her side. She was strong and in good health. Heinrich's parents were older, with his father's bad heart to consider.

Sophia left them a few minutes later, went straight to the Sisters of Mercy chapel, and lit candles for each of them, and Heinrich's parents, and even Theresa's baby. She went home after that, and her father was waiting for her, with an anxious expression.

"It's all set," she said simply. She felt drained.

"When?"

"Tomorrow night. I'll work tomorrow, and I'm going to go with them as far as the border, in case Theresa goes into labor on the way." He nodded, and learned a lot about Sophia that night.

"You could get shot, and killed," Thomas said with tears in his eyes. He could lose both his daughters. But there was no other choice. Either try to escape or wait to get arrested, and maybe wind up in one of the killing centers being euthanized as traitors to the Reich, "undesirable citizens." The Nazis were killing people for less. "Just make sure you come back," he said, with a lump in his throat.

"I will, Papa," she said, hoping she was telling him the truth. He had had no idea until then how brave she was, and as she thought about what lay ahead, neither did she.

Chapter 4

Sophia put in a full day's work at her father's hospital the day they were to leave. She went home after work and changed into hiking clothes, and wore the sturdiest boots she owned. Her father came to say goodbye to her and hugged her close. Theresa had come to see him that afternoon at the clinic, and he held each of his daughters tight before letting them go. They were the only family he had, and he fully understood that he might lose them both. He almost told Sophia not to come back and to stay in Switzerland with Theresa, but they weren't Jewish, and she had no risk. And selfishly, he knew, he wanted her back with him.

A friend of Heinrich's, whom he trusted, picked Sophia up. Heinrich and Theresa were already in the car with him, and he drove them to the restaurant where they were meeting

Claus. They ate before they left, and then slipped out a side door and got back in the car. Their papers were in order, and there was nothing unusual about them. They were five friends going on a holiday. And a young couple with a pregnant wife gave them an appearance of wholesome innocence. They drove from Berlin to Munich that night on the Reichsautobahn. It took them six and a half hours, and they arrived at two in the morning. Theresa slept the entire way. They switched drivers then and drove two and a half hours from Munich to Mengen, which was as close to the Swiss border as Claus felt they should get without drawing attention to themselves. It was almost five in the morning, and still dark, and Heinrich's friend left them then to drive back to Berlin. The others walked into a wooded area on foot. They were headed to Blumberg as their journey began in earnest toward the Swiss border, to the town of Schaffhausen on the Swiss side, and from there to Zurich. They walked in silence for three hours, until the air began to get cool, the path was steeper, and the sky turned blue in the morning light. They were still far enough from the border that there were no patrols yet. Claus was confident as he led the way. He had come this same route several times before. They stopped for water and something to eat from their supplies. There were thick bushes all around them, and tall trees. Theresa didn't complain, but Sophia could see that she was tired. It was a rough journey for a heavily pregnant woman, and she had almost tripped several times over tree roots. Each time, Heinrich caught her. He stayed very close to her.

They walked for the next twelve hours, stopping as seldom as possible and never speaking except in whispers, and then Claus finally let them rest for the night in an area of dense trees and vegetation. He cautioned them not to speak, lest there was someone in the woods to hear them. There were no patrols in the area because the trails were so narrow and hard to follow. No vehicles could be used, and even the patrol dogs didn't like to go there. Claus had come this way successfully before. On the second day of their journey, Claus woke them before daybreak, and as they stood in a clearing they could see the Hoher Randen mountain on the German side. They were close to the border and pressed on again. It was only a six-hour hike to Schaffhausen now, and freedom.

Sophia then saw the little cabin Claus had told her about, where he would leave her. They hadn't come across a single patrol. Sophia saw Theresa rub her stomach when the baby kicked her, but she hadn't gone into labor, which seemed miraculous. And she never complained, as Heinrich helped her as best he could. Even Sophia was exhausted by their fifteen-hour march the day before. But they were almost there now. They only had about another six hours left to walk, and Heinrich and Theresa would have made it to safety. They had to leave Sophia now.

The two sisters cried and hugged each other, and Sophia watched them go, as Claus led them through the woods. Sophia sat in the trees and bushes near the cabin, eating sparingly from the supplies that Claus had left her. All she could think of was her sister walking the final miles to safety, and Heinrich with her.

It was nine o'clock that night, after a long, anxious day alone in the woods, when she heard a rustling in the bushes, but there was no sound of patrol dogs as Claus appeared. Sophia cried when she saw Claus walk into the clearing, looking for her. She sprang out of the bushes and burst into tears, as she leapt into his arms.

"They made it?" she asked him, and he smiled as he nodded.

"We never got stopped, no one ever saw us. They'll be all right now. There's a road near where I left them, and the village is nearby. He can call his brother in Zurich to come and get them. The war is over for them. They can wait there until it's over for the rest of us in Germany." Sophia was relieved for Theresa, but it was a strange thought knowing that she and Heinrich would be living in peace and safety while Hitler and his monsters were destroying Germany and invading the rest of Europe.

They rested that night, and left before dawn the next day, taking a faster, steeper, harder route without Theresa to slow them down, and they were back in Mengen that night. They were unscathed, untouched, and as safe as anyone was in Germany. They went to a beer garden for something to eat. Claus called a contact he had in the area, who came to get them. There were a group of soldiers drinking at the beer garden who paid no attention to them. Now they just looked like a young couple out together. Their hiking clothes and hiking boots attracted no attention, and Claus's contact arrived quickly, and drove them to Munich after they ate, where another contact in Claus's network picked them up and drove them back to Berlin on the Reichsautobahn again. This time his contact was a young woman. She drove fast on the way back. They reached Berlin by five A.M. The whole journey had taken three days round trip. Claus picked up his own car and left Sophia at her front gate. When she walked into the house, her father walked out of his bedroom, saw her, and started crying and couldn't stop. He held her and smoothed down her long straight hair and looked at her. She looked like she had gone camping with friends, although her legs were aching. She cried too when she looked at him.

"I thought I'd never see you again," he said hoarsely. "Heinrich's brother called yesterday. They're tired, but safe, and she hasn't had the baby." It was a miracle. Claus had saved them. She had infinite respect for him, and they hadn't run into a single German patrol on the way.

"And Heinrich's parents?" she asked, as they went to the kitchen. She dropped into a chair, and her father handed her a cup of tea a few minutes later. "Are they okay?" she asked, and saw the look on her father's face, and knew before he told her.

"They took them yesterday. Their cousin was right, and Heinrich was smart to want to leave immediately. The SS has been looting the house all day. They have trucks in front to load the art into. The neighbors saw his parents being taken away. They'll be treated as common thieves now, Jews who have no right to own property. I drove by but I didn't stop to inquire. It's best to stay away. I heard it from one of their neighbors."

"What will happen to them now?" she asked sadly.

"They'll be sent to a camp like the other Jews. There's nothing we can do for them. At least their sons are safe now in Switzerland, and your sister and the next generation." It was the best they could hope for in the circumstances. Theresa couldn't imagine Heinrich's elegant mother in a concentration camp, or his father. It was unimaginable what had happened to Jews in Germany. Thomas couldn't imagine them living long in the conditions they would be facing.

"Did anyone ask about me?" Sophia asked, nervous about what would happen now.

"A police captain came to speak to you yesterday, looking for Theresa. I told him that we hadn't heard from Theresa and Heinrich in many days, and found it odd, and that you were on your rounds, checking on postsurgical patients at their homes, and wouldn't be back for several hours. He lost interest in less than an hour, and he told me that the von Ernsts had turned out to be Jews, and the Reich had reclaimed their home and its contents. He said that he felt sorry for me that my daughter had married a Jew, and I told him that we didn't know, and it was very unfortunate. Then he left. I don't know if he'll come back, but at least we know Theresa is safe, and they can't do anything to us because they fled. We're still here, doing our jobs. They'll leave us alone."

Sophia told him about the journey then, and how smoothly it had gone with the guide they had. And then she took a long bath, went to bed, and slept until she had to go to work on an afternoon shift.

The next day, it felt odd to be performing ordinary tasks again, assisting her father in surgery, checking on patients, and wearing her uniform as though nothing unusual had happened. The police didn't come again, and there was no further news of Theresa's parents-in-law. Within a week, a colonel had moved into Heinrich and Theresa's beautiful new home, and Thomas heard through the grapevine that one of the generals had moved into the von Ernst mansion and all of the art had been given to the Führer for his private collection. It didn't surprise Thomas. Heinrich's parents had some very fine art and were important collectors.

The day after she came home, Sophia went to the convent and had a private meeting with Mother Regina. They spoke for a long time, and Sophia told her what had happened, and that her sister and her husband had reached safety.

"You were very brave to go with them," the Mother Superior said to her. "You could have been killed if you had run into a patrol at the border."

"I wanted to go with her as far as I could. I was afraid she'd give birth on the way. And I might never see her again."

"Probably not until something changes here, or the war is over."

"We're not at risk because of who my father is, and all the important patients he has. They can't reproach us for anything," Sophia said confidently. "His owning the hospital and being an important surgeon, even to the SS, protects us. Theresa and Heinrich were in danger because his father turned out to be half Jewish," she said simply, and the Mother Superior nodded.

"No one is entirely safe here anymore," she said wisely, which was why Sophia had come to see her. She had made a decision on the long hike to the border and back, that if she was spared, and survived, she wanted to follow the path that had been beckoning her for years. She was sure of it now, that it was the right one for her, although she knew her father wouldn't be happy about it. But in the insanity they lived in now, it was the only thing that made sense to her.

The Mother Superior told her to discuss it with her father, and then they would talk about it some more.

It seemed like an easy decision to Sophia now, and no one was going to talk her out of it. She had felt during all those days in the forest that her mother had been following them and keeping them safe, and that she would approve of her decision, even if her father wouldn't. It was the only way Sophia thought she would find the peace she was seeking and had longed for all her life. It was the only answer that made sense to her now, in a world which no longer made sense in any way.

She went to one of her dissident meetings the next day, to look for Claus, and he was there. They smiled when they saw each other and it struck him again that she was beautiful, but there was always something about her that made her seem out of reach. She thanked him again for what he had done for Heinrich and Theresa. He had saved them, and their baby. If they had stayed in Berlin, they would have been wherever Heinrich's parents were now, and their story would have had a very different ending.

Sophia and Claus left the meeting together that night, friends forever. Claus watched her drive away, and he sensed that she was a woman with a powerful destiny. He didn't know what it was, she had only just begun her journey to find herself, but he was certain it would be something important.

Sophia missed her sister every day now. They were very different and hadn't seen each other often since her marriage, but it had been comforting to know that Theresa was somewhere nearby. Now she wasn't, and wouldn't be for a long time, if ever. All that socializing with the High Command, and his father's contributions to the Reich, had brought them nothing in the end except danger and misery, and the loss of all the material things that had been so important to them.

Sophia turned twenty-one the week after she got back. The police had come to see her that day, to ask about her sister, and Sophia told them she knew nothing, except that Heinrich had a brother in Switzerland, and they had enough money to pay someone to get them there, but she had heard nothing since they disappeared, which was credible enough that they left her alone after that. And they had been polite and respectful to her.

The night she turned twenty-one Sophia told her father her plans, and he was as shocked as she had expected him to be. She said that she was going to enter the convent to join the Sisters of Mercy. She told him about Edith Stein, and how she had always been an inspiration to her, and more so than ever now, after what she'd seen for the past few years. Sophia said she was going to be a nursing nun, and work in whatever Catholic hospital they assigned her to.

"How am I going to manage without you?" he said. "With one daughter maybe gone forever, or for years until the war ends, and now you disappearing into the convent to be a nun. You're too young to make a decision like that." He was deeply unhappy about it.

"I'm happy there, Papa. It suits me. It's a good life for me."

"Don't you want to have a husband and children one day?" he asked her, and she shook her head with a quiet smile.

"Being in the convent makes me feel peaceful." Peace wasn't easy to find anymore. He didn't want to argue with her, but he was profoundly saddened by her decision.

"Can I come to visit you?"

"Of course." She smiled at him. "You're busy anyway. You won't even notice that I'm gone."

"Yes, I will. Especially in surgery. You're a very fine nurse, Sophia." But the world offered her no lures she wanted. She had no attachment to material things, and never did.

What she cared about ran much deeper, working with the poor, saving children from the Nazis now. It was all the things that Edith Stein personified. She had been an activist and a dissident and still was, and Sophia didn't intend to give those things up either. She was just going to live differently than she did now. She knew her sister wouldn't have approved of it either. But it was right for her. She had no doubt in her mind. And she had a feeling her mother would have approved. Her mother had understood her.

She told Mother Regina the next day that she had spoken to her father, and they made plans for her to move to the convent.

She moved in the day that the Germans locked a hundred and sixty-five thousand Jews into the Lodz Ghetto in Poland. The Sisters of Mercy prayed for them. She officially became a postulant ten days later, on May 10, 1940, when Germany invaded France, Belgium, Holland, and Luxembourg, and Winston Churchill became the British Prime Minister. The Reich had just devoured another big hunk of Europe, and Sophia had begun her life as Sister Anne. It was exactly the life she wanted. The first time her father saw her in her habit, he cried.

They walked around the convent garden together and talked about the war and all the countries that were occupied by the Nazis now, and they wondered where Heinrich's parents were. There had been no news from them to anyone. Sophia wondered if they were dead. They wouldn't be useful for hard labor in the camps. Thomas wondered if they had been euthanized at one of the killing centers, or just murdered more crudely like so many others. They had no status or useful connections to protect them now. They would just be considered Jews, with no privileges and no rights, all of their possessions and money taken from them. There was no way to know or find out where Heinrich's parents were, and whether dead or alive.

Thomas worked harder than ever once Sophia moved to the convent and became a postulant. Mother Regina had assigned her to St. Joseph's Hospital to work in the children's ward, and she loved the work. The hospital was modern and only twelve years old. Twice a week on her way back to the convent after work, she went to the same meeting of dissidents she had attended for years. She justified it to herself knowing that she hadn't taken a vow of obedience yet. The other nuns didn't know she went there, but it meant too much to her to give up, and she was sure God didn't want her to.

The first time Claus saw her in her habit, he was shocked.

"When did that happen and why?" he asked her, and she laughed.

"I started thinking about it when my mother got sick five years ago. I always knew this life would suit me and I was right. I made the decision finally on the walk to Switzerland with you."

"Well, don't sign your life away yet, you might change your mind one day, when the right man comes along." He knew that he wasn't it, but they were friends and he worried about her, and admired her. She had more courage than anyone he knew. And was faithful to her principles. "I wish you'd told me. I'd have tried to talk you out of it."

"I don't think a man could change my mind," she said.

"You're too independent to be a nun," he said, and she laughed again. "Do the nuns know you come to these meetings? Do they know you're here tonight?"

"No," she said. "But I'm sure God does, and thinks it's all right. It's our secret." She was smiling and looked happier than he'd ever seen her before. But he still wasn't convinced that she had made the right choice, even if she did look happy and at peace now.

"Can we still be friends?" he asked cautiously.

"Of course. You can come and visit me on Sundays. I have to ask permission, but they'll let you. It's not a cloistered order."

He smiled as he looked at her, wondering where their respective paths would lead them next. Just knowing her was interesting. All he had to do now was get used to calling her Sister Anne, and he thought that he could do that. For however long she stayed a nun. He wasn't convinced it would be forever, but it was a safe place for her now. Sophia was convinced it was the right choice for her, even if Claus wasn't.

70

Chapter 5

Sophia settled into her new life in the convent with surprising ease. It gave her everything she had longed for all her life, and combined what meant most to her. She enjoyed her life in community, as she had suspected she would. Living with like-minded women with the same goals was both comforting and exhilarating. She no longer had to hide her religious beliefs, and Mother Regina was a strong spiritual director for her. They spent many hours discussing the religious issues which Sophia had pondered for a lifetime, with no one to share her views and philosophies. She soaked up the Superior's answers to her questions like a hungry plant desperate for water. The religious answers to her deeper unspoken questions were like water for her soul.

She continued to attend dissident meetings when she could get away with it, and only missed a few. It was the one thing she didn't share with the Mother Superior, because she knew she wouldn't agree. But like her role model, Edith Stein, Sophia had strong beliefs about Germany, the war, and the Reich, and the destruction they were wreaking, the people they were destroying and killing, the lives they had shattered. At the meetings, she could speak out freely, without fear of being reported or chastised, or punished, and worse.

Her father came to see her dutifully every Sunday and looked aggrieved when he did. He still couldn't understand why Sophia had chosen a life in seclusion and given up her prospects as a beautiful young woman. It made no sense to him, but she had always been different. He recognized that now. She was even less like her sister Theresa than he had ever suspected. Having a husband and children meant nothing to her. She lived to help others and wished that she could save them all. She had a tender heart, but no wish to give it to a man. She was devoted to the human race as a whole, and willing to sacrifice herself for what she believed. She was a strong, brave woman, stronger than he'd ever known. Her dangerous walk to the Swiss border to save her sister showed him a kind of love he'd never understood and he readily admitted that she was more like her mother than like him. He was a scientist, not a saint, but he thought his daughter was.

Through an old patient of his, who came to visit him unexpectedly, Thomas had news of Heinrich and Theresa. Their baby had been born in Zurich in June, a month early, probably due to the rigors of the walk from Germany to Switzerland. He was a big, healthy boy. They had named him Thomas, after him, which touched him deeply, and he wished that he could see his first grandchild, but there was no hope of it until after the war, if then. Who knew what the conditions would be at the end of the war, and who would win. The British were putting up a fierce fight, but Hitler's war machine seemed unbeatable at the moment, like a man-eating beast devouring whole countries and forcing the population to submit to their rules and beliefs.

Thomas was glad now that Theresa was leading a comfortable, familiar life in Switzerland, and he knew that Heinrich would take good care of her. He was an honorable man. His patient informed him, discreetly, that Heinrich's older brother was helping them. They were living with him for the moment, and at his father's suggestion, Heinrich had had the foresight to place money in Switzerland right before war was declared, so he had funds to rely on. And even if they lost everything in Germany, both brothers would be financially sound afterward, unless the sky fell in on the whole world. But failing that, their investments in Switzerland would protect them. They would lead a very different life in

73

Switzerland now than the people they had known in Berlin, some of whom had lost not only their fortunes, but their lives, their children, their livelihoods, their homes.

It was also a very different life that Sophia was living now with the Sisters of Mercy. Thomas knew that Theresa would have been shocked if she had known, and disappointed for her sister. She had always envisioned both of them married, with children. Sophia had chosen a very different path, and Thomas could only hope that she would change her mind one day. She was still very young at twenty-one to follow such a Spartan path for life.

They were only able to exchange letters with Theresa from time to time, and they didn't dare put anything significant in the letters. Thomas didn't even dare tell her that Sophia had moved to the convent when he wrote to congratulate her about her son and wish them well. He didn't want to bring attention to Sophia. The Nazis were not fond of Christian religious fanatics either, and several members of the church, both priests and nuns, had been arrested and sent to labor camps if they weren't ardent supporters of the Führer. He wanted to be their god, not just their ruler, and punished anyone who disagreed with him. Thousands had been imprisoned for differing political views as well. It was a time to keep your head down, say little, and make yourself as unremarkable as possible, which was Thomas's goal. All he wanted to do was treat his patients and continue the work he had always engaged in. Even more so now, with Sophia in the convent, his work was his only interest, and he only went home to sleep at night. He ate all his meals in the hospital cafeteria. His housekeeper almost never saw him anymore.

One thing Sophia readily admitted was that working conditions at St. Joseph's Hospital were far less comfortable than they had been at her father's ultra-comfortable, luxurious hospital, where they had state-of-the-art equipment, all the supplies and medicine were abundant, surgical conditions were ideal for the physicians, patients, and nurses, and the patients were of the highest caliber, either important military men seeking expert private medical advice in addition to what the army offered them, politicians of high rank, or socialites with wealth and education. Although he hadn't planned it that way, Thomas's patients were the most elite in Berlin. He dealt with educated people, which made his job easier.

At St. Joseph's, Sophia dealt with simpler people who didn't always understand the procedures or their illness even after it was explained to them. Even some of the doctors were less highly trained and were rude to the nurses, and although the hospital was relatively new, some of the equipment was antiquated. The staff had no choice but to overlook the conditions and offer the best care they could in the circumstances. Sophia was deeply shocked by some of the forms they had to fill out, to eliminate an undesirable element of "hopeless cases" according to standards set by the Reich, and not medical practitioners: children who were too ill and had been since birth, some with deformities that could even be fixed, like club feet, which she had seen her father operate on and repair many times in his hospital. Any sign of mental instability or retardation, elderly people showing signs of dementia, however slight. The Führer wanted a perfect race of flawless people and would accept nothing less. Nurses, doctors, and midwives were required to report any deformities or anomalies, mental or physical, "for life unworthy of life," for the good of the Fatherland. The direction and appropriate forms came from the Reich Health Ministry. It applied to all patients, both children and adults. A panel of "experts" would then evaluate each case, and three plus marks on a form was a death sentence, either by lethal injection, or starvation until they succumbed. For adults, they didn't waste time starving them, and administered lethal injections. No anomalies were to be tolerated, no defects, no substandard conditions, even those which might have been cured over time. It was part of a pet program of the Führer's, code-named Aktion T4, designed to purify the master race. He had instituted the program in 1939, only weeks after war was declared, and all medical personnel were ordered to participate. And by 1940, all Jewish patients were removed from all institutions and killed.

Sophia systematically failed to report any malformations, conditions, or anomalies that would draw attention to patients who might be subject to the rule. And she had never been caught so far, for failure to report. She knew that killing patients was frequent in all hospitals in Germany now, including the one where she worked. It was a cruel, inhuman selection process, and not mercy killing as the Health Ministry claimed.

Sophia was outraged every time she heard of one and had tried to erase a red plus on a report she had seen for a bright three-year-old boy who was partially deaf, but the plus sign had been written in red ink and she couldn't remove it. The child had disappeared from the pediatric ward the next day. They hadn't bothered to wait for starvation, and the parents had been heartbroken. They had been told that he had died in the night from a heart defect he didn't have. Sophia was off the night he disappeared. She would have taken him and hidden him at the convent if she could get away with it, but she knew she couldn't, and there were so many patients like him, both young and old, and of all ages. Too many to count lately, as euthanasia was becoming a common, acceptable alternative to treatment, decided by zealous doctors, sometimes even by medical students. It was all about Nazi politics, not humane, compassionate, responsible medical treatment. Coming from her father's highly dedicated, medically advanced private hospital, it was a shock to Sophia, and fanned the flames of her silent hatred of the Nazis. For the sake of the convent, her father, and even her own safety, she kept her views to herself, but they ate her up each time she encountered an inhuman situation, and made her ever more faithful to her hidden group of dissidents.

She was leaving the hospital one evening after her shift. To save gasoline and support the war effort the nuns were driving less than they used to, and the Sisters of Mercy were allowed to take the bus when they left work. Sophia left the bus long before her stop, on a different route, and walked to her meeting on her way home. It was always easy to explain that she had been delayed at work, and the meetings didn't last long. She took a familiar seat at the edge of the room, jotted down a note of something she didn't want to forget, felt someone sit down next to her, saw a familiar voluminous black skirt beside her, and looked up to see Mother Regina sitting next to her, her hands folded in her lap, her gaze straight into Sophia's big green eyes. She didn't know what to say at first. She felt like a child who had been caught stealing or cheating on their homework. She had been lying about where she went twice a week, ever since becoming a postulant of the order.

"I'm sorry," was all she could think of to say at first, and Mother Regina nodded and whispered to her.

"I wanted to see where you go every week, twice a week, on Mondays and Thursdays. I didn't think it was like you to do it to avoid your shift in the laundry." She smiled indulgently, and Sophia decided to open her heart to her.

"This is important to me. It's a moment of sanity in the world we live in now, and knowing that others feel the same."

"Our views in the convent are not so different from yours, Sister. But it would not be wise for us to express them, it might cause pain or danger to others we don't wish to harm."

"Will you forbid me to come here?" Sophia asked her, wanting to be obedient, but not sure she could be on this one important point.

"I want to hear what they say. That's why I came."

The discussions that night were slightly less inflammatory than usual, but painful nonetheless, stories of Jewish neighbors who had been dragged away, their houses burned, their children beaten in front of them, and fathers shot and killed, stories from other cities, Jews being forced to live in ghettos, which were being systematically sealed, and the residents starved, bombed, or murdered, in order to eliminate thousands of Jews at one fell swoop. It was sickening as one listened, and Sophia gave a brief account of the Aktion T4 "mercy" killings she had become aware of, in many cases killing healthy children with problems that could be cured, children who were starved or killed by injection, often Jewish children, but not always.

The Jewish children were deported to die in camps with their parents. The smell of death was heavy in the air by the end of the meeting. Claus cryptically reported six very pleasant trips to the market that week to buy fresh vegetables, which meant something only to the initiated. It meant that six children had been successfully removed and taken to safety, either in hiding, or to another location, by people active in missions to save them, just as he had helped Heinrich and Theresa to escape. Mother Regina asked Sophia to explain it when they left, and she did, and told her about their trip into the mountains to save her sister and her husband in April, when she decided to enter the convent.

She introduced Mother Regina to Claus before they left, and he was intrigued to see her with another nun and wondered if she was under some kind of supervision now. Sophia couldn't explain that the Superior's visit had been a surprise to her too.

"They're all brave people," Mother Regina said solemnly as they walked to the bus afterward. "At another time, I might have called it foolhardy, but we need people like them now, to save those we can, and there are too few. And you want to be one of them? I assume you've done some missions yourself?" she asked Sophia directly. Sophia wondered if she was going to ask her to leave the convent. She didn't want to, but she couldn't sit helplessly by doing nothing either, when the opportunities arose to help someone and they asked her. Particularly Claus. She owed him so much, for her sister's safe escape.

"I would like to," Sophia said honestly. "I've done very little so far, but I help where I can." A bus ride with a child, waiting with them in a dark cellar until other help arrived, taking a child to a nearby city under a blanket in her father's car. She'd had a few missions she had completed successfully, and she wanted to do more.

"You realize that if you take great risks, you put all of the sisters at the convent in danger."

"I do, and I don't want to do that. But if I can help in small ways, I would."

Mother Regina smiled for a moment as she looked at her. "You sound like Sister Teresa Benedicta of the Cross," she said, which was the religious name Edith Stein had taken as a Carmelite. Sophia considered it a great compliment. "Be careful and be wise, for your sake as well as ours. If something happens, there is nothing we can do to save you. The Reich barely trusts us as it is. We can't jeopardize the order

81

for you. Only the brave want to do what you long to do, Sophia. A wise priest once told me that God doesn't canonize the foolish. Be as careful as you can be, and I will pray for you," she said, as they boarded the bus that would bring them close to the convent. They sat side by side. Sophia looked out the window, thinking of what Mother Regina had said. In essence, she had given her blessing to Sophia to continue to attend her meetings, and to do whatever missions they asked her to do, without taking undue risks that would put the sisters in the convent in danger. She knew it would be a fine line, and these were wartime rules, but she was grateful for the freedom, and reached over gently and held Mother Regina's hand. The two nuns exchanged a knowing look and got off at their stop a few minutes later, walking back to the convent. It was everything Sophia had hoped for. She was a nun now, and was free to follow what she believed in, and help wherever she could. To outsmart the deadly Nazis and cheat them of even a single death was her mission, and her reason for living now. Mother Regina had given her an incredible gift. She understood that it was something Sophia had to do. In Mother Regina's opinion, the cause of freedom needed more people like her. Only the brave could do it and Mother Regina was well aware that Sophia was braver than she knew.

* * *

Only the Brave

The summer seemed longer to Theresa in Zurich than it did to Sophia in Berlin. Mail out of Germany was erratic, but since Switzerland was neutral, eventually letters got through. Heinrich made Theresa use a post office box, in case a letter fell into the wrong hands and the Gestapo instantly had their address. But there was nothing they could do to them here. They had seized everything the von Ernsts had in Germany, all their possessions and valuables, their bank, their fortune, and their home, but Heinrich felt it was a small price to pay for freedom. The greatest loss was his parents. They still had no idea where they had been taken or what had happened to them after their arrest, and Heinrich feared the worst. His older brother Bernhard was not optimistic that they would survive whatever they were experiencing and might already have succumbed or been killed. Neither of his parents was suited to a labor camp, his father with his heart condition, and his mother having been pampered and protected all her life. She came from an aristocratic family as wealthy as his father's, and hardships were unknown to both of them. And what one heard about the concentration camps where Jews and dissidents were being sent was terrifying.

What consoled Heinrich now was the love of his young wife, and the birth of their son Thomas. He was a beautiful blond baby from the moment of his birth and looked like

Theresa with the same big blue eyes and ready smile. He laughed and giggled within a month of his birth.

He had been born in a luxurious private clinic in Zurich, similar to her father's hospital, so nothing was unfamiliar to Theresa. The birth had been hard because the baby was big, but she had gotten through it, and was thoroughly enjoying him. As she held him in her arms to nurse him, she thought of her mother and sister, and wished that they could see him, and had been with her at the birth. It had been harder to go through it alone, with only nurses, but after the two-day trek to reach safety in Switzerland, she felt as though she could face anything. She had never been as frightened, or so physically challenged and exhausted, in her life. On doctor's orders, she had stayed in bed for a week after they arrived in April. Thomas had been born two months later, three weeks before his due date. He couldn't wait to be born, and no harm had come from arriving a few weeks early.

Theresa was constantly surprised by how much she missed her sister. She wanted her advice, or to tell her something, and there was suddenly an aching void in her life, balanced by Heinrich and the baby, but a man and an infant were not the same as a sister. She realized now more than ever before how wise and stable her sister was, and what a support she had been to her after their mother got sick, and since she had died. Sophia was always the voice of reason, which had irritated Theresa profoundly in her teens, wanting more freedom, but she saw now the love that had been behind every rule and scolding.

Her father had managed to share with her in a letter at the end of the summer that Sophia had entered the convent after they left. Theresa was horrified by the idea of it at first, that her sister would take vows of poverty, chastity, and obedience, which sounded horrible to her, but she realized in some part of her that it suited Sophia, who had been indifferent to material things all her life, and cared more about others than herself. She had lavished that capacity for love on her sister, and would do so now, on the poor, in the hospital where she worked, and on strangers. The concept was totally foreign to Theresa, but she knew it wouldn't be to Sophia.

She worried about her father too, who had no one to take care of him now, with Sophia living somewhere else, although not far away. And she knew how hard their father worked. Like Sophia, he only thought of others, in his case his patients, and not himself. At least he had his hospital to keep him busy, but she was sure he must be lonely now without his daughters near at hand.

Heinrich had just bought them a very pretty house on the lake, which she was decorating lavishly, and he always indulged her. There was a whole floor for the children they intended to have, and an enormous garden. Her dressing room was the size of their bedroom in Berlin. Theirs was not a life of deprivation while they waited out the war in the peace and safety of neutral Switzerland. She had wanted to go to Paris to do some shopping, but the Germans had occupied Paris since June, and it was no longer safe. She was disappointed they couldn't go, and Heinrich and his brother were shocked and saddened that France had fallen, and that others would suffer the losses they had. Jews in France were already being rounded up to be deported, homes and art were being seized, and the country was being plundered. The French had signed an agreement with Hitler, acceding to the occupation and trying to minimize the damage, but Heinrich and his brother were sure the effects would be enormous, and loss of life would follow, as it had everywhere else.

Theresa tried not to think of the dangers of war whenever she thought of Sophia and her father, and instead she kept her warm memories of them close to her heart, as she watched her son grow.

By October, four months after his birth, she was pregnant again, and she and Heinrich were delighted. Their peaceful time in Switzerland seemed like the ideal time to build the family they wanted, in idyllic surroundings, in their new home. Heinrich's older brother was married to a woman with ill health, and they had no children, so they were enchanted to see the babies arrive to bring joy to their lives, and the promise of new life.

The war seemed unreal and very distant to the von Ernsts in Zurich. Looking at the mountains and the lake, it was hard to imagine the hardships and dangers of daily life in Berlin. Even more impossible to visualize Sophia's life as a nun. It all seemed so far away now, and the only reality for Theresa was her baby, her husband who made her so happy, and their new home. And Heinrich kept the ugly details of the war from her whenever he could. She had already been through enough, in his opinion, with their escape to Switzerland. She didn't need to hear the stories he did that weren't suitable for her ears. He wanted her second pregnancy to be even smoother than the first, without the shock of having to flee when she was six and a half months pregnant. And as long as he drew breath, he intended to protect her from any unpleasantness, and treat her like the beautiful jewel she was. It was a far cry from the life of Sister Anne, with the Sisters of Mercy, working among the indigent in a public hospital, attending secret meetings of Nazi dissidents, and occasionally transporting Jewish children a short distance in Berlin or somewhere in Germany to pass them along to someone who would bring them to safety at great risk to themselves, and literally risking death as punishment each time she did. But if Sophia could have seen, or even imagined, her sister's life in Switzerland, she would have been happy for her.

Chapter 6

In November, a month after Theresa became pregnant with her second child in Zurich, news spread in Europe of both the Krakow and Warsaw ghettos being sealed off, which was a familiar tactic now, to isolate the people who lived there, all Jews, and kill them en masse while they were trapped in the ghettos. There were twenty thousand Jews confined to the Krakow Ghetto, and four hundred thousand in the Warsaw Ghetto. It was the Nazis' hope to wipe out over a million Jews between the two cities, an incredible number of men, women, and children to annihilate, trapped with no escape, and doomed to die.

Hearing about it, Sophia's heart ached for all of them, but especially the children, for whom they could do absolutely nothing, sitting in Berlin. They discussed it at a meeting she attended with Claus. He had been on a long mission some-where in Europe, which he said had been successful. All she knew was that it involved getting a group of children in France to safety, and he had been working with the French Resistance, which had become very active ever since the German occupation in France.

She had been on a few short missions herself recently, one which took her to Wiesbaden, the other to Munich, but she couldn't travel long distances and stay away from the convent for long. It was the only thing Mother Regina had asked her to be careful about, and she accomplished each mission in a day, came back to the convent the same night, and explained her absence as a double shift at the hospital, which no one questioned. Only Mother Regina knew her secret, which protected them all as well.

The war news was distressing when Germany bombed Coventry, England. Hitler was determined to occupy England, whatever it took to do it. The nuns added the English bombing victims to their prayers at Vespers that evening, which the Nazis would have taken a dim view of, but which seemed direly necessary to them, and Mother Regina agreed.

A few days later, Thomas Alexander, Sophia's father, had an unexpected visit. Colonel Gerhard Schmitt of the SS came to see him representing the Reich Health Ministry. He was charming at first, and praised Thomas for the high caliber and standard of his work, which Thomas knew was only a graceful introduction to whatever it was he wanted.

"I believe that one of our very illustrious generals, a patient of yours in fact, paid you a visit some time ago about the Führer's Aktion T4 program. He is particularly interested in that project, and it is a great honor for him to ask you to help him implement it. I'm sure you're sensitive to the compliment he has paid you, and your hospital setting is ideal for it. In fact, my mother-in-law had surgery here two years ago, for her gall bladder. You accomplished it very successfully, and she raved about the care she received here, particularly by you. Our whole family is indebted to you.

"And now we would like your assistance to support the Führer in this venture. You can of course carry out his request at our centers where we handle ordinary cases, but for the more important ones, your hospital will be most suitable." He flashed an evil smile as he explained to Thomas what he wanted, and Thomas felt his heart race as he listened. He remembered perfectly the general's visit, and what the Aktion T4 plan was. It was wholesale murder in the form of "euthanasia"—"mercy killings"—"for the good of the Fatherland." However they explained it to him, or dressed it up, Thomas knew that he was not going to do it for them, under any circumstances. What he couldn't figure out was how he was going to deliver that message in a palatable way they would accept without considering it an act of treason on his part. He listened to Colonel Schmitt explain to him what a simple thing it would be, and how much it would please the Führer.

In the end, there was nothing he could do except decline, as simply and as honestly as he could.

"I understand that the Führer feels this is an important program, but I took an oath when I became a doctor, and this goes counter to everything I promised and believe, and how I've practiced medicine for more than thirty years."

"Would you defy the Führer's orders?" Colonel Schmitt asked with a look of astonishment. He had little beady eyes that made Thomas nervous, and he clearly expected a response.

"If I understand you correctly, Colonel, this is not an order, it's a request, and it is something I simply can't do, for the Führer, or even for a patient. I've had patients who've begged me to euthanize them. I'm a man of principle, and I respect the oath I took. I just can't do what you suggest."

"Is that your final answer?" the colonel said harshly, and stood up abruptly in Thomas's office.

"I'm afraid it is," Thomas said calmly and firmly. "It has to be. I can't euthanize children because they have a defect, or someone because they don't agree with our current policies, or are Jewish, or an old person whose sight or hearing is failing, or even if they have dementia. Would you want someone to euthanize your mother-in-law because her gall bladder was malfunctioning?"

"If she was a traitor to the Reich, I would. Those who don't represent our race in its absolute ideal form need to be eliminated. They don't belong here."

"We all belong here, Colonel. I'm not a religious man, but I have a profound respect for human life. I have dedicated my entire career to preserving and protecting those lives. I can't turn my back on that now."

"I was giving you another chance," the colonel said, glaring at Thomas. "The general was very angry that you denied him when he asked you."

"I'm sorry. Euthanasia is something I simply cannot do." The more Thomas said it, the more he believed it. What they wanted him to do was an abomination, an outrage, a crime against humanity. He would rather give up practicing medicine than euthanize one man, woman, or child certainly, who had nothing or very little wrong with them, and didn't deserve it. Even if someone was terminally ill and suffering he couldn't do it. In that case, he would make them as comfortable as he could, as he always had, not kill them. They wanted to turn him into a murderer, and he stood up and looked the colonel in the eye.

"I'm sorry, Colonel," he said, and the colonel turned on his heel, marched out of Thomas's office without a word, and slammed the door behind him. Thomas wasn't even afraid of the reaction this time, as he had been the first time. It was the only answer he could give them. There was no other choice in his mind.

The response was swift this time. After the colonel's visit, Thomas continued seeing his patients as usual—lawyers, bankers, a member of the Reichstag, the Republic's legislature, a well-known socialite, and two of his patients' children. He didn't mention the visit to anyone, or what had transpired in the meeting. The whole idea disgusted and horrified him.

Two days later, a car with four members of the Gestapo arrived, and two SS officers in a separate car. They had sent the highest-ranking officers to arrest him. They strode into his office while he was at his desk.

"Do you still refuse to follow the directives of Aktion T4?" the senior officer asked him, standing in the middle of the room. "And refuse to obey the Führer's orders?"

"I do refuse," Thomas said calmly, feeling as though there was a film happening in front of him and not real life. "The directive violates the oath I have taken as a physician and would force me to take actions that I cannot perform as a doctor."

"Take him," the Kommandant said to two soldiers who had appeared in the room. "You're under arrest," he said to

Thomas before he stormed out of the room, as the two soldiers grabbed Thomas roughly, dragged him across the room, and pushed him down the stairs, where he fell into the hands of more soldiers waiting for him. He was still wearing his white doctor's coat. They tore it off him, threw it on the floor, and trampled it as they dragged him out, as horrified nurses and orderlies watched.

"You're not a doctor anymore," one of the officers said. "Your license has been revoked, by order of the Führer. You are a traitor to the Reich, and a disgrace to the Fatherland." As he said it, Thomas wondered if they were going to euthanize him. But whatever they did to him, he still knew that his refusal to kill innocent people for them was right.

They pushed him roughly into one of the police cars waiting outside, and all of the cars sped off within minutes. The nurses huddled inside the hospital, wondering what to do now. There was no one to direct them. At six o'clock a truck full of soldiers and two SS officers arrived. They walked up to the reception desk, and the senior officer spoke to them coldly.

"The hospital is now closed. Release your patients immediately."

"What should we do with them?" one of the nurses asked, looking frightened. They had been worried about Dr. Alexander all day and wondered what crime he had committed.

The patients knew nothing about it and had been told that the doctor had important meetings and would be back tomorrow, which they hoped would be the case. Now it was clear that wouldn't happen. It wasn't a misunderstanding he could clear up. The soldiers unrolled posters that said CLOSED in bold letters, and taped them to the doors and the façade of the building.

"Send the patients home," one of the officers answered the nurse's question.

"Some of them are too ill to be moved, and had surgery too recently," another nurse explained. They had come down from other floors when word spread of what was happening.

"Then call ambulances and send them to other hospitals," the second officer said more humanely. "You have an hour to get everyone out." The receptionists at the front desk got busy immediately calling for ambulances and calling hospitals, while nurses and orderlies rushed to the upper floors to prepare the patients. Some of them called their families and within minutes, their relatives started to arrive. Those who were able to walked out or were taken in wheelchairs. The patients who were too ill to move easily were lying on gurneys in the hallways, with blankets over them and their belongings in suitcases next to them. Their relatives came as quickly as they could. The hospital had been emptied of patients in under two hours, as the soldiers told them to hurry and get out of the building.

One of the patients asked an officer if Dr. Alexander was Jewish. It was the only explanation for what had happened, and how quickly they were forced to leave.

"No, he's a traitor to the Reich, to a criminal degree," he said in a strong voice that everyone could hear. No one said a word after that, and all the patients were gone finally, as the nurses cried at what had happened.

"Now the rest of you go too, and don't come back here. Take your belongings. You worked for a criminal. If you come back here, you'll be arrested for consorting with criminals." They scurried to get their things then. There were nearly fifty of them, including cleaning and clerical staff, though most of them were nurses in starched white uniforms, or blue ones with white aprons and white caps and black shoes.

They left the building in a mass exodus, glancing over their shoulders at the soldiers and officers who stood watching them go. They were all unemployed now and they had no idea what had happened to Dr. Alexander. They wondered if Sophia had been arrested too, by association, because she was his daughter. They walked away from the hospital to catch their buses. Some of the nurses had their husbands pick them up, and said they'd explain it later. It had been a wonderful place to work. The soldiers locked the doors behind them. They had their orders. There had been some discussion about whether to remove the equipment, but in the end the decision was not to.

They searched the house adjacent to the hospital, where they knew the doctor lived, and removed some sculptures and paintings, and then returned to the hospital to follow their orders. Another truck full of soldiers arrived, and a brigade of firefighters. Then the soldiers went through the hospital floor by floor, smashing everything with axes, throwing instruments on the floor, turning over beds. Machinery was hacked beyond use or recognition. If Thomas Alexander returned to his hospital, there would be nothing useful left or in working condition. When every floor had been vandalized, they set fire to it, and left the building. The firefighters kept careful watch to make sure the fire didn't spread to neighboring houses, but there was considerable space around with the gardens. Then they went to Thomas's home and repeated the process. His house was smaller than the hospital, so it didn't take as long. The two buildings created an enormous fire, which lit up the sky in bright orange with clouds of smoke rising. Once everything was burning, the soldiers and officers left, and the firefighters remained to control the blaze if necessary. People had come out into the street to watch the two buildings burn, and the firefighters shouted at them to go back to their homes. People were shocked that no one was trying to put out the fire. It didn't dawn on them at first that it had been set intentionally.

The fires had been set by eight-thirty, and by nine o'clock the blaze lit up the neighborhood and you could feel the heat at a great distance, although it was a cold November night.

The nuns were about to go upstairs for the night after their evening prayers, when one of them looked out the window and saw the flames leaping toward the orange sky, shooting sparks and black smoke billowing above the fire.

"Oh how terrible, there's a fire in the neighborhood. It looks like a bad one." The others came to see what she had noticed, and they gasped when they saw it. Sophia was one of the last to get close to the window and guessed instantly the direction that the fire came from. Without asking permission, she bolted from the building and took off at a dead run. She was there within minutes, her worst fears confirmed. Her father's hospital was being burned to the ground, and their home next to it.

"Oh my God," she said as she stood next to the firefighters. "What happened to the patients? Did they get everyone out?"

"They left two or three hours ago," one of the firefighters answered her, as they stood and watched the buildings burn.

"And the doctor? The staff?" They looked at her strangely. "Why aren't you putting the fire out?" No one answered.

"There's no one in the building," one of them finally said, not wanting to be rude to her since she was a nun. "You should go home, Sister, there are a lot of sparks flying. You don't want your habit to catch fire. You should go back to the convent." He knew there was one just down the street. The other nuns had started walking toward the burning hospital by then, curious, confused, worried, and Mother Regina was among them.

"What happened to the doctor? This was a private hospital," Sophia asked the firefighter closest to her.

"He was arrested this morning," he said in a flat voice, and Sophia felt like she was going to faint for a minute, as Mother Regina arrived next to her and put an arm around her.

"Let's go home, Sister," she said to Sophia quietly. "It's dangerous here," she said, holding her tight, and Sophia understood her. It was why the firefighters weren't fighting the blaze. Mother Regina had guessed what had happened when she saw them, and she led Sophia away. Sophia didn't resist her, and the other nuns followed. Sophia cast a glance at the house she had grown up in, that her mother had decorated so beautifully, and which had been a warm home for all of them. It was nothing but a flaming skeleton now. There was nothing left of it, and the hospital was still burning white hot as they all walked back to the convent in silence.

Mother Regina led her into her office so the others wouldn't hear them. She sat Sophia on a chair, handed her a glass of water, and closed the door, and then sat down at her desk to talk to her. Sophia was staring at her blindly, in shock at what had just happened.

"They were letting the house burn, Mother, and the hospital."

"I know. I saw that." The Mother Superior could guess that they had set the fire, or someone had.

"They said my father was arrested this morning. How do I find out where he is and what happened?"

"I'm not sure. I'll try to find out tomorrow. It could be dangerous to ask. I'll see if Father Weiss knows someone. Do you know if your father was involved in any dissident activities?"

"No," Sophia said, dabbing at her eyes, from the smoke and the emotion. She felt overwhelmed and the Superior could see it. "He wasn't interested in politics, just medicine and patients." Mother Regina didn't ask if they were Jewish, she was sure they weren't. But something very serious had happened to cause such a violent reaction. The firefighters had clearly been told to let the fire burn until the building was reduced to ashes. But more importantly, Sophia needed to know what had happened to her father, and if she was in danger now too. They needed information.

"Don't go to your meeting next time," she warned Sophia, "until we know what happened." Sophia nodded, and a little while later, Mother Regina walked her upstairs and put her to bed in her tiny cell with the narrow bed and the thin mattress. You could smell smoke in the air now, and they could see from the windows that the fire was still burning brightly.

After prayers the next morning, Mother Regina called Father Weiss, who said mass for them, and asked him if he could find out what happened. He wasn't sure he could, but he promised to try, as discreetly as possible.

He called back at noon. All the other nuns were at their jobs, and Sophia was alone in the convent with Mother Superior. She had called in sick at St. Joseph's and stayed at the convent to wait for news.

Father Weiss told them what he had learned. He called a sergeant he knew and had gone to school with. The sergeant told him the doctor in question had been arrested for treason. He had refused a direct order from the Führer, which was usually punishable by death. He didn't know if it would be in this case. Father Weiss said that the sergeant believed the police still had Dr. Alexander, and he had heard they might be sending him to Sachsenhausen, a concentration camp just outside Berlin, and eventually relocated to Dachau, near Munich, or directly to Dachau in the next few days, after interrogation by the police had been completed. That usually meant torture. Father Weiss didn't add that detail, but Mother Regina could figure it out for herself. The priest added that the doctor must have made the High Command furious for someone of his stature to be so harshly punished, particularly since the Reich needed doctors, as so many Jewish doctors had been forbidden to practice and sent to concentration camps. It was all he knew, but sending Thomas Alexander to a camp was a certainty. The only question was which one. And Mother Regina was grateful to know that Sophia's father was alive.

Both camps he mentioned had a reputation for harsh treatment and a shockingly high mortality rate. The priest mentioned that Dachau had an infirmary staffed by inmates, and since he was a doctor, it seemed more likely they'd send him there. Dissidents of the Nazi regime were frequently sent to Dachau, and there were said to be close to twenty thousand prisoners housed in thirty-two barracks. It was the first camp that had been opened. Prisoners were sent there for forced labor, and there was a crematorium. Whichever camp he was sent to, it was easy to deduce that Thomas would be facing hard times and would be lucky to survive.

Mother Regina delivered the news as gently and simply as she could, and Sophia cried as she listened, trying to guess what cataclysmic event had resulted in such a violent reaction. It was hard to imagine. Her father had been loved and admired by all, even the High Command of the Reich, but clearly he had been given an order that he had refused to comply with, and she felt sure it had been something that he considered a crime against humanity. Although he hated the Reich, he was never an obvious dissenter, and many of the highest officers of the Reich were his patients. Now he was being sent to a concentration camp for hard labor. She just prayed that he'd survive it. There was nothing she could do now except pray for him.

She spent the rest of the day in her cell, praying and thinking about him. He was a good man and didn't deserve what was happening to him. She couldn't imagine her life without him and was afraid she would never see him again.

When Thomas arrived at the police station, after he was dragged from his office, he was taken directly to the head of the SS in Berlin, and the Director of the Health Ministry was there waiting for him. Thomas Alexander's refusal to cooperate with the Aktion T4 program had gone straight to the top. There was no hiding from it now. They didn't attempt to convince him this time, they reminded him that it was a direct order from the Führer and asked him if he was willing to comply or defy the Führer. They reminded him that a refusal was punishable by death. It was a frightening reminder but it didn't change his mind. He was willing to go to his grave to protect the oath he had taken as a doctor, and he was not going to start murdering people to satisfy the Führer or anyone else. He was quiet and polite, and respectful, but also firm and clear. He was then led out of the room, and taken to a cell where four police officers beat him senseless and kicked him mercilessly with their boots. Then he was left in the dark for many hours while he drifted in and out of consciousness. He tried to keep track of how long he was there but every time he passed out, he had no idea how long it had taken him to wake up again, and his grandfather's gold watch, which he wore daily, was gone.

He thought it had been two days when he regained consciousness and was fully awake. There were no windows in his cell, and they had left him in darkness, so he had no idea what time of day it was. They hadn't fed him since he'd been there, but he wasn't hungry. His whole face was caked with dried blood, his lips were parched and cracked. His lower lip had split from one of the blows. He could tell that he had several broken ribs, he wasn't sure how many. He thought maybe four, which made it hard to breathe, and one eye was swollen shut. He took a careful inventory in the dark, and wondered what they were going to do now, possibly kill him, but strangely he wasn't afraid. He knew his response to them had been right. The only one he was worried about was Sophia. He didn't know if they would take revenge on her as well. He hoped not, and was grateful that she was no longer working with him and was living at the convent. In the end, that had been providential and might save her. It was too late for him to be saved now. He backed into a corner, and leaned against the wall, waiting to hear his fate at their hands, whether a firing squad or another beating.

It seemed like he had sat there for a long time when they opened the door, and shone a light in his eyes, which blinded him. "Stand up!" a male voice shouted at him. It took him several minutes to comply with the broken ribs. Finally he stood, but couldn't see beyond the light to who was shouting at him, or how many there were. "Move!" the voice shouted again, and Thomas wasn't sure in what direction but walked toward the light. Several hands grabbed him at once and shoved him, and he stumbled, and gasped from the pain in his ribs. He was pushed through a door into a brightly lit hallway, and his one good eye adjusted as he squinted, and followed two police officers, with two more behind him. He followed them through a maze of hallways, and down a flight of stairs into a garage. Police cars were lined up, and he was pushed into one of them. They hadn't bothered to handcuff him, as he wasn't an escape risk. They knew who he was, and he wouldn't get far if he tried. And he was in no condition to run, thanks to them.

He watched the city slide by, wondering where he was going and if he would ever see Berlin again. Or how much longer he'd be alive. Maybe they were taking him to one of the killing centers for Aktion T4 where they administered the lethal injections. He almost didn't care, except for Sophia. He didn't want to leave her alone in the dark world that Germany had become.

They drove just out of the city to an industrial freight station. There were freight cars lined up and waiting on the tracks. Thomas guessed that they were sending him to a concentration camp, he didn't know which one, and it didn't matter. They told him to get out of the car. He had no coat on and it was freezing, and to make matters worse, it started to snow.

A handful of soldiers walked over to them, carrying machine guns, and looked Thomas over with disgust.

"We have another passenger for you," one of the police officers said, "for the first-class carriage," and the soldier laughed.

"It's already full, but we'll find him a seat."

"When do you leave?"

"Tomorrow night. We have some stops to make on the way. We'll get there by morning." The police officers handed him a large envelope with Thomas's papers in it, and one of the soldiers slid open the door of the freight car and pushed Thomas with his gun. "Get in!" he told him roughly, which made his broken ribs shriek with pain again. Thomas gritted his teeth and did as he was told, and saw that there were two or three dozen men already crowded into the freight car. Some were wearing suits, and one was wearing a naval uniform of some kind. There were three priests. They didn't look like criminals, but they looked battered and tired. Thomas slid along the wall of the car, as the wind whipped in around them, and then let himself down into a sitting position. He couldn't have stood for much longer. And once the door closed again, some of the men talked to him. They were mostly professionals, some lawyers, a judge, two doctors. They had all defied Nazi regulations in some way and committed crimes against the state. It explained the police officer's comment about the first-class carriage, not so they could be treated better than the others, but perhaps because they had some designated use for them when they arrived at their destination. It was only an educated guess, and maybe a hope for survival.

"Do you know where we're going?" Thomas asked one of them after they had exchanged information for a few minutes.

"No, but I'm guessing Dachau. I heard the soldiers talking about traveling south. They have an infirmary there, with inmates as the doctors, so maybe they'll keep you alive," the man said to him. There was no food on the train, and Thomas could no longer remember the last time he'd eaten. There was a slop bucket full of excrement in a corner. The stench was strong, of bodies and fear and the slop bucket.

"How long have you been here?" Thomas asked them.

"Four days." Thomas nodded, and curled up in the cold, warmed by the bodies pressed next to him in the crowded car, and eventually fell asleep. He woke up in the dark to the sounds of hundreds of feet on gravel, men calling out, soldiers shouting, doors opening on the other freight cars, and Thomas realized that they were filling all the cars with men being deported to the concentration camps. There was grunting and calling and shouts of pain as the soldiers pressed them in, filling each car well past maximum capacity so the men could hardly breathe. Their car filled with enemies of the state from various professions really was a first-class carriage compared to what the others were enduring. Thomas could hear them moaning, and some crying out in despair, as the soldiers continued to fill the train through the night and the next day. And then finally at dusk, the day after he got there, the train started to move toward their destination. They still didn't know where they were going and wouldn't until they got there. They had been given no food or water. They were just cattle now, men whom the Reich treated like animals, and would slaughter if they wanted to. They were nothing now, and no one. Some of them had been respected, successful men, but they were just cargo now, on the train to hell.

Chapter 7

The train stopped three times that night to load more
men on the train. They kept shouting that they couldn't
breathe as the soldiers shoved them in, to bursting point.
The doors would close and the train would move on. And it
stopped for the fourth time in the morning. The men couldn't
see out of the train so they didn't know where they were.
The judge who had been on the train with Thomas said he
was sure they were near Munich and going to Dachau. It
made sense since Dachau was the main concentration camp
for political prisoners, which technically Thomas was. His
personal form of dissent had been to refuse to euthanize
people, particularly those who had nothing wrong with them.
It was also the main camp for Christian religious prisoners,
which explained the priests on the train. They had admitted

during the train ride to preaching against the Führer from the pulpit, and had been reported.

The train was moved to sidetracks to get it out of the way, and when the doors opened it looked like there were several thousand prisoners. Thomas wasn't sure how many, but a lot. When they got out of the freight cars, there were several bodies left on the floor, men who had died on the way, either crushed, or ill, or too old and frail to survive without food or water for several days. Thomas was still shivering in his suit and trying to adjust to the cold. They were forced to march for several miles until they reached the gates of the camp, with the words "Arbeit Macht Frei"—"Work Makes You Free"—on an archway. It was a labor camp, and only the fittest would survive.

There were thirty-two barracks, and several additional buildings, one of them being the infirmary, where Thomas assumed he'd be assigned. There was a prison block and two crematoria, and surrounding the camp a wall, a ditch, an electrified barbed wire fence, and seven guard towers surveying the camp. There was also an area set aside for executions by gallows or firing squad. Dachau was also used as a training center for SS concentration camp guards. It served multiple purposes.

The new arrivals were quickly marched to a barracks where they would surrender their clothes and any valuables and be given the regulation prison pajamas they would wear, which were even thinner than anything they were wearing. They were allowed to keep none of their own clothes, and they were given boots of any random size, whether they fit or not, boots that had been worn by others who might have died in them. Thomas tried not to think about it. They were forced to shower, deloused, had their heads shaved, and were assigned to their barracks. The camp was originally designed for five thousand men. There were more than twenty thousand there now. Bunks were in short supply, latrines and toilet facilities were inadequate. It was a shocking adjustment for those who had been living well and had had seemingly normal lives a few days before. But this was their reality now, for whatever crimes they had committed against the Reich.

After they'd gone through all the steps of the introduction process, they were given lunch, which consisted of a cup of watery soup, and a small ration of water. Thomas's stomach revolted immediately, and he threw up. He was told that breakfast would be watery ersatz coffee, and lunch and dinner were a cup of the soup he'd just thrown up. There was no more substantial food than that. They would have to survive on it, or die, which thousands did.

They received their job assignments after that. The laundry, the kitchen, the construction detail, the rock quarry,

113

the burial detail, the gravel pit, road construction, and the infirmary. Not surprisingly, Thomas was assigned to the infirmary, as was one of the other doctors who had arrived with him. The third one was assigned to road construction. He was older and very slight, and Thomas couldn't help wondering how long he'd survive.

When he saw the infirmary, Thomas was shocked by how inadequate the supplies were: a modest supply of bandages, medicine stores that were more empty than full, some rusty instruments and nowhere to sterilize them, beds without mattresses for the patients. Conditions were unclean, supplies almost nonexistent, and the few men lying on the beds there with a thin blanket over them looked like they were blazing with fever. One of the men showing Thomas around whispered, "They don't come here till they're nearly dead. If they see that you're sick before that, they shoot you, so nobody comes." Thomas nodded and saw the evidence in the men who were there, with glazed eyes and bad coughs. One of them was coughing blood into a filthy towel. It was light-years away from the conditions he was used to, but they would have to use what they had—his knowledge and skill, if nothing else. He was informed by the prisoner in charge of the infirmary that he would be an orderly for the first three months, assigned to cleaning the floors and bed pans, of which they only had two. He would be assigned medical tasks after they saw what he could do. He didn't argue with him. There was no point.

He didn't bother drinking the soup for dinner, and lay on his bunk with the two men he was sharing it with. He was too tired by then to care how cold he was, or how hungry, or how much his ribs hurt. He knew that if he ate now, his stomach would revolt again. He had gone too many days without eating to be able to eat normally all at once, but there was nothing normal to eat anyway. All the real food went to the officers and guards, not the prisoners. Every man he saw there was down to a skeleton weight with deep sunken eyes, and bones that protruded everywhere.

He went to sleep thinking of Sophia that night, and Theresa, when they were younger. He smiled thinking of his two little girls, and how sweet they had been. Thinking of them now would keep him alive, and he was hoping to bring some comfort to the sick, starving men he had seen that day. It was the only consolation for being there, and a useful purpose for his final days, which he suspected now these were.

Once Sophia's father was sent away, Christmas became a nonevent for her. Father Weiss was able to confirm through his sergeant friend, who checked with the records office, that Thomas had been sent to Dachau, near Munich, in southern Germany.

Only a year before, she had celebrated Christmas with Heinrich and Theresa. Their father had been working, as he always did, and Theresa had told her she was pregnant. In the past six months they had fled to Switzerland, their son had been born, Heinrich's parents were in a concentration camp somewhere, if they were even still alive, and her father was in Dachau, his beautiful hospital destroyed, their home burned to the ground. Sophia didn't walk past it anymore. It was too painful for her, the memories too strong, the losses too severe. No one knew why her father had been sent away, only that he had been considered an enemy of the Reich and arrested for treason.

She had lost her entire family except for a sister she might never see again. In a letter she was able to send Sophia, Theresa had sent a photograph of the baby. He looked just like her. And another photograph of the three of them in front of their splendid new home on the lake. Sophia had no home anymore, and everything she owned had burned in the fire set by the SS the day her father was arrested. Her whole life, as she'd known it all her life, had gone up in flames. It strengthened her ties to the Sisters of Mercy. They were the only family she had now.

Mother Regina had continued to turn a blind eye to the meetings Sophia went to. She didn't fully approve, but she knew that Sophia needed them. And she continued to disappear for a day or two here and there, working with Claus to spirit away children who had been hidden now for several years. Some of them had been infants when their parents were deported. They had lost whole families before they ever got to know them. And several times, danger had come too close, and the people who were hiding them had to send them on to someone else, which was where Sophia was useful to Claus. As a nun, she appeared to be innocent and trustworthy, and several times she had nearly gotten caught, and then miraculously the Fates had intervened and she had brought the children he entrusted to her to safety.

A deep friendship had formed between them in the last year. He was still sorry she had become a nun, but he felt like a brother to her. She had lost her sister and both parents, in a practical sense, but Claus was always there. She could rely on him. He admired her strength and her perseverance. Despite everything she had lost, she wasn't bitter, and she worked harder than ever to help others, working long hours at the hospital, like the other nuns, and was fearless and never turned a mission down when he asked her. She poured her heart and soul into everything she did, and never hesitated to risk herself, to the benefit of someone else. She admired Claus for what a good person he was. He never talked about it, but she knew that he had helped hundreds of children and many adults by then, just as he had Heinrich and Theresa.

She invited him to the convent for Sunday dinners, since she knew he had no family either, but he never came to see her anymore in case he was being watched. His missions had become more daring, and he didn't want to bring danger to her door by associating with her, if he ever got caught. Mother Regina thought it sensible of him.

Sophia worked late on Christmas Eve, all through the day on Christmas Day, and late into the night, with a child with pneumonia. His fever finally broke late that night. If she had followed the Health Ministry rules and reported him officially, they would have euthanized him rather than wasting medical treatment on a sick child who might not survive. The Nazis would rather kill him. Sophia had never reported a single patient to the Health Ministry, and all the children she nursed had survived.

She was glad when the holidays were over. They were too bittersweet to think about now. She was glad that the year had ended and a new one was beginning, and hoped that the war would end soon.

In Dachau, Thomas almost forgot that it was Christmas. He worked in the infirmary that night, tending to two men who had pneumonia, although he was only assigned to wash the floors and handle the laundry. They were all suffering from severe malnutrition, and the cold. In their weakened state, it was hard to fight off any disease, and pneumonia was a common cause of death among the prisoners. Thomas could tell that one of the men wouldn't make it through the night, and he sat with him so he wouldn't die alone. He stole some medicine for him that was reserved for the officers, to make him more comfortable. He didn't get caught, so he took some more for the other man. He was younger and stronger and Thomas thought there was a chance that he'd survive.

The sicker one died peacefully in his sleep that night, as Thomas watched him, and kept him warm with two extra blankets, one of them his own. And the younger one woke in the morning, free of fever, and smiled at Thomas. His name was Erik.

"Thank you, I think you saved me."

"No, you're just stronger than the miseries here. You're going to make it through and be free again one day. This won't go on forever," Thomas said, trying to give him hope as well as strength, and Erik's eyes looked bright and alive for a minute.

"Thank you. Are you a doctor?" he whispered, and Thomas nodded. "Mostly a surgeon, but I have nonsurgical patients too. Or I did. I have a hospital in Berlin." He didn't know that it no longer existed. "Where are you from?"

"Hamburg." Thomas didn't ask how he had wound up there. It no longer mattered. They were here.

"You're a good doctor, if you can cure people here."

"I didn't cure you," he said modestly, "I just kept you warm. Your own body broke the fever." Erik was young and wanted to live. Thomas could tell. Once the prisoners lost the will to live, they were dead within days or weeks. They had to be fighters against the forces against them. They had watched the other man carried out that morning, to be buried in a common pit with others who had died in the last few days, over Christmas.

Some of the men in the barracks had sung Christmas carols, and they had heard the guards and officers singing too. It was a strong sound which warmed them and made them sad at the same time. Their homes were so far away, and the war seemed endless, and the conditions they lived in were so cruel.

Erik left the hospital the next day and came back to visit Thomas in the infirmary from time to time, just to talk for a few minutes. He lived in the barracks next door to Thomas's, and sometimes they drank their watery morning coffee together. Erik worked on the construction detail, and was built for it. He was tall with broad shoulders and strong arms, but the rest of him looked like a skeleton. He had begun to lose his teeth from malnutrition. Two cups of thin soup per day was not a diet anyone could live on.

The two men were friends now, and Erik talked to him about things Thomas hadn't thought of in years, like soccer. Erik had a wife and two little girls in hiding in Hamburg. His wife was Jewish, which was how he had come to Dachau. He was arrested for being married to a non-Aryan and helping her escape. They didn't find her or his daughters, but they found him, and deported him, and sent him to Dachau. He said he didn't mind as long as his wife and children were safe. He didn't know if they still were, but he prayed for them every day. And he wanted to stay alive to see them again. Thomas wanted to see Theresa and Sophia, and his new grandson.

Sophia sat staring at the front page of the newspaper she saw at the hospital on New Year's Eve. There had been a huge bombing raid in London, by the Luftwaffe. The Reich was declaring it a major victory, as Sophia stared at a photograph of a mother holding her dead child in the rubble. The German news services had picked it up from the British press, and were bragging about dead children and lost homes. The attack had been brutal, and the article said that the Luftwaffe had brought England to its knees. And to what end? Everyone was suffering and no one was winning. She put the newspaper on the table where she'd found it and went back to work. She had more than enough to do during her long shifts.

Her life was a merry-go-round of activity now, which was

a blessing. Her chores at the convent, her nursing work at St. Joseph's, her meetings twice a week, and the occasional missions she did for Claus and his group, escorting a child, or hiding with one for a few hours until the next person could pick them up and get them to safety, until they had to be moved again.

By April, she hadn't heard from her father since he'd been deported. It had been five months, which seemed like an eternity to her. She didn't know if he was dead or alive. The one thing that comforted her was his usefulness as a doctor. It seemed unlikely that they would kill him if he was helpful to them, which he certainly was.

She had had two letters from Theresa, whose pregnancy was going well. She had friends in Zurich now, and loved it and their new home. The baby was due in July. She had been married for two years, with one child and another on the way. Sophia marveled at how normal her sister's life was when she read her letters. It was like there was no war at all. She said she worried about their father too, but Sophia could tell that none of it seemed real to her. In a way, Sophia envied her, but she couldn't see herself living that life, giving dinner parties, and playing with her son, waited on hand and foot, pampered by her husband, feeling safe in their beautiful home, and never doing anything useful for others. It was a very self-indulgent life.

Sophia lived every day hoping she had done enough, wishing she could do more, aching with worry and fear for her father, wishing she could save every child the war and the Nazis had orphaned, wanting to cure all the world's ills, and wishing she could make it a better world, with no idea how. She was twenty-two years old and had the weight of the world on her shoulders. She never got the chance anymore to do what young women did, flirting and wearing makeup and pretty dresses, dancing with a man she loved. That had always been Theresa's life and not hers. She didn't miss it, but she hated feeling so old, and worrying so much about ills she couldn't cure. She had read some of Edith Stein's writing and noticed that she felt the same way. However much of herself she gave, Sophia always felt it wasn't enough, and wished she could give more.

In May she took her vows as a novice. She would still have to take her final vows one day, the ultimate commitment of her life to Christ as a nun. But the novitiate was her first big step into the church as an adult, a grown-up choice she had made and believed in. She wore the full veil of the order with her habit now, over her starched white coif, instead of the shorter veil of a postulant. Her habit reached the floor, and she wore a gold wedding band on her right hand, as a sign of her commitment. She was bursting with excitement and pride at the mass where she and three other postulants became novices. They celebrated at lunch afterward. Mother Regina poured each of the nuns a small glass of wine, and it was very festive.

In May, warmer weather had finally reached southern Germany. Even in the camp, it looked like spring. A team of prisoners had been assigned to plant flowers around the Kommandant's house. There was a vegetable garden, planted for the officers, and the prisoners stole a carrot, an onion, or a tomato, or whatever they could. The penalty for doing so was death, but some risked it anyway, and died with their prize in their hand when they were shot.

Even though the days were sunny, Thomas had been coughing for months. The cough seemed to grow more severe as the weather got warmer and he got thinner. He had been sharing his meager food rations with those he felt needed them more. He was still an orderly in the infirmary, but the other prisoner-doctors asked his advice, and recognized that he was more experienced than they were. He knew a great deal about the diseases that plagued them, although most of them were due to malnutrition, exhaustion, unhealthy conditions, and the severe beatings that the prisoners endured. He had set bones several times, and convinced the guards to let him make casts, saying that the prisoners could still work with a cast on. Their bones had gotten brittle from lack of food. Thomas was known by many of the prisoners, and even respected by the guards. One of them had even consulted him in secret for a problem his wife was having at home. And Thomas's advice, without even examining her, had saved her. He had correctly guessed what the problem was, although her own physician had missed it. She recovered within weeks after Thomas told the guard what medication she should ask for. She did, and it worked. The guard had brought Thomas a piece of meat and a loaf of bread in thanks. Thomas had quietly given them to someone else he thought needed it more.

His cough persisted all through May into June, and he started running a fever at night, but didn't report it to anyone. There was nothing they would do anyway, except shoot him. One prisoner more or less didn't matter to them. At first he thought he might have typhus, which had been epidemic in several other camps, according to the guards. Or maybe tuberculosis. But finally he realized that his body was just giving out. Seven months in Dachau had taken a brutal toll. He began coughing blood and could no longer keep food down. He hid the symptoms from everyone, even his bunkmates. He wanted to write to Sophia and Theresa but knew the letters would never reach them. He loved them so much more than he had ever been able to tell them when he was so busy and had so much to do.

He sat in the sunshine for a few minutes before dinner that night, and a guard hit him with the butt of his rifle and told him to get back to work. He could feel a rib break when the guard hit him. The pain was severe, worse than usual. He gave his ration of soup to someone else and went to bed as soon as it was allowed. He was coughing blood when he fell asleep, and smiled thinking of his daughters. Beautiful Theresa, and so serious Sophia, his two beauties, and Monika. He could feel her beckoning to him, and he wanted to see her again. And with a last cough and a rush of blood onto his bed, he held out a hand to her, and went to join her.

His bunkmates found him an hour later, in a pool of blood in their bed. One of the other doctors suspected that a broken rib had punctured his lung, or maybe he had just died of starvation. Through all seven months in Dachau, Thomas had been kind and generous to everyone, and polite to the guards no matter how badly he was treated. The men in his barracks cried when they saw him, but he looked peaceful. They wrapped him in a blanket one of them gave up for him, and they carried him to the pile of bodies waiting to be buried the next day. He was just one more. Erik stood near, watching him, with tears rolling down his cheeks. "Goodbye, my friend," he said, and walked away.

Only the Brave

They reported his death to one of the guards, and he wrote down Thomas's number to report it to the Records Office. They kept thorough notes on all the prisoners who died. Erik and the others knew that he would be remembered for as long as they lived, however long that was, which none of them knew. But at least Thomas was free now.

Chapter 8

Theresa's baby was born in July, on schedule this time, another boy. He was smaller than Thomas had been, and the birth went quickly. She was holding him in her arms the first time Heinrich saw him, and he looked at his wife with a proud smile.

"You're getting good at this," he praised her, and he had a handsome son. Theresa was only twenty years old, and Heinrich had just turned thirty. They named the baby Wilhelm after Heinrich's father.

"Next time, I want a girl," she pouted prettily, and he put a sapphire bracelet on her wrist. Bernhard and Ursula came to visit her the next day, with gifts for the baby, a silver cup and spoon, and a teddy bear. Theresa was already up and walking around her hospital room and wanted to go home.

The baby nurse was holding the baby, and Theresa's hairdresser had come to do her hair. Heinrich couldn't wait until she could go out again and they could see their friends. Her room was full of flowers from those who had heard the good news.

She wrote to Sophia from the hospital, and the letter arrived at the convent in August, after it passed the censors, but there was nothing objectionable in it. It was all about the baby, and the birth, and Heinrich. Theresa still sounded like a little girl to Sophia, who smiled when she read the letter. She existed in another universe from Sophia, and always had, but more so now, married to a wealthy man. He still had no news of his parents' whereabouts. His lawyer in Zurich had told him that there was no way to find out where and how they were until after the war. But it had begun to seem less and less likely that they had survived. Life in the camps was too hard for people their age. Sophia and Theresa were in the same situation, unable to find out anything about their father, although they at least knew to which camp he'd been sent. Heinrich didn't even know that.

Sophia was busy at the convent and the hospital in September, and time seemed to be rushing past in her daily life with so many chores and so much to do. But the war news had been dragging, nothing seemed to change, just more countries falling into the Nazis' hands.

Greece and Yugoslavia had surrendered to the Germans in April. The Luftwaffe had bombed London mercilessly in May. The British took revenge on Hamburg the next day. The German Navy had sunk the British ship HMS *Hood,* and three days later, the British Navy had sunk the *Bismarck,* the Germans' largest battleship. At home in Germany, Hitler's generals, led by Göring, were preparing the Final Solution, to eradicate all Jews from the face of the earth. But in a broader sense, there was more happening abroad than at home.

The Jewish children who had escaped the first roundups had been in hiding for two or three years by then. It had been two years since war was declared. Claus was busier helping to blow up munitions depots and supply trains than moving hidden children around Germany. He had been missing meetings lately, engaged in dissident activities, away from Berlin. Sophia still attended the meetings faithfully, and she missed seeing him when he wasn't there.

In October, the German army was active on the Russian Front, advancing on Moscow, and the Russians were a formidable opponent. The British were refusing to be defeated by Hitler, protecting their island with courage and determination. There was a lot to keep track of in the world, and Sophia tried to stay well informed. The news in Germany was increasingly depressing, with concentration camps overflowing and Jews exterminated in massive numbers whenever possible.

She saw Claus at a meeting in October. He looked tired and thinner, and she hadn't seen him in two weeks.

"Where have you been?" she asked in a whisper when he sat down next to her. She noticed that his fingertips were blackened, and guessed that he'd been working with explosives.

"Don't ask," he whispered back. He looked distracted at the meeting, but there was nothing new to hear. They were talking about even more restrictive laws for the Jews, and the gas chambers at Auschwitz. The Führer and his generals were obsessed with his plan, called "the Final Solution," to obliterate all Jews from the planet, and they were confident they could achieve it.

Claus followed her out when they left the meeting and stopped walking for a minute. "I hate to do this, Sophia, but can I ask you a favor? I have a kid I've moved four times in six months. He has no family and we're all he's got. The neighbors are nosy everywhere I've put him. He's seven years old, and he's been in hiding for three years. I got a call tonight, and I have to move him. But I need to be in Wiesbaden tomorrow, I'll be driving tonight."

"Where is he?" He hadn't asked her for a while.

"Right here in the city, not far from you. If you move him for me tonight, I'll take him to Munich to a long-term situation when I get back. I need to get him to a friend now, who will keep him for me. She has three kids, he'll get lost in the crowd, and she'll keep him out of sight."

"Okay, where is he?" Sophia asked again. He wrote down the address in a simple code they used, and she shoved the piece of paper in her pocket. He looked serious when he said goodbye to her. "What are you up to?" she asked him. "You look worried." She knew him well after years of friendship.

"I've been doing some big stuff lately. High-stake gains, big wins, a little stick in the wheels of the SS, but riskier than usual."

"Don't do anything too crazy," she warned him.

"If I don't, who will?" he asked seriously. "We all have to be a little crazy to stop them, or they'll win in the end." It was a daunting thought, and she knew he was willing to risk his life for what he believed in.

"Just be sure you come back."

"Don't worry, and if I don't get back, my friend will take the boy to Munich. She has the details and the contact. I just have to get him to her."

"I'll take care of it," Sophia promised. She went back to the convent then, intending to slip out again that night. The person who had the boy was expecting her at ten o'clock. She didn't have far to go with him, once the streets were empty and there were fewer people around, but with patrols, nothing was as simple as it looked.

She didn't know why, but she decided not to wear her habit that night. A nun riding around on a bicycle at ten o'clock would look more suspicious than a young woman. She kept a set of black clothes in a small suitcase under her bed for missions like this one. She slipped into black trousers, a black sweater, and a black jacket. The nights weren't too cold yet, but it was chilly. She was going to take one of the nuns' bicycles and say the boy was her brother if she got stopped. Her official papers were still in her own name, not her religious name, which was convenient in a case like this.

No one stopped her when she left the convent. All the lights were out, and she didn't see Mother Regina watching her from an upstairs window with a worried frown. She could guess what Sophia was doing, and she said a prayer for her as she saw the bike disappear down the street, with no lights on it, and the slim figure in black fading into the night.

The woman who opened the door to Sophia at the address Claus had given her looked elderly and kind, like an ordinary grandmother. The boy had been with her for a few weeks, but she was afraid her neighbors were watching her, and she didn't want to risk the child. She had no children and wasn't worried about herself. She introduced Josef to Sophia, and he gave the woman a fierce hug before he left and said he would come back to stay with her after the war. He thanked her for the cookies she had made him. She had tears in her eyes and hugged him tight. He was nicely dressed and was taking nothing with him, except a small teddy bear named Fred tucked into his jacket.

The two women exchanged a serious look, and Sophia put him on the bike in front of her so he wouldn't slip off the back. She stood up to pedal and he had the seat. They didn't speak, and she chose the streets carefully, aware of where the main patrols usually were. It took them fifteen minutes to get to the address Claus had given her. They slipped into a garage as prearranged. The woman was waiting for them, and Josef disappeared as soon as he thanked her. And Sophia took off again, mission accomplished. Terrifying but easy. Nothing was really easy anymore. There was risk in everything.

She was almost back at the convent when a police car with its light off came out of nowhere and stopped her. The officer who got out of the car asked to see her papers, which were in order, and she handed them to him. She was sorry now she hadn't worn her habit, but she didn't want to attract attention or be hampered by it on the bike and could move more freely without it. He looked carefully at her papers to make sure she wasn't a Jew, and asked where she'd been.

She said she'd gone to see a sick friend. He handed the papers back to her with a suspicious look, but he didn't stop her, and she could hear them following her at a distance. She didn't know whether to go back to the convent or not. He might find that even more suspicious, and if she said she was a nun, what was she doing out of her habit? She decided to go back anyway, as it was safer than riding around aimlessly on the bike. She drove the bicycle into the convent garage, left it there, let herself into the house with her key, hurried upstairs to her cell, and quickly put away the clothes she'd been wearing and put on her convent nightgown. She lay in bed for a long time, wide-awake with her heart pounding, but nothing happened, and after a while she fell asleep.

She got up with the other nuns in the morning, dressed, and went to Matins, their first round of communal prayers for the day. After breakfast, she was helping to clean up the kitchen when a police car pulled up in front of the convent. One of the sisters opened the door, and two SS officers asked to see the Mother Superior.

Mother Regina gave Sophia a quick questioning look when she walked into the kitchen, and Sophia shook her head, to let her know nothing had happened the night before. She had been stopped, which she couldn't say with the other nuns around. But the officers had let her go.

Mother Regina was calm and pleasant when she spoke to the officers in her office. One of them said that a young woman had been seen riding around the neighborhood the night before, after ten o'clock, and had let herself into the convent. He wanted to know if she was aware of it, who the woman was and if she lived there.

"Probably one of our postulants," Mother Regina said with a smile. "They're very young. They're not part of the order yet, and they're not used to our restrictive lifestyle. And some of them don't make it much further."

"Her name was Sophia Alexander," the officer said, consulting a small notebook he took from his pocket. "Is she a postulant?" he asked pointedly.

"A novice, just one step further. And a very dedicated nurse," the Superior said, vouching for her, as Sophia waited nervously in the kitchen. "She may have had a difficult case at the hospital yesterday and needed some air. It's irregular, I'll admit, but these are young women, and troubling times. I'll speak to her and see that she doesn't wander around late again. I apologize, Captain."

"May we speak to her?" he said, not easily diverted.

"Of course. She hasn't left for the hospital yet." She went to the kitchen and whispered quickly to Sophia. "What happened last night? I saw you leave."

"I got stopped by a patrol on the way back. I was alone,

they never saw the boy. But it was late, and I was in street clothes. I thought it would be safer." Mother Regina nodded.

"They want to talk to you. Stay calm," she warned her. Sophia followed her to her office, looking serious and contrite. The SS officers seemed surprised to see her in her habit. She looked very dignified.

"What were you doing out so late last night?" the captain asked her as soon as she sat down.

"I was going to see a friend. I didn't realize how late it was, and when I did, I turned back."

"Were you wearing your habit?" he challenged her.

"No, I wasn't."

"Why not?"

"Sometimes I don't, if I go to see a friend," she said, looking apologetically at the Superior, who nodded. "I haven't taken final vows yet. And it's hard to ride a bike in a habit."

"Are you any relation to Thomas Alexander?" the captain asked her, his voice harsh, and Sophia was startled by the question.

"He's my father," she said softly. He had thrown her off balance with the question.

"I'm sure you're aware that he was arrested for treason against the Reich, sentenced to hard labor, and sent to Dachau."

"Yes, I am," she said, looking devastated, which was genuine.

"And your sister and her husband fled Germany to avoid

arrest. He's a Jew. His parents were deported." He had done his homework. "You have a colorful family, Miss Alexander. And what about you? Are you a nun or simply masquerading as one, and a criminal like the rest of your family, committing crimes against the Reich?"

"No, sir, and I am a nun, and a nurse." He stood up then, and so did Mother Regina.

"I can vouch for Sister Anne wholeheartedly. I've known her since she was a young girl, before she came to us to enter the order."

"I'm sure a nun's habit is an excellent disguise for any criminal. Traitors come in all shapes and guises these days, even young women dressed up as nuns. Heil Hitler!" he said, and saluted them both. They returned the salute, and Mother Regina escorted him to the door. "We'll be back," he said ominously, and Sophia was shaking after he left.

"Oh goodness, Mother, I don't want to cause you any trouble."

"You won't, but you can't go out again like that," she said sternly. "It's too dangerous for you, and for us. I'm sure you'll get out of it this time, but you can't engage in secret activities, or go to the meetings anymore. They might follow you back here." Sophia nodded, knowing that the Mother Superior was right, and that she had been lucky so far, for three years.

She was about to leave for work when there was a call on the convent line, someone asking for Sophia. She almost panicked when Mother Regina told her, and she took the call in the Superior's office. Sophia didn't recognize the voice and the caller didn't give a name. It was a woman, and she was crying.

"I thought you'd want to know. Claus was killed last night. He was setting explosives on some train tracks. They saw him and shot him. He always told me to call you if anything happened. I'm sorry," the caller said, sobbing.

"So am I," Sophia said, her eyes full of tears, and she hung up then. The other woman was already off the line. Beautiful, sweet Claus who had taken Theresa to safety was gone. He had died trying to stop the Nazis one more time from destroying the country he loved. And he had been too brave for his own good. "My friend Claus died last night," Sophia said to Mother Regina after she hung up.

"Nowhere is safe anymore. Everything and everyone is dangerous," Mother Regina said. "You have to be satisfied with your life in the convent now, or you'll be the next one who's killed, or one of the children you transport." Sophia nodded, unable to speak as she thought of Claus. They might have been lovers if she hadn't entered the convent. Perhaps the woman on the phone was his lover. He never talked to her about women, and he had always been a little bit in love with her, or maybe a lot, while she loved him as a brother and a friend. It was a huge loss. Another one. The war had cost them so many friends and loved ones.

She went to work then with a heavy heart, worked all day, thinking of Claus, and came straight back to the convent afterward on the bus. When she got there, the same SS officers were waiting for her in Mother Regina's office. The Superior looked pale when Sophia walked into her office after she summoned her. The other nuns looked frightened.

"We have considered your case, and your family history," the captain said coldly. "Your sister ran away, rather than facing her crime of marrying a Jew, and he escaped with her. Your father refused a direct order from the Führer and in doing so, committed treason, and is now an incarcerated criminal. And what will you do? Will you run too, and go to your sister, wherever she is? Switzerland, probably," he guessed accurately, "where her husband must have been hiding money, defrauding the Reich by doing so. Her father-in-law was a Jew too. He and his wife died in Sachsenhausen, executed two days after they got there. Your entire family are criminals, Miss Alexander, and I believe you are too. Your nun's habit doesn't fool me. I am certain you're an enemy of the Reich, like your father and sister. You're under arrest, before you can continue any subversive activity you may be engaged in. You belong with other political criminals like you. We have places for people like you now, not behind convent walls. We have stronger walls to keep you from harming the Reich. You are coming with us." Sophia looked shocked and Mother Regina more so. She tried to object but the SS captain wouldn't listen. He was convinced of Sophia's guilt.

Sophia knew he wasn't wrong. He just didn't know what she'd done for the past three years, helping to hide Jewish children and escorting them to safety. Whatever punishment they meted out to her now, it would have been more severe if they knew the truth. She was being punished now by association, for her sister's flight, for Heinrich being a quarter Jewish, and for her father's alleged treason, which she still didn't believe, and never would. In fact, her crime was worse than the others, and she had done it many, many times in the past three years, with and without Claus and other dissidents. She had been terrified when the captain started speaking, but she wasn't afraid now. In her heart of hearts, she knew how many times she had broken their laws, which were a crime against humanity. Hers were a crime against a madman who had seized the country and was destroying it, and killing thousands of people, even children.

Sophia stood silent and tall, as the junior officer grabbed her arm and led her from the room in her habit. Tears ran down Mother Regina's cheeks. She could only imagine what they would do to Sophia now. The other nuns had gathered in the hall, worried, and they saw Sophia go with the two SS officers, to an unknown fate, but one she was willing to endure. She had no regrets about a single child she had saved, even if they didn't know about them. She did, and was proud of every child she had taken to safety, and she would do it again if she could. She looked back once at Mother Regina and the other nuns before she left, and she smiled.

"I'll be back," she said quietly. One of the nuns said later that Sophia looked like a saint.

"God bless you and keep you," Mother Regina said as the door closed behind her, and a minute later, they drove Sophia away.

All the nuns could do now was pray for her, that she'd survive whatever punishment they devised. All the officers could prove was that she had been out late at night. She had committed no crime that they knew of. But nowadays they shot and killed people for less. People were arrested and tortured for mere suspicions without proof. And there were Jews who had been killed for far less, even for sport, and police and soldiers were encouraged to do so. One fewer Jew was a gift to the Reich and the Fatherland. Sophia wasn't Jewish any more than her father had been a traitor, but she hated everything the Reich stood for, and was willing to die trying to stop them from harming even one more human being.

She thought of Claus as they pushed her into the car and locked the doors, and whatever he had done on the train tracks, he had been willing to die too, ever since it all started. For Sophia, it had been a decision, like the one to embrace the religious life. She couldn't stem the tides of history, or stop them, but she could commit herself heart and soul to do whatever she could, one human being at a time. And if they killed her, her life would have served a purpose. It was the only way to change an ugly, dangerous world—one step, one human being, one life at a time.

Chapter 9

They took Sophia to police headquarters for further interrogation, to see what they could get out of her. They questioned her for four hours, relentlessly, with three SS officers facing her, and circling her ominously. Then they tore off her habit, and left her naked in a freezing cold stone cell, with a bucket of urine and excrement in the corner, and on the floor as well. The cell smelled foul and she was shivering. She kept moving to try and stay warm. They had gotten nothing from her. She stuck to her other story that she had gone to see a friend, and turned back when she realized how late it was. Their insistence in questioning her assured her that they knew nothing about her clandestine activities, and they never mentioned Claus. She said repeatedly that she was a real nun, a novice, even though she had broken the rules and gone out late at night to see a friend. They never asked who the friend was, and didn't seem to care. There were no Jews left in the neighborhood. They had combed it thoroughly for the past three years, and they were certain there were none left, even in hiding.

Random searches and tearing the residents' houses apart had exposed everyone concealed in attics and cellars, storage areas, closets and secret rooms and passageways. Whole families had been sheltered by neighbors who had been punished for it, and a team had gone to the convent that afternoon and found nothing. They had searched Sophia's belongings thoroughly. There was no evidence, but their suspicions were strong. She was just the kind of young traitor who would try to undermine them, and they didn't need more than suspicion to incarcerate her and punish her and send her to a labor camp. Her fate was sealed now, and she knew it, but if this was God's plan for her, she was willing to endure it. It was what Edith Stein had said in her writings as well. It was their sacrifice to honor God, and they embraced it willingly, without hesitation.

Sophia said repeatedly in the interrogation by the SS that she had committed no crime. They didn't believe her and tried to trip her up and intimidate her. The more she resisted and refused to be cowed by them, the angrier they got and the hungrier to punish her for whatever she wasn't admitting.

They didn't believe in her innocence for a minute—she was too calm, too sure, too brave, especially for such a young woman, unless she was burning for a cause she didn't voice. They could smell a zealot for a holy cause from a mile away, whatever she said. And she would die for it if they chose. It was up to them now.

They sent two soldiers in to beat her and torture her as she waited naked in her cell. Had she been wearing her habit, it might have intimidated them, but naked she was just another woman, another criminal. She wondered if they were going to rape her, and tried to brace herself mentally for it, but they didn't. They slapped her hard and punched her and pulled her hair. They slammed her head into the wall until it bled and punched her in the face and kicked her. She was covered with blood when they left, but she was conscious, and she lay on the cold floor and drifted into unconsciousness, thinking of her father and what he must have endured, and Claus, who must have died quickly when he was shot. He had been willing to die to save others and honor the country he loved, and so was she.

She woke up when she was kicked again, and they threw cold water on her to bring her back to consciousness.

"Get up!" an SS matron said harshly. Sophia had no idea how long she'd been unconscious, and now she was wet as well as cold. The matron threw some clothes at her that they had taken from others when they were arrested, and she told Sophia to put them on. The skirt was too big and too short since she was tall and slim. There was a blouse that was dirty and smelled of sweat, and a pair of shoes that were too big. Sophia had no idea where she was going and didn't ask if she was to be interrogated again, or tortured, or moved to another place. It didn't matter now. Her body belonged to them, but they would never have her mind or her heart or soul. She knew the Sisters of Mercy would be praying for her.

Two matrons escorted her from the room, and she went quietly. She knew her hair was in disarray and caked with blood, but it was short now to wear under her veil. There was blood on her face and on her legs. The water had washed off some of it but not all. They took her to a locked area, and there was a truck standing by, with other women in it and guards standing around. They led her to it and pushed her in. There were a dozen other women in the small police truck, sitting on the floor, in the same condition she was in, some even worse, with teeth missing from the beating, one with a broken nose. Some of them said nothing, but they nodded as she got in. There was no way to tell who or what they were now, or who they had been. They were the victims of the Nazis, at their mercy now. Sophia wondered if they were being taken to one of the killing centers she had heard about. If so, it would be simple and fast, by lethal injection or gas. She knew that some patients from St. Joseph's had been sent there.

They sat in the truck for another hour, and two more women were pushed in, and those already there moved over to make room for them. One of the women had passed out, and another one had vomited. Then finally, the doors were locked, and they drove away. The windows were blackened so the women couldn't see where they were going, and most of them didn't talk. A few whispered to each other. One of them was crying about her children, who had been taken away separately. And one was visibly pregnant.

Sophia sat quietly and could feel all of her wounds and bruises during what she guessed was a two-hour drive, until finally they stopped, the doors were pulled open, and they were told to get out by soldiers training guns on them. They had arrived at an enormous encampment with a staggering number of barracks and buildings. There was a high wall with electrified barbed wire surrounding the whole camp. Other trucks had arrived at the same time, and about a hundred women were pushed toward the reception center, where their heads were shaved and they were showered, deloused, and given the camp pajamas. A colored triangle was roughly sewn onto Sophia's prison pajamas—there were red, purple, green, yellow, and black ones to indicate political prisoners, Jews, Jehovah's Witnesses, "asocials," and common criminals who had broken Nazi laws. Sophia was designated in the last category for breaking Nazi laws, so her triangle was green. Others had a letter in the center of their triangle to indicate their nationality. Since she was German, she had no letter in the green triangle. Each nationality had a letter, each category of criminal a different colored triangle. Everything was systematic and relatively well organized, as the women were shuffled from one part of the reception center to another.

"Where are we?" Sophia asked quietly of the female guard who handed her the prison uniform, which were thin pajamas.

"Ravensbrück," she said. "You're here to work. You look strong," she said. Sophia had heard that it was the largest camp for women in the Reich, fifty miles outside Berlin. It had been open for two years, mostly for political prisoners, and they had built a smaller men's camp nearby that year. Sophia learned from the guard who gave her the green triangle that there were ten thousand women there, although it had been built for six. And when they were finally taken to their barracks, she discovered that each barracks had been built to house two hundred and fifty women and now housed close to two thousand. They slept three and four to a bunk, with many on the floor with no bed or blankets at all. There were three toilets for the use of each five hundred women, with no doors on them. The level of humiliation and degradation and overcrowding was so great that no one seemed to care about doors on the latrines. The day began with roll call at four A.M. Weak ersatz coffee followed, and then work, with no breakfast. Lunch was watery soup served at noon in the barracks, and dinner was the same soup again. Sunday was their day off from hard labor. Some of the women were assigned to factories with barracks onsite, but most worked at the camp. Beatings were used as punishment and there was a prison block for those who resisted or didn't comply. The guards used dogs to attack the prisoners when they felt like it. Disease was rampant, often from the water, which another prisoner told Sophia to beware of. There was a camp doctor whom the prisoners never saw until they were nearly dead. And another prisoner whispered to her, when she saw the pregnant young woman among the new arrivals, that babies born there were killed at birth, or shortly after. It was another vision of hell.

Sophia was assigned to a bunk with three women already in it. They had just returned from work and were crowded together on the thin mattress talking softly. One of them smiled when Sophia approached.

"Welcome to the Ritz," a redheaded woman with a French accent said. "Don't worry, we'll make room. You don't get fat here. We all fit, and we get more blankets like this, with four to a bed." She seemed good-humored and Sophia guessed

151

that she was pretty when she was clean, had had enough to eat, and hadn't lost several teeth. She guessed her to be about forty. She learned later that she was twenty-three, a year older than Sophia.

The other two were German women. All were categorized as common criminals according to Nazi law, having committed minor offenses. The Frenchwoman had been married to a Jewish musician. She was a singer and had come from France to marry him, her only crime. He was in Auschwitz, and her name was Josephine, Jo. The other two were Hedwig, called Hedi, a dark-haired thirty-year-old artist from Berlin who had been making and distributing posters maligning Hitler and the Reich, and Brigitte, a pretty blonde of twenty-five who had been a model, accused of prostitution for sleeping with a Jewish doctor. Tamar, on the bunk below, was a college professor from Cologne, accused of treason for not following the teachings of the Reich. None were criminals any more than Sophia was, but all were accused of anti-Nazi crimes. Tamar was older than the others, who were in their twenties but looked much older now. She had snow-white hair, was forty-four, a widow, and had a son who had been in law school when she was arrested. He had been arrested too, and she didn't know where he was now, another camp, possibly Dachau, but she wasn't sure. There was no news or correspondence between camps, only word of mouth from new prisoners arriving from other camps, often the bearers of bad news. But so far, Tamar thought her son was still alive. He was young and strong. Sophia thought she didn't look well, and she had a noticeable wracking cough that was echoed by others in the barracks. The other women were skeletons, but their spirits seemed hardy, given the circumstances. It was what kept them alive, despite malnutrition, hardship, and disease.

"And you?" Hedi asked her. They were curious about new arrivals.

"My father is a doctor, he was arrested for treason, his hospital destroyed, and sent to Dachau. My sister fled to Switzerland with her husband, who is a quarter Jewish. And I was out late at night a few days ago, and they think I was doing something I shouldn't, but they haven't said what. I'm a nurse." She hesitated for a beat and then added, "And a nun."

"You're a nun?" Jo said, shocked. She had freckles which stood out on her face now, she was so pale. "And they put you in here?"

"Yes. Guilt by association, as the daughter of a traitor."

"Your sister is lucky she got out," Brigitte said. She was the model accused of prostitution for her affair with a Jewish doctor. "How did she get to Switzerland?"

"She walked, six and a half months pregnant. I went with her to the border, but I came back. I didn't want to leave my father alone. That was before he got arrested. So I went back to Berlin, and then I entered the convent."

The others were intrigued by Sophia and the fact that her religious status hadn't protected her.

"There are a lot of religious prisoners here," Tamar said, and then had a coughing fit. It sounded like bronchitis to Sophia. A lot of people around them were coughing.

"I would hate to be a nun. No makeup, no high heels, no men, no dancing," Jo said, and they all laughed.

"I was out without my habit, which made it worse. I'm still a novice, I haven't taken my final vows. I've been in the order for a year and a half."

"And you like it?" Hedi asked her. All of them were talkative and intrigued by her. Tamar was a little less so because she seemed sick.

"I do. It's the right choice for me. I like living in community with other women."

"Then you'll love it here," Jo said. "It's just like the convent, except for the beatings and the dogs. Be careful of the dogs. They use them to terrify us. I hate dogs."

Sophia had missed dinner by the time she arrived, but the warm welcome she got from her bunkmates and Tamar on the bunk below made it less terrifying, and they gave her all the information they could about what to be careful of, which guards were the most dangerous, and which the most lenient, how to get to the toilets before everyone else, which meant giving up an hour's sleep and getting on line at three instead of four A.M. They tried to guess what jobs she'd be assigned to. Tamar had a lucky job, doing office work, entering information about the inmates in ledgers. Jo was on a construction crew, paving roads with twelve other women. Hedwig worked in the laundry, and Brigitte cleaned latrines.

"Maybe you'll get an office job," Brigitte said hopefully, trying to encourage her. She had no job to go back to if they survived. To get her to give up her Jewish doctor boyfriend, they had burned her face with cigarettes to torture her, and left scars, which ended her career as a model. But so had the lack of food, harsh treatment, and diseases that were rampant in the camp. Sophia could see on their faces and in their eyes what they had been through, and was stunned by the strength of their spirit, and their support of each other. And right from her first day there, Sophia had four friends.

The days were as long and hard as her bunkmates had warned her, and as she had expected. Their shared information made life easier, but the hardships were as severe as they and others told her. Sophia was assigned to the tailor shop, which made the prison uniforms, and uniforms for the SS. Ravensbrück also received most of the confiscated luxury items, like fur coats and fancy clothes confiscated from Jews in Berlin and neighboring towns, which were then passed on to officers' wives if they wished them. They had to be checked and repaired if necessary, before being sent back to Berlin.

Sophia had no great needlework skills, and making the SS officers' uniforms was painstaking work. She worked a fourteen- or fifteen-hour day and often missed her evening meal of soup, while she tried to finish a uniform in fabrics that were stiff and hard to work with. And her supervisors were exacting and demanding and critical, and often made her start again.

Other women were lent to factories who hired slave labor from the camp. They frequently lived in barracks outside the camp near the factories, but punishments were harsher there to prevent escapes. One of the factories made electrical components for rockets. And some of the older women knitted sweaters and warm scarves for the army. Everyone had a job, and everyone worked hard with no gratitude or praise. Brigitte was elated when she got transferred to a job in the kitchen washing dishes after a year of cleaning latrines.

As hard as they were, their jobs helped pass the time from one day to the next. They had Sunday off, which most of them spent lying on their bunks, getting ready for another week of forced labor, and some of them slept all day, and didn't have the strength to do anything else.

Sophia had just finished an SS uniform with relief after three unsuccessful attempts, for an officer in the records office where Tamar worked. He had come for a fitting, and it still hadn't fit him properly the last time he tried it, and she hoped it would this time. She had pricked her fingers dozens of times, and the sewing machines they used were antiquated. It was the week before Christmas, and she knew he needed it for the Officers' Dinner in two days.

He arrived to pick it up at the end of the day, and she knew she'd miss the evening meal of watery soup if she stayed, but she had to know if she got it right this time, or if she'd have to work all night to correct it. So she waited, and he showed up minutes before the tailor shop closed. His name was Hans Mahler, and he was a young lieutenant who looked like a poster for Nazi Youth. He was tall, blond, and would have been movie-star handsome if he hadn't been a Nazi. Knowing what he represented and the punishments he undoubtedly delivered, Sophia was disgusted by him. But she was unfailingly respectful when she saw him.

"Good evening," he said politely, "I'm sorry I'm late. My commanding officer kept me at the office too long, and I couldn't leave." It was the kind of thing you'd say to a friend, not a slave.

"It's fine," she said. She always had the feeling that he was checking her over, and his deep blue eyes bore through her.

She kept her gaze down and handed him the uniform on a hanger. "I hope I got it right this time."

"I'm sure you did, Fräulein." The courteous greeting surprised her.

"I'm not much of a seamstress," she admitted with a smile intended to apologize for her clumsiness, not to woo him.

"Should I try it?" he asked, and she nodded.

"I think you'd better, to make sure it fits." She had made the shoulders too tight the first time, and the pants too big and too short the second. Making a uniform was not simple.

She pointed to a little curtained-off area where he could put it on, and he took it with him, and then pulled back the curtain with a broad smile after he tried it.

"It's perfect! Even the pants are right this time." And she could see it herself. He looked strikingly handsome, and the uniform made him look even more so, much as she hated to admit it. It fit him perfectly, and he approached her with a grateful look and lowered his voice. "I look better than Hitler!" he said, and she laughed and meant it.

"That's not hard. You look better than a movie star. Your commanding officer will be impressed."

"He's a beast," he lowered his voice further. "He treats me like one of the prisoners," he said, and she wondered if he actually knew what that felt like, between the dogs and the beatings and no solid food.

"I hope not," she said to be kind. "I'm sure he'll give you a promotion when he sees the suit."

"He doesn't like me," he shared with her. "He's kind of bad-looking, and he has a bad scar on his face from the last war. He hates anyone younger and better-looking than he is." The lieutenant seemed very young and innocent as he confided in her.

"Just be nice to him, even if he's not. And compliment him on something, how well he does his job, or something you like about him." She was speaking to him as a nun, not an inmate, and for a minute the roles were reversed, and without meaning to be, she was in control of the exchange.

He smiled gratefully at her and signed off on the suit.

"I think you're right. I never thought of him that way. No one likes him, not even his dog. It bit him last week," he said and laughed, and so did Sophia. She loved the idea of one of the guards being attacked by his dog. It served him right. "I don't like the dogs either," he confessed, "they're hard to manage, and they get out of control easily. I have a German shepherd I love at home, but I don't like the dogs here." He suddenly sounded almost human to her, which was an eerie feeling, given their respective roles at the camp, he as an officer and she as an inmate. And she looked like any other woman to him, not a nun. Her hair had grown since she'd been there and came to her jawline now. And the hardships of the camp hadn't ravaged her looks yet. Her friends had been there longer and it had taken a toll, particularly their grossly inadequate diet of watered-down soup. She offered up her constant hunger to God, and found it helped.

"Thank you for the excellent uniform," he said to her before he left. He lingered for a moment and then came back to where she was sitting, tidying up her worktable before leaving for the night. He came very close to her and frightened her for a minute, and then slipped a hand into the pocket of her prison uniform and left something in it. She reached in to see what it was, and found a full-sized bar of chocolate. She looked up at him, stunned, and afraid too.

"I can't take this," she said, her hand shaking as she held the tantalizing chocolate. It even had nuts in it, she could almost taste it, just looking at it. "They'll kill me for this if they find it, or if the dogs smell it on my way to the barracks."

"The dogs don't want to eat chocolate. They want to eat you," he said. "It's to thank you for doing such a good job, being so kind and working so hard on it. I know it wasn't easy. What job did you do before you came here?"

"I'm a nurse," she said shyly. It was the longest conversation she'd had with a man in years, other than her brother-in-law or her father or Claus.

"And probably a very good one. They should use you in the infirmary, but they won't. The job assignments are always crazy here."

"I've never been very good at sewing," she admitted, still worried about the chocolate.

"Well, you are now. You can get a job as a seamstress after this. Keep the chocolate, you've probably missed your dinner by now," he said guiltily. She took it out and looked at it again, and thanked him with starving eyes. "Goodnight, Fräulein, and thank you," he said, and carrying his new uniform, he left. Sophia hurriedly put the chocolate bar on her lap and broke it into five equal parts. She was going to share it with her bunkmates and Tamar. There was a nice-sized piece for each of them. These were riches beyond belief. She knew she shouldn't accept it, but she couldn't resist. Even if they killed her for it, it was worth it.

She put it back in her pocket, divided now, and still in the wrapper, which she'd have to find a way to dispose of later, without getting caught. She turned off the lights in the sewing room and hurried back to her barracks. Jo, Hedi, and Brigitte were curled up on the bunk. Others were talking, or already asleep early after a hard day's work. The lights in the barracks were dim, and Tamar was lying on her bunk with her eyes closed. Her bunkmates were lined up for the latrine, which would take a long time.

Sophia was smiling when she joined them.

"Where were you?" Hedi asked her. "You missed dinner, if you can call it that."

"I had to wait for a uniform to get picked up," she said,

161

and hopped onto the bunk with them, and cuddled up close. She slipped her hand in her pocket then, took out the first piece, and slipped it into Hedi's hand, then did the same with Jo and Brigitte. Their eyes grew wide when they realized what it was. And then she leaned down and slipped the fourth piece into Tamar's hands. She put it straight in her mouth with a look of amazement, and Sophia ate hers. All five of them were silent as they let the chocolate melt in their mouths with an ecstatic expression, and Jo whispered to her.

"Where did you get it?"

"It was my tip for the uniform I got right on the third try."

"Jesus, it's fantastic," Brigitte said.

"If you weren't a nun, I'd be suspicious of what you had to do to get that," Jo said, and they laughed.

"Only sewing, I promise," Sophia said. It was like a Christmas present from another world. "I was afraid the dogs would tear me apart if they smelled it on my way back."

"It would have been worth it," Jo confirmed, and Tamar looked up from her lower bunk and gave them the high sign. They had a secret and could have been punished severely for it, but nothing had gone wrong, nothing had happened. Sophia viewed it as a minor miracle, and a gift from God. The others just hoped it would happen again one day.

Chapter 10

The day after the Officers' Dinner, Lieutenant Hans Mahler came to the tailor shop again.

"I came to tell you that you were right," he said in a low voice. The others had all gone to lunch and she hadn't left yet, but he was careful anyway. "I complimented my boss on how well he looks in his uniform, and how well he does his job, and he invited me to spend Christmas with him and his wife at his house." He grinned at Sophia victoriously and she smiled at him. Officers of the High Command were given houses just outside the camp, and had their families with them. And Lieutenant Mahler's boss was second in command, and he was his aide.

"And I want to order another uniform," he said. "He admired how well mine fits. I told him he should have you make him one. Maybe he will. Thank you for the good advice," he said.

"Thank you for the 'tip,'" she said cryptically, and he laughed. He had had another idea and wondered if she would be willing.

"An inmate cleans my quarters, a poor girl from Linz. She doesn't clean very well. If you do it, we could talk," he said, blushing, "and I could leave you some food." It sounded to Sophia like a form of prostitution, cleaning his house in exchange for food, and whatever else he had in mind. He clearly liked her. She was tall and graceful with a good figure and a pretty face, and even in the prison uniform, he thought she was beautiful.

"Lieutenant," she said, and he stopped her.

"Call me Hans. When no one is around of course." She nodded, not sure if she would.

"There is something I need to tell you, that you don't know about me. And thank you for the very generous offer. I'm not just a nurse, I'm a nun too." He stared at her in disbelief, speechless for a minute.

"A nun? Seriously? You've taken all your vows? How old are you?"

"Twenty-two. I've taken the first ones, not the final ones. I'm a novice." He looked relieved.

"Then you can still change your mind."

"You can always change your mind," she said quietly, "but I don't want to. I've always wanted to be a nun."

"That's ridiculous and a terrible waste. You're beautiful and you're smart. You should marry and have children."

"God got me first." She smiled gently at him, which made her even more desirable. "I'm married to Him."

"No," he corrected her. He was Catholic too. "You're engaged. You can break an engagement if you meet someone else. It wouldn't need a divorce."

She laughed at the analogy. "I just thought you should know, with your kind offer to clean your house."

"The other woman comes twice a week. Maybe I could have you one day, and her one day, so no one is suspicious."

"And what would you like me to do, in addition to clean the house?" she asked him directly, and he blushed. He was actually well brought-up and treated her with respect even though she was an inmate of the camp. To him, she was just a very beautiful woman, and he loved talking to her. She was smart, and kind.

"That would be up to you," he said respectfully. "I know what my wish would be, and maybe in time. . . . I won't force you to do anything you don't want." Oddly, he looked a little like Claus, both tall, blond, Aryan, aristocratic-looking men, at opposite poles politically, and now poor Claus was dead. And Hans was very much alive.

"Thank you," she said gratefully. He could have raped her if he wished or done any number of horrors to her, and she knew he wouldn't. He was technically and practically her enemy, but she trusted him. And cleaning his house would mean food she could share with the others. "It sounds interesting, and since it would only be once a week, maybe they would let me keep this job."

"I can arrange it," he said. And then he looked serious for a moment. "Your records say that your father was a traitor and defied the Führer's orders. What did he do?"

"I don't know exactly," she said. "I think it had to do with something medical that he wouldn't do. My father is very principled." A shadow crossed his face then. He wanted to be sure her father hadn't been part of a plot to kill the Führer, or something equally serious.

"Maybe it had to do with Aktion T4," Hans said, guessing randomly. "The euthanasia program, of 'undesirables,' 'for the good of the Fatherland.'"

"My father would never have done that," Sophia said, and Hans nodded. "They destroyed his beautiful private hospital, and our home, after he was arrested."

"They're not kind to traitors. And I looked at your records. You were out late at night, that's all? Your records say you were suspected of illegal activity, but it doesn't say what."

"That's all. They said they expected the daughter of a

traitor to be one too. And my sister escaped to Switzerland with her husband when he discovered he's a quarter Jewish."

"They don't forgive that. So now you're paying for their sins," he said, sorry for her.

"And my own, whatever they are. Not very serious ones." It wasn't entirely true, but it was best if he believed that.

"I can tell. You're not listed as a nun, you know," he told her.

"I haven't changed my identity papers since I joined the Sisters of Mercy, and I'm Sister Anne."

"You are Sophia Alexander to me. Remember, you're only engaged to God, not married," he teased her, and they both laughed. He hadn't convinced her, and she knew he never would. No matter how nice he seemed, he was a Nazi officer at a concentration camp. She hadn't lost sight of that, no matter how handsome he was, and how much he wanted to help her with privileges and food. And more, if she let him. "I'll see about getting you the assignment to clean the house," he said, and then he had to go back to his office. "And don't forget the second uniform."

"Yes, Lieutenant," she said, smiling at him, and waved as he left. He was beaming. He had a plan, and loved the idea of being alone in his house with her. Sophia knew what she was doing was wrong, but he was offering food she could share with her friends, and maybe other favors down the line. She wasn't going to do anything bad or have sex with him, and she liked him, as much as was possible given who he was. The prisoners did what they had to do to survive here. She felt lucky to have met him, and grateful for what he wanted to do for her. But she was never going to love him, or sleep with him, no matter how handsome he was.

Hans was smiling when he went back to his office. He wasn't going to rush her, but he knew he had met the woman of his dreams. And one day, she would forgive him for his job during the war. He could tell she was a kind, generous young woman and she'd forgive him, he was sure. He was no fan of the Führer's either. He had no choice in the matter. He was a soldier and had to do as he was told.

The request to have Sophia clean his house once a week went through quite simply. He filled out a form, made out a request for a change, and it was approved. And the other young woman kept the job once a week. No one challenged it. They didn't care which prisoners cleaned his house.

Sophia started right after the New Year. She continued to work in the sewing rooms, and his second uniform fit perfectly now that she had learned what to do.

She was allowed to leave work at noon on Fridays, in order to clean his house. He had a small cozy place to himself, and he was impeccably neat. He was there the first time she went, having arranged something for himself that allowed him to leave his office early. She looked nervous when she arrived, but no one was there except Hans. He looked meticulously immaculate, and she had tried to look as clean and orderly as she could in the prison uniform. The first thing he did was walk her into the kitchen and open the refrigerator and the cupboards.

"Eat whatever you want," he said generously, "just don't make yourself sick." She couldn't believe all the good things he was offering her. Fruit and vegetables, milk, eggs, a ham, orange juice he squeezed himself, fresh bread. They were on rations, but the SS were generous with themselves. With his encouragement she made herself fried eggs and a slice of ham, a piece of toast, and drank a glass of milk. She felt slightly sick the first time, unaccustomed to eating anymore, but she kept it down, and was stunned by his generosity. She took slices of bread for her friends, and some slices of ham, and two oranges. Thanks to him, she could keep all five of them alive, and eat a real meal once a week herself. It was the best gift he could give her, life force for them.

In gratitude, she cleaned his house until it was spotless. He admitted that he gave food to the other young woman too, though not as lavishly, but always some fruit, or bread, or a slice of ham, or some sausage.

When she finished cleaning the house, he made tea for both of them, with honey, and they sat and talked for an hour, like normal people in another world. He was twenty-seven years old and had been studying economics in Berlin when he got drafted into the army when the war broke out. He wanted to work in finance after the war, like Heinrich. His father was a lawyer. Hans was the kind of young man she should have met long ago and never had. And now he was an officer in this hellhole where untold horrors happened, and unimaginable suffering was inflicted on the prisoners on the Führer's orders.

Sophia knew she would never be able to get past that no matter how kind he was, or how well he fed her. He didn't believe in many of the principles of the Reich, but he was still following orders to inflict harm on others. She couldn't bear the thought.

Hans told her about the news of the outside world at times. He told her that on December seventh, the Japanese had bombed American military installations in Hawaii. The United States and Britain had declared war on Japan the next day. Then Hitler declared war on the United States three days later. That was shocking news. And he told her that German U-boats were sinking ships off the east coast of America, which surprised Sophia too.

Their arrangement worked well. Sophia spent a whole afternoon at his home once a week. Hans was usually there, gazing at her, wishing he could put his arms around her and go to bed with her. She was true to her vows, but they talked a lot, and she ate. There was a lot she liked about him. He was responsible and honorable and a kind person, but also a Nazi, which she couldn't stomach. He didn't like the war either, or Hitler, but he was loyal to Germany and his commanding officers.

She had never heard anyone speak of him as part of the mistreatment of prisoners, but he was there, still a Nazi and part of the SS. She and her friends were benefiting greatly from the food he gave her. It always had to be small enough so she could carry it without being noticed, which she hadn't been so far. She and her four friends looked better and had more energy now, and Tamar wasn't coughing as much. She still didn't look as well as the others, but she was older. Age was not an advantage at Ravensbrück. You had to be young and fit and have endurance to survive. So far they all had, now thanks to Hans.

Sophia was lying on her bunk on a Sunday in April. She had been in the camp for six months by then, and Hans had been feeding her and her friends for four months, since she started cleaning house for him. If it had been discovered, he would have been shot. He was risking a great deal for her.

Hans had said he wished he could see her on Sundays, since

they were both off, but there was no way he could without exposing their friendship. That would have to wait until after the war. He had his heart set on more than that eventually, or sooner, once they knew each other better. For now, he was trying to respect her vows, which was hard. Sophia had just turned twenty-three, and she was surviving the hardships of the camp that they had to endure, in part thanks to him, but also due to her own strength and will to live. She refused to give up and let the brutal treatment by the Nazis kill her. Hans wanted to protect her as best he could, but there was only so much he could do without putting them both in grave danger.

She was lying next to Jo on their bunk when she had an idea and whispered to her. "Do you want to get out of here?"

"Of the barracks? You mean for a walk?" Jo whispered back, not sure why they were whispering, except if Sophia had another chocolate bar from the lieutenant. His gifts, which Sophia shared equally among them, were making life almost tolerable for them. Jo had the hardest job of all on the construction crew. And a new rule had been put into effect two weeks before, whippings as punishment, to incite the women to work harder. The whippings were vicious, and it was something more for Jo to worry about and endure.

"No, I mean out of *here*," Sophia said more precisely.

"The camp?" Jo said even more audibly, and Sophia nodded.

"There has to be a way. There are five of us, we can figure out something." Some of the camps had been declared impossible to escape from, but with so many of the inmates with outside jobs, there had to be a way to confuse the guards at some point and slip away. Sophia was convinced of it. Jo nodded excitedly.

"I'm game. I'd rather risk it and die, than stay here." She had no idea whether or not her husband was still alive. Since he was Jewish, there was a strong likelihood he wasn't, although none of them ever said it. "What about the dogs?" The soldiers used them to find people if they tried to escape.

"Let's think about it," Sophia said.

It took her a week of constant thinking. She whispered her idea to the others in bed one night, when all four of them were huddled together on their bunk, under their blankets. "On the nights when there are night shifts at the factories, we slip out with them, and get on the trucks. The guards don't watch them that closely, because they're the most trusted inmates here. We make our escape from the factory. They don't take roll call on the trucks or when they get back. I asked. We take off from the factory. They may not even notice until the next morning, when we miss roll call. That gives us a head start."

"To where?" Hedi asked. "And in what?"

"To anywhere. On foot, just as far and as fast as we can get."

"In our prison uniforms?" Brigitte whispered, dubious of the plan, but anxious to escape too. But the plan had to be a good one.

"I have access to the closet," Sophia reminded them, where all the fancy confiscated clothes were, which came from rich Jewish women, and which were then offered to the wives of the SS High Command. There were some spectacular clothes there, with fancy labels from big designers. "I do all the repairs before they go back to Berlin for the wives to pick through them." They had never thought of that. "We can look like ordinary women and then disappear. We can wear them under our uniforms on the way to the factory." They all fell quiet then, thinking about it.

"We'd have to walk a long way to get out of the area and hide somewhere. We have no papers," Jo said.

"I have some contacts," Sophia said softly. "They can get us out of the area, maybe to the Swiss or French border. I can call them once we're out. We can hide in wooded areas and forests along the way." They talked about it for a long time and then fell asleep. None of them were sure, and it was a daring plan, not easy to pull off, but not impossible either.

Sophia talked about it to Tamar the next day. They wanted to include her, although she was the least healthy and would have the hardest time keeping up, but they wanted to offer it to her. She was the quickest to agree.

"I want to do it," Tamar told Jo and Sophia. "If I don't get out of here, I'm going to die. I just get sicker and sicker lying here. Will you really let me go with you?" They both nodded.

"We won't go without you," Jo said, and Sophia agreed.

"We have to figure out which factory truck we want to join, I think the one with the greatest number of workers." And often they didn't use the dogs on factory nights, because the inmates allowed to work outside the camp were known to be trustworthy.

"When do we want to do it?" Tamar asked, and Sophia was quick to answer.

"June. It's warm. Six weeks from now. We need time to plan, and I need to steal the clothes, that'll take time too. We'll go on a Friday night—the guards are more relaxed on Fridays. And I go to Hans on Fridays, I can get enough food to last us for a couple of days or longer if we stretch it."

The plan was taking shape in all of their minds. They each had suggestions to contribute. What they would need most was courage to see the plan through, no matter how dangerous or frightening. The only way to do it was to keep going no matter what happened, even if they got hurt or shot at or attacked. The only reason to stop was if they were killed, which could happen too. But if they made it, they were free. It was enough to make them risk anything. Their eyes blazed with hope at the thought of it.

"What about your boyfriend?" Hedi asked Sophia.

"Who? . . . oh . . . I can't ask him. They would put him in front of a firing squad for sure if they found out. And he's one of them after all. We can't take that risk." They all nodded agreement and dropped the idea of enlisting Hans's help. It was one thing to smuggle food to them, and an entirely different thing, of unthinkable magnitude, to help them escape. He would be shot as a traitor for sure. Sophia doubted he would do it. She wasn't going to try. In the end, no matter how kind he was, or how much he liked her, the women were prisoners, and he was a guard.

May was the prettiest month Sophia had seen so far in Ravensbrück. There was a gentleness to it, a warm light. The weather wasn't hot yet, but warm enough, with sunny days and balmy nights. It meant that June would be even better, which would be good for them when they made their escape. They were almost ready and had refined the details of their plan. Sophia already had most of the clothes they needed but not all. She had them hidden at the back of a closet in the sewing room. She needed shoes they could walk in, and even run if they had to, and she had found those too. They had tried to think of everything, and had made steady progress to put the plan in place. It made them all nervous but they were excited too. Tamar was particularly hopeful.

She could almost smell freedom in the air. She had been at Ravensbrück for more than two years.

Sophia was sitting with Hans in his garden on a Friday afternoon. She had already cleaned the house, and no one could see into his garden. They were enjoying each other's company, and she told him it was a special day.

"Why? You've decided to give up your vows?" he asked hopefully, teasing her. He brought the subject up often, to no avail so far, but he hadn't admitted defeat yet, and never would.

"No, it's my father's birthday." She smiled at him. "I hope he's all right." She'd had no news since his arrest, and it had been eighteen months. "You would love him, he's such a good person, a good man. He's a man of principle," she said, as a cloud crossed Hans's eyes, and she saw it. It was just a glimmer, but she'd known Hans for six months and she had just seen something that struck fear in her heart. "What?" He was silent for a long time. "Have you heard something?" Her heart was beating faster while she waited for him to answer.

"Sophia," he said, and gently took her hand in his. "When I looked at his arrest record and asked you about it, I saw something," he confessed.

"What?" She clutched his hand so tightly it hurt him.

"I didn't want to tell you. It was in the records. He died in Dachau last June." He said it so softly she could hardly hear him. She let out a cry and he held her as she sobbed and then looked at him again.

"Are you sure?" He nodded. "Did they kill him?"

"No, it said he died of illness. Lung disease."

"Why didn't you tell me?"

"I didn't want to take away the little hope you had. It's so hard here. I didn't want to make it even worse for you. And I didn't know you that well when I saw the notation. It's in your file now. I've wanted to tell you since then, but there's never a good time. Every day is hell here, for you and the others. I didn't want to make it worse."

"You've made it better," she said sadly, with tears still on her cheeks. "I might have died before this, just from starvation." She was still desperately thin, but the sustenance he provided gave her strength and kept her going, and her friends too. It was minimal, and only once a week, but still an enormous, life-saving gift. All the others had nothing and there were dozens of deaths every day. And now her beloved father was gone. She had no hope of ever seeing him again. But at least she knew the truth. She was sure Theresa didn't know either. She would have to tell her when she saw her or spoke to her again, which might not be for a very long time, unless their escape was successful, and there was a very slim chance of that.

Sophia sat quietly in the May sunshine then with Hans,

holding hands. He put an arm around her and she leaned against him. Some of the strength had gone out of her, hearing the news, which was what Hans had been afraid of. He would have kissed her if he dared, but he didn't. He just sat there, holding her, and desperately sorry for her as she grieved the man he would never meet and she would never see again. The price of war was too high.

Chapter 11

Only a few days before Sophia and her friends were to make their escape, the British sent a thousand bombers for a massive air raid on Cologne, and did a vast amount of damage. All of Germany was talking about it, and the Reich was outraged, disregarding their own bombing raid on several historic cities in Britain five weeks before. But Cologne was a harsh blow for the Reich. News of it even filtered into the camp at Ravensbrück, although Sophia and her bunkmates were focused on their plan. Everything was in place now.

She had chosen the wardrobe carefully, and it looked like everything would fit. There was nowhere private for the others to try it on. Sophia had tried hers in the sewing room when no one else was there. She had chosen a simple cream linen skirt, and a pale blue cashmere twin set. She looked like a lady going to a tearoom to meet a friend when she tried it on, and she laughed. It had been so long since she wore anything even remotely like it, before her habit, and prison pajamas. She had picked a black cotton pantsuit with a jacket and simple white blouse for Tamar, which would be easy to wear under the prison uniform, red slacks and a black sweater set for Jo, summer dresses for Hedi and Brigitte that they could stuff into their prison pants, and flat shoes for all. The sizes were a guess but looked right. She had even picked purses for them, which they could put in the bags in which prisoners took water to drink while they were on the job at the factory. They would all look like nice respectable house-wives. It had been a challenge to find simple daywear—there were far more evening gowns and fur coats in the mass of confiscated items from wealthy Jewish women being sent back to Berlin for the wives of the High Command to choose from. And she had found some coins in each of the purses, which she was going to use to call people in the network once they reached a safe place to do so.

Sophia and her four friends all went to work that morning as planned, with no diversion from their usual schedule. They had answered roll call at four A.M., and Sophia went to Hans's house after lunch to clean, as she always did on Fridays.

She was quieter than usual and he noticed it, but he knew she was still mourning her father. Learning that he was dead, and had been for a year, was a hard blow. He went through some papers on his desk while she cleaned, and she finished quickly. He offered her food, but she said she wasn't hungry, which was slightly unusual.

"I'll take a few things to the others," she said, and she diligently sliced some bread and ham, and oranges, and took a few biscuits and chocolate bars. Hans's cupboards were well stocked. The best foods were reserved for the officers.

"Are you having a party?" he teased her, and she smiled shyly. "Take whatever you want." He was always generous with her. She wrapped all the ham and bread carefully in wax paper, put it in a small paper bag, and put it under her prison shirt, so it didn't show. It was their only food supply for their escape, and he was their only source of supply.

They chatted for a little while, but she didn't want to linger for too long today. She seemed very serious to him, and she put a hand on his arm before they left his house at the end of the day.

"Thank you for always being so good to me, Hans." He thought there were tears in her eyes when she said it, still upset about her father.

"I care about you a great deal, Sophia. I hope you know that. And I'm so sorry about your father. Maybe I should have told you sooner. I just didn't have the heart."

"It's all right," she said. "Maybe you were right. I don't think the SS knew he had died when they arrested me, or they would have said something."

"They probably didn't know, or they didn't want to tell you. They would have had to check with Dachau, and they wouldn't bother to do that unless someone inquired about him. Sometimes that information travels faster between the camps, with transfers and new arrivals, before it goes to the central records bureau in Berlin, and the news gets upstairs. He obviously wasn't a great danger to the Reich, so once he was arrested, they paid no attention to it after that." But they had put him in a concentration camp anyway, until he got sick and died, if that was really how he died. She'd never know that for sure either.

Sophia was solemn as Hans walked her partway back to her barracks, and he went to check on some papers he was waiting for at his office, and then went home. As always, after she'd been there, he missed her. He loved talking to her. Her spirit seemed to linger in the house after she left. He made something to eat, and then noticed that she had left her water bottle, which was important to the inmates. It was a small bottle they used to collect their water allotment for the day, and they drank it sparingly since it was all they got. He knew she would need it long before he would see her again and didn't want her to be without it. He finished his dinner and was going to take it to her afterward.

At the barracks, Sophia and the others had dressed under their blankets, and were wearing their stolen clothes for the road under their prison uniforms. They were all so thin that two layers of clothing wasn't even noticeable. They each had a bag the inmates made from scraps for their water bottle, and their new shoes were at the bottom. Sophia was carrying the food in hers. She noticed that she had left her water bottle at Hans's but would have to do without it. She couldn't go back for it now.

The factory workers left at six-thirty for an all-night shift. They'd had their ration of soup by then and were ready for work. Sophia and her group stayed close together. No one questioned them or found it unusual that they were going to the factory that night, the other four were already on the truck, and Sophia was about to climb up, when Hans came running up with her water bottle, called her name, and she turned and he handed it to her. He was surprised to see her at the trucks with the factory workers, and she was equally startled to see him.

"You forgot this," he said, and she looked shocked. He

stared at her strangely, startled at the look on her face. "Where are you going?"

"We were assigned to some extra work tonight," she said vaguely, and she was normally so honest that he could see instantly that she was lying.

"No, you weren't," he said in a low voice so that no one else could hear. "Sophia, what are you doing?" He looked like the SS officer he was for a minute, and then his face softened, as other women from the barracks continued to get into the truck, and Sophia needed to be on it, or her friends would leave without her.

"Hans," she said, and his eyes stopped her.

"Don't do something crazy," he begged her. "They'll kill you if they catch you."

"I don't care." Nothing was going to stop her, not even Hans.

"I have to report you," he said in a whisper. His eyes were begging her to stay so he didn't have to. As usual, there were no dogs there. Hans was the only thing that could stop them.

"No, you don't," she said in a strong voice. "You don't believe in them either. This madness will be over one day, and you'll be back in the real world of sane people. Don't do anything now you'll regret later." He didn't answer her, but she looked hard at him, and then walked to the truck and jumped in. It pulled away a minute later, and he was still standing there watching her. She could still see his eyes and the torment in them, torn between his sworn duty and his feelings for her. If he warned the guards now, she and her four friends would be killed. If he gave them some time, they could still escape when they got to the factory, and if he didn't report them at all, they might reach freedom. She didn't know what option he would pick. Between his heart and his conscience and the insane government he had sworn loyalty to. And if they suspected he was part of Sophia's plan, in collusion with her, they'd kill him. He had hard choices to make, between love and duty, her life or his, sanity or madness. She was shaking as she sat in the truck with the other workers, and Jo leaned over to ask her in a whisper.

"Why was he there when we left?" She had never trusted him. To her, he was just another Nazi.

"I forgot my water bottle at his house, he brought it back to me," she whispered back. Jo nodded and said nothing, but she had seen that they had both looked like they were about to cry. Something had happened. But Sophia had gotten in the truck anyway, and he hadn't stopped her.

When they got to the factory, all the prisoners got out of the trucks and the whole group walked toward the building, ready for a night's work, Sophia and her group went left when the others went right, and no one paid attention.

They hid in some bushes in the parking lot, pulled off their prison uniforms, shoved them deep into a trash can, and hurried onto the street that led to the factory, walking down it with determination and a fast step, in the shoes Sophia had stolen for them. None of them spoke. They cut across a park and down another street, headed toward a wooded area on the edge of the town, and didn't stop until they were well out of sight. Then they sat down on some logs to catch their breath. They had been walking fast for half an hour. They sat there and looked at each other. Tamar couldn't talk, she was so out of breath, but they had made it. No one had stopped them. Hans hadn't alerted the guards as they left, and no one on the trucks realized that they didn't belong there.

"Oh my God, we did it!" Jo said, stunned. "We look like a bunch of rich ladies who ran out on lunch in a fancy restaurant." She had noticed that her red skirt said Dior and her black sweater set Chanel.

They all laughed, and Tamar could breathe again. She had a rattle in her chest.

"Hans could still report us. He may have already. We'd better keep moving," Sophia said, and they continued deeper into the forest and walked for another two hours. They felt safe then—there were no sounds of patrol dogs in the distance, no sirens or gunshots or shouts. They really had made it.

Their destination was a little town called Windberge, which Hedi had suggested. It was a two-day walk from Ravensbrück, which would be less arduous than any day they had survived in the camp. And once there, in Saxony, there were countless small villages where they could seek refuge. Claus had had a contact there that Sophia was going to call. She knew that Claus had placed several children in the vicinity. It was a peaceful rural area of farms and agriculture.

They had no travel papers, so they had to stay out of sight and away from checkpoints and patrols. When they had walked for two hours, Sophia took charge. "Let's try and sleep for a while," she suggested, and the others agreed, "and we'll start again before the daylight." They took small sips from their water bottles and lay down on the leaves on the ground. They had no blanket to lie on, but the ground was soft and the night was warm.

They slept for a few hours, woke up early, while it was still dark, and were eager to move on. By morning, the camp would know that they'd escaped when they didn't answer roll call, and there would be search parties and patrols with dogs looking for them. The five women had to put as much distance as they could between them and the camp. And they had two days of walking ahead of them.

They had to wake Tamar, but she was alert and willing when she woke up. She couldn't walk as fast as they could, but she

189

pushed as hard as she was able, and they took turns giving her a supporting arm when she got too tired to move faster.

"Don't worry about me," she insisted. "Just keep going, I'll catch up." But she was pushing herself to her limits, and they knew it, and weren't going to abandon her, even if she slowed them down.

In the flat shoes Sophia had gotten them, they walked all day, despite blisters, tired legs, aching feet, and rough terrain. They stopped once to eat Hans's food, but they were used to hard labor now with very little sustenance to fuel them, and they kept going. Sophia guessed that they had covered about forty miles that day, according to their plan to stay in the country and go where it would be easier to hide and ultimately fit in. But they needed papers before they could take the risk of running into patrols.

On the morning of the second day, they had stopped at a village, and Sophia went to a phone box, used the coins she had brought, and dialed a number she still remembered, a friend of Claus's she had met a few times at meetings. Max was one of Claus's prime contacts when he needed new papers for a child, in a different name. And Max had been transporting children since the war began. He ran a group that had been doing it now for several years. He had been an artist and engraver before the war and had been using his skills to create papers so people could escape.

She gave him her first name, and the code word Claus had given her, and he recognized her immediately. She told him where she was. He didn't ask and she didn't tell him she was on the run, but he guessed it because she'd called him.

"Where are you headed?" he asked her.

"Windberge. I think we can get there by tonight, on foot. There are five of us, all women." He gave her more precise directions for their walk that day, where there were forests, and they could navigate safely.

"Call me when you get to Windberge, I'll have someone meet you there. I want to get you to Ahnsbeck, to a convent called St. Blaise. I'll meet you there with everything you need. You'll be safe there for as long as you want. I'll have the papers with me. We can take the pictures when you get to the convent."

"I can't thank you enough." She had tears in her eyes when she said it. "And, Max, we have no money," to pay for their travel papers. All they had were the coins she had left, to call him.

"Neither do I." He laughed. "Let's say I'm doing it in memory of our friend Claus. He would come back and haunt me forever if he thought I wouldn't help you."

"Thank you." The women had another day's long walk ahead of them. And Max repeated that the nuns at St. Blaise would take care of them, and they would be safe with travel papers in their new names.

They continued walking after the call and were soon in another forest Max had described. The area they were walking through wasn't highly populated, and the terrain was easier than the day before.

Sophia and the three younger women had gotten used to the pace of the forced march and Tamar was visibly struggling to keep up. Her health had deteriorated in three years in the camp, with the trauma, the beatings, the starvation, the illnesses she had managed to stave off, and those she had succumbed to. Sophia suspected as a nurse that she had problems now with either her lungs or her heart or both. But Tamar was still continuing gamely.

They all talked very little to save their strength. They were looking rumpled now, but the quality of the clothes they were wearing served them well, and lent respectability to them any time they had to cross an open road to get to another wooded area. They were a funny little group of women you'd expect to find playing bridge, except that their hair was somewhat bedraggled, short but not shorn, their faces were very pale, and they were shockingly thin. But from the distance, they looked normal. None of them even had a hairbrush, and they hadn't seen lipstick since they'd been arrested and sent to camp. At close range, they looked a little dubious, from afar, they looked fine. But they saw no one on the way.

They stopped for lunch and ate the last of Hans's ham. There was still bread and biscuits left, and an orange they sectioned carefully and shared, and then they walked on. By nightfall, the towns and landmarks Max had mentioned began to appear, and they knew they were approaching Windberge. They were almost there when Tamar fell twice, and they could see that they could force her no further. They found a place to stop in the woods, and Sophia volunteered to walk into the small village to call Max so he could send his contact to pick them up.

There was a road close to the forest, but no sound of cars. They were sure they were safe there, as they lay on the ground, recovering from the long walk that day. Tamar fell asleep, exhausted. Sophia could hear the rattle in her chest as she slept. Sophia was about to set off to walk to the village to find a phone to call Max, when suddenly they heard the roar of a motor, men's shouts, and the barking of dogs. The men were laughing loudly between shouts. All four women sat frozen in terror, the men in the car sounded drunk. The car stopped and the men flashed searchlights into the forest. At first Sophia thought they were looking for them, and then their uproarious laughter made her realize that it was a standard patrol of young soldiers and they'd been drinking, and were having fun, and had nothing else to do. The sounds became more frightening once their vehicle had stopped.

They got out, there was more hilarity, their patrol dogs were barking furiously, and if they unleashed them, Sophia and the others knew the dogs would find them. They were very close. Instead, the soldiers shouted into the forest, fired some shots, and drove on. The danger was gone, and Jo turned to signal to Sophia with relief, but didn't see her. She had disappeared. And then Jo looked down and saw her lying on the ground. At first Jo thought she'd fainted, from fear or exhaustion. They turned her over and saw a large bloodstain spreading on her chest. One of the soldiers' random gunshots had hit her. Sophia had been shot.

Jo looked at Hedi and Brigitte. "What do we do now? We can't take her to a hospital, how do we find a doctor?" Sophia was their leader and the others looked panicked.

Brigitte ran to the road, to see what was nearby, if there was a house or an inn, on the other side of the road. Tamar slept through it all. They didn't want to wake her to tell her the bad news, so they let her sleep.

Brigitte was back minutes later and reported to Hedi and Jo. "There's a farm a little distance away. If they call the police, the police will send us back, or to someplace worse, like Auschwitz."

"We don't have any choice. If we don't get a doctor for Sophia, she'll die," Jo said, watching the blood spread through Sophia's pale blue sweater.

Brigitte volunteered to stay with her, and Hedi agreed to go to the farm alone, so they didn't all go and frighten the people who lived there. They were five women showing up out of nowhere at night, clearly on the run from somewhere, and one of them was shot and bleeding. Not exactly the kind of group you want to invite in. Hedi set out alone, running, and reached the farmhouse in minutes. All the lights were out, the house was dark. She could hear cows bleating, and there was a full moon overhead. She knocked on the door and no one answered. She waited and knocked harder, and a light came on. A few minutes later the front door opened and a dour-looking middle-aged woman stood staring at her with a wary expression. Hedi wasn't sure what to say, but all she could do was bare her soul to this woman and beg for help and pray that she didn't betray them. They were at her mercy.

"I'm so sorry to disturb you," Hedi said, feeling frightened of this woman and what would happen if she called the police. "I need your help," she said, near tears. They had come so far, and she didn't want to get caught now, and sent back. "My friends and I are lost. We've come a long way. There are five of us and one of us is hurt," Hedi said simply. It had the ring of truth as the woman looked her over.

The woman stared at her, wondering if it was some kind of trap. "I'm here alone with my children, my husband died last year, in Russia." She looked as though she had seen a lifetime of hard times.

"Do you have a barn where we could stay? And is there a doctor somewhere nearby? We're on our way to Windberge to meet a friend, and from there to Ahnsbeck, to the convent of St. Blaise."

"They're not real nuns. They're Protestants," the woman said sourly. It was the least of their problems. "Where are your friends?"

"In the woods. We'll have to carry the one who's hurt." Hedi didn't want to say she'd been shot.

"All right, you can sleep in the barn tonight, but you have to go tomorrow." She was nicer than she looked, and Hedi said they'd be back in a minute. She ran to the woods to where she had left the others, to tell them, and found Jo and Brigitte crying.

"Is she okay?" Hedi asked, panicked.

"Tamar is dead," Jo said in a strangled voice. They had seen so much death, but it still mattered, and they were so close to freedom, but not there yet. "She died in her sleep."

"Oh my God. We can stay in the woman's barn. She wants us out tomorrow, but we can get to the convent, if we can move Sophia. We'll have to leave Tamar tonight and come back tomorrow." She didn't want to lose two of them. They had no choice but to leave Tamar for now. They gently moved her behind some bushes. She looked like she was sleeping.

Hedi and Brigitte took turns carrying Sophia through the woods and across the road to the farmhouse where the woman was waiting for them. They were an unholy group, carrying Sophia, unconscious and covered with blood. They wanted to get out of sight quickly in case the soldiers came back that way.

"Where's the fifth one?" the woman asked, and there was nothing to say but the truth.

"She's dead," Hedi and Jo said in unison. The woman didn't say a word and led them to the barn. She used a pitchfork to scrape the straw away, which revealed a trapdoor they helped her open. They carried Sophia down the stairs and laid her on a narrow bed. There were a table and chairs, and the woman lit a lamp on the table, as they all looked at each other. She saw the bloodstained sweater Sophia was wearing. The white skirt was smeared with it too.

"I'll call the doctor," the owner of the farm said. Sophia hadn't stirred. "You can trust him," she added at the look of panic in their eyes. They had been lucky with the farm they chose.

Hedi, Brigitte, and Jo sat at the table in the lamplight and watched Sophia, and a short while later, the trapdoor opened again, and an old man with gray hair and a weathered face carrying a satchel came down the stairs with the woman. She said his name was Dr. Herman. She introduced herself then as Ulla.

The doctor walked over to Sophia, raised her sweater, and examined her. "How long ago was she shot?" he asked them.

"About half an hour ago," Jo answered. "It was a patrol, they were drunk. They didn't know they shot her, and neither did we until we saw her on the ground."

"The bullet just grazed her and exited through her arm," he said after he examined her. "She's in shock. You need to keep her warm. The wound looks worse than it is." He bandaged Sophia and she stirred when he was finished.

She opened her eyes and asked the others in a weak voice, "Did they find us?"

"No, we're fine, except you got shot by the patrol." There was time to tell her about Tamar later.

The doctor had packed the wound with antibiotic powder, which was all he had, bandaged it, and given her something to sleep, and he told them to keep it dry, keep her warm and let her rest, and call if the wound started bleeding again. And then he left with Ulla.

"Do you think she'll report us?" Hedi asked Brigitte with a look of terror. She couldn't go back to Ravensbrück.

"No. If she were going to, she'd have called the police

instead of the doctor." They were too tired to think now, and in shock themselves.

"We have to try to get to that convent tomorrow," Jo said. Without papers, they were dead if they ran into another patrol. "We should call Max in the morning, if Ulla lets us use her phone." The farm looked dirt-poor. And they had to go back for Tamar, if the nuns could help them.

They took turns watching Sophia all night, and in the morning, Ulla brought them fresh milk from the cow and some bread. She let them use her phone, and Sophia gave them the number to call Max. They called him and he promised to send someone to pick them up and take them to St. Blaise.

When they went back to the barn, they told Sophia about Tamar. They were all sad about her, but death had become too familiar and not a surprise. Two hours later, Max's contact arrived, and asked for his "sisters." He came in a battered truck. It was old but functional. The convent was two hours away. They thanked Ulla and left. Sophia was wrapped in a blanket, and the others rode with her. They had left Tamar in the woods until the nuns could help them deal with her. They felt terrible leaving her there, but they had no choice for now, and she was out of sight.

There were six warm, welcoming nuns waiting for them at St. Blaise, with Max. They helped them get Sophia to a safe room in the basement. There were children running all through the house, twenty of them, according to one of the nuns.

"They've been here for a year, all orphans," Mother Paul, the Mother Superior, explained to them, and Sophia was sure that they were all Jewish, with false papers. She remembered now Claus mentioning the convent to her. This seemed like the one he had told her about. They never turned him down for a child in danger.

All four women spent the day in the basement beneath a trapdoor, waiting for Max to finish the papers after he took their pictures. At the end of the day, he appeared with five impeccable sets of travel papers, signed and stamped by the Reich. They had new names and identities, and credible documents. The two young men who worked for the nuns brought Tamar back from the woods wrapped in a blanket, and they buried her in the convent cemetery that night, with her friends present to say goodbye. The ground was hard, but the young men were strong and dug the grave.

It had been a harrowing three days since the women left the camp, but they felt as though they had been born again. Sophia's arm was in a sling, and they had dinner with Max and the nuns that night, after they put the children to bed. The four friends were sad about Tamar, but at least she had seen freedom again, even if only for two days. She hadn't died in her bunk in Ravensbrück, or been shot, and her soul was free at last.

The others had decisions to make about where to go, and what to do now. The nuns said they could stay as long as they liked. Sophia made a decision that night, the same one she had made before. Jo wanted to go back to the unoccupied part of France and wait for news of her husband there, if he survived Auschwitz. Brigitte had relatives in Munich whom she trusted and knew would take her in. And Hedi wanted to try and get to Portugal, which was neutral. Some of her artist friends were living there. Germany felt too dangerous to her now.

Max left the next morning, and Sophia spoke to Mother Paul after he left. She was the kind Mother Superior who had taken them in so generously. Sophia had her arm in a sling and explained to her that she was a novice of the Sisters of Mercy in Berlin, but she didn't want to go back there and cause trouble for them. They might be under surveillance now, "although I've been gone for eight months," she explained. It felt more like eight years that she had been in Ravensbrück, or eight centuries. Or a lifetime. Freedom felt unfamiliar now, and it felt comforting to be back in a habit again, even if that of a different order.

"I don't want to be a burden to you either. I've been doing work similar to yours for three years."

"We don't transport the children, they come to us, from many different sources," Mother Paul explained, "all over Germany. We keep them as long as they need."

"I think some of the children I escorted came here," Sophia said quietly. She felt at peace there. The moment she entered a convent, she felt at home, and as though it was where she was meant to be. She had felt that way all her life.

"They probably did come here," Mother Paul said about the children. "You're welcome to stay with us, Sister. We're not Catholic nuns though. We're Protestant, if that makes a difference," she said openly.

"None at all, Mother," Sophia said, "if you don't mind."

"We'd love to have you. I think God brought you to us. We can use another pair of hands." Sophia's were willing ones, as was her heart. She had brought three of her friends out of captivity to safety, and the fourth one was at peace. She thought of Hans then, and wondered if he had reported them, and suspected he hadn't, or the patrols would have been after them quickly and relentlessly to recapture them, punish them, and maybe kill them. He was a kind man, but she knew it would never have been possible between them. The pull back to the convent was too strong for her, but he had helped her survive Ravensbrück. She wasn't sure she would have without him, and he had allowed five of them to flee to safety, which redeemed him to some extent for the atrocities of his superiors and the orders he was duty-bound to follow. She didn't love him, but she was deeply grateful to him.

"It's settled then? You'll stay with us, Sister?" Mother Paul asked her. She was only ten years older than Sophia, but she was mature for her years. It was a small convent, with only a few houses in Germany. She explained to Sophia that the previous Mother Superior had died just after war was declared, and Mother Paul had been asked to step into her shoes, which she had done efficiently, as Sophia could see.

"I'd love to stay, Mother." Sophia thanked her, and Mother Paul assigned her a small cozy cell, with a view of the countryside, the farms, and the woods they had come through. It seemed like a safe place to sit out the war, until the country returned to sanity, especially now that she had viable papers. They were flawless, even if fake. Sophia thought of the countless lives Max had saved with the papers he provided.

Sophia told the others in the morning that she was staying, and they were happy and sad to hear it. Happy for her, because she seemed so at ease to be back in convent life. She was wearing the habit of the Protestant order since she didn't have her own. And her friends were sad too, because they thought she was such a wonderful young woman and she deserved a fuller life, one more like theirs.

"You never know," Jo said wisely, looking very French,

even in the donated clothes the nuns had given her, which were too big for her. The clothes she had worn to escape in had been covered with Sophia's blood, so they burned them. "One day, a dashing man may come along and sweep you off your feet." She smiled. "But please God, not a Nazi," Jo added, and they laughed. Jo had never approved of the lieutenant's pursuit of Sophia, even though he sent them food which Sophia shared with them.

The others were planning to spend a week or two at the convent, make their plans as best they could now, and then leave. They would be sad to leave Sophia when they did. She had led them to freedom with her daring plan and stolen fancy clothes, but most of all her courage to do it. Only someone very brave could have done what she did. And without her determination and perseverance, they would never have tried.

The night of Sophia's escape from Ravensbrück, Hans Mahler had to make one of the hardest decisions of his life. He had wrestled with his conscience and his duty, and what he owed his country, and his superiors. In the end, a slim young woman had won not only his heart but his mind and his honor, and he had remained silent. Their absence had been duly noted at roll call the next morning, and no one ever knew that he had discovered the plan at the last minute the night before. Sophia had changed something in him, and opened his eyes, in the short time he knew her. She had stayed true to her vows and her beliefs the entire time. She was the strongest spirit he had ever met, a holy woman, he thought now. He knew he would never forget her. His heart ached for her, but he understood now that she could never have been his. And saving her life and the lives of the other four women had changed him, and he hoped atoned for some of his sins, committed in the name of the Reich. All he wanted now was for the war to end. And he hoped that Sophia and her friends were safe.

Chapter 12

Hedi, Brigitte, and Jo were so comfortable at St. Blaise and the nuns so kind that they stayed for several weeks, longer than they expected, tasting the delights of freedom again, and recovering from their escape. They went for walks in the rolling hills, played with the children, helped in the kitchen, and did errands for the nuns in their ancient truck. It startled them to see Sophia in her habit now, and they teased her about it. It was better than her prison uniform, but Jo thought her so beautiful, it irked her to see her hide her womanhood in a habit. She thought her too young to renounce the opportunities life hadn't even given her yet. She was twenty-three years old and hadn't given life a chance. To Sophia, it felt like a homecoming when she put on the habit of the Order of Saint Blaise. She felt safe in it, and protected. It was one of the many things she had missed at the camp, along with freedom, and food, and safety, and sleep, and being able to be warm at night. There had been so many things she missed, and so many hardships. She thought of the other inmates often, and how many of them died of illness and abuse every day.

She enjoyed playing with the children at the convent and read stories to them. Jo played the piano for them and taught them songs before she left. She wanted to go home to France and had borrowed a small amount from the convent to get there. They had a small fund to help the needy. She was from Paris, but with the German occupation for the past two years, she couldn't go home. Now she wanted to settle in the remaining free zone in France. It was part of the agreement the French had signed with the Germans. It was a small area in the south, governed by Marshal Pétain in Vichy. She wanted to get out of Germany. It had nothing but bad memories for her.

Brigitte felt the same way, but she had nowhere else to go. Her modeling career was over, with the scars on her face the SS torture had left her with. She didn't have parents, and her aunt and uncle had offered to house her in Munich and give her a job in their restaurant. They knew what happened to her because of her Jewish boyfriend, and had sent her the money to come to Munich and stay with them when she contacted them from St. Blaise. It wasn't the life she wanted, but she had few job opportunities now with her damaged face, and anything was better than Ravensbrück. She was grateful to be alive. She didn't think she'd run into anyone she knew in Munich, so she felt safe there with her new identity and new name. And her aunt and uncle were willing to house her, even with false papers. Max's forgeries were excellent and had never been questioned. She was going to ask a doctor to try to improve the scars on her face. And she had told her aunt and uncle that she would rather die than go back to Ravensbrück.

Hedi was going to meet up with her old artist friends who had moved to Lisbon, which seemed like a safe place to her. One of them had offered to lend her the money to get there, and she was going to stay away from political art and satire in the future.

Only Sophia was staying close to home. She didn't call or write to her sister, because she didn't want anyone to be able to trace her to the convent. She hadn't written to Mother Regina in Berlin for the same reason. And she didn't want to sit the war out in Switzerland with Theresa and Heinrich in their elegant home. Although she hadn't said so openly, she had sensed from Mother Paul that they still engaged with others to move children to safety, and she was willing to risk that again. She wanted to. She felt it was her mission, although she had paid a high price for it for nearly the past year.

She hadn't chosen to be a nun for the easy life she would lead, but for the good she could do in the world.

She was sad when her friends left at the end of July but she was grateful that they had all reached freedom together, except Tamar. The beatings she had weathered, and the harsh conditions and starvation, had just taken too great a toll. They would never know what happened to her son now, but Sophia prayed he was still alive and would survive the war. There were so many like him, that no one knew where they were or what happened to them, and so many who would never come back. Some of them were so young, their lives cut short in concentration camps all over Germany and Poland, Auschwitz being the most dangerous among the camps now, where thousands of inmates, mostly Jews, were being exterminated. There was little chance of survival there.

Five weeks after her old bunkmates left, a Dutch nun came to the convent to bring two children to safety, and told the nuns what had happened to Sister Teresa Benedicta of the Cross, Edith Stein in secular life. She had been arrested in the Netherlands at the beginning of August, with her sister Rosa and two hundred and forty-three converted Jews. They had been briefly incarcerated in Amersfoort and Westerbork concentration camps in Holland and had been sent to Auschwitz subsequently. Sister Teresa had been put to death three days after she arrived. All of the nuns were deeply saddened to hear it. She had been a brave, admirable woman and seemed like a modern-day saint to Sophia. Sister Teresa was one of the most profoundly spiritual and religious people whose work Sophia had ever read, and she was deeply moved to learn of her death. Stein had been willing to die for her beliefs for years, and had never hidden. And now they had killed her. But in Sophia's opinion, hers was a voice that would never be silenced. She had talked to her father about Edith Stein too. Sophia considered her one of the great intellects of their time, and a powerful activist for noble causes. She had taken a firm and outspoken stand against the Nazis, and was killed for it.

Mass murder of Jews was being committed at Auschwitz in the gas chambers, and Edith Stein was just one more victim, but a strong and outspoken voice against Hitler nonetheless.

The rest of the war news that summer was mostly about battles in Russia and North Africa, and an American air attack in Europe, vilified in the German press. And later in the year, Sophia read of the Reich's outrage that the British Foreign Secretary had spoken of the Reich's mass execution of Jews in Auschwitz as something horrific, instead of praising them for it, and thanking them.

Sophia's months at the convent of St. Blaise had been peaceful since her heroic escape from Ravensbrück. She had gained some weight and looked healthier. The nightmares she'd had for months had begun to recede, and she enjoyed her time with the children. No new orphans had arrived since the two Dutch children, and Sophia felt guilty that she wasn't doing more to counter the atrocities of the Nazis, but Mother Paul thought she should rest. Her life in the peaceful countryside was doing her good, after eight months of trauma and torture. She went for long walks alone, and walked along the edge of the woods in Ahnsbeck, which was a small, peaceful, medieval town. It was only four hours' drive from Berlin but seemed light-years away.

She felt mildly guilty too about not using her nursing skills, but the nuns needed her help for small tasks at the convent, and she was happy to assist them. She helped make Christmas decorations with the children, and she and the nuns knitted sweaters for the children and made small gifts for them. It was a very different Christmas for her than the year before in Ravensbrück.

A month later, early one morning, after Matins with the other nuns in their small community, she was walking along the edge of the woods, and heard an odd sound, a moan like an injured animal or bird. She looked around and didn't see anything on the ground. Then she heard the sound again, just above her head, looked up, and found herself standing just below a parachute that had gotten caught in the tree branches, with a man dangling from it who appeared to be unconscious.

She was frozen in place for a moment, and then called up to him softly, not wanting to draw the attention of anyone passing by. She didn't recognize it, but the man's uniform didn't look German to her. The man wearing it looked dead or unconscious, and only the soft moans he occasionally made suggested that he was still alive. She took another look, picked up the skirts of her habit, and ran back to the convent as fast as she could to find Mother Paul. She had to run a long way. She had walked a good distance from the convent.

Mother Paul was helping the other nuns to make the children's beds. They had just gotten up and were downstairs having breakfast. Sophia came to her quickly and asked to speak to her alone, and she told her what she'd seen.

"I don't think he's German, and he's still alive. We need to cut him down before someone finds him."

"American, maybe," Mother Paul said, frowning. "They bombed Wilhelmshaven last night. I heard it on the wireless this morning. I'll get the boys." Andy and Arthur, two strong young men from neighboring farms who helped them with heavy tasks, were there. Both had been rejected by the army. They had seen the children come and go from the convent for many years, guessed what the nuns were doing, and had always been discreet. The nuns knew they could trust them.

Both of the young men had been trying to move a heavy piece of rusted old farm equipment behind the chapel.

213

Mother Paul found them quickly, and told them to bring the truck, a tarp, and a couple of sharp knives. Sophia had gotten blankets. From what she had seen, they would have to cut the man out of the tree and dispose of the parachute.

With the two boys and both nuns in the truck, they drove to where Sophia directed them, parked a little distance away in a clump of trees, and then walked into the woods, where Sophia looked up and pointed. The flier was still there, and no longer moaning. She assumed he must have spent the night there and was probably half frozen.

"Andy, you need to get up the tree and cut him down," Sophia said in a soft voice, directing the younger, more agile one, who was still of an age to climb trees, "and Arthur and I will catch him when he comes down." The young men were seventeen and twenty and strong enough to get him down. The airman appeared to be lifeless, and Sophia could already see that one leg had bled through his uniform, but it was impossible to assess from the ground how badly he was injured, or even if he was still breathing. He looked dead.

Andy shimmied up the tree with ease and cut the strings attaching the man to the parachute. "He's going to come down," Andy warned them, and Arthur braced himself to catch the man, with Sophia ready to help and holding blankets to cover him. Arthur made a masterful catch, as though the airman were a rag doll, and they could see the American flag patch on his flight suit and the stripes of his rank. He never regained consciousness as Arthur carried him to the truck, laid him on the blankets Sophia spread out, and covered him with the tarp so he was hidden from view. Andy then went further up the tree to free the parachute and cut it out. He had all of it down in minutes and joined them at the truck, while Mother Paul watched the entire operation. Sophia felt for a pulse and the airman still had one although it was weak and thready, and he felt ice-cold to the touch. She was suddenly reminded of the night she had helped her father warm the little Jewish boy who was being hidden and concealed himself in the icy pond on Christmas.

"Let's get back to the convent fast," Sophia said. And as soon as they did, Mother Paul instructed Andy to bury the parachute, and he got out a shovel to do it, while Arthur carried the airman down to the cellar safe room, hidden under the floor. It was where Sophia and her bunkmates had been hidden until Max had finished their travel papers and new identities. The room was completely hidden. Arthur eased down the stairs carrying the big man, with Sophia right behind him, and Mother Paul brought two lamps down and lit them. They didn't provide a bright light, but Sophia could see enough to examine the man. She rubbed his hands to try and warm them, kept the blankets around him, and unzipped his flight suit carefully, not sure what she'd find, or even if he'd been shot before he exited his plane.

His body was intact, from what she could see, barring internal injuries which she couldn't assess yet, but his left lower leg was covered in blood, and his ankle bone was protruding. He had a compound fracture, and she had no way of knowing how long he'd been hanging there. She suspected he was suffering from hypothermia as well. That combined with shock and whatever had happened in the plane and right after, there was a good chance he wouldn't survive.

She turned to Mother Paul and spoke in a calm voice. "We need a doctor." The nuns had one they trusted in Ahnsbeck. "Tell him we have a compound fracture of an adult male, probable hypothermia, possible internal injuries, and maybe a concussion. He's unconscious and has a weak pulse." Mother Paul nodded and left quickly. The nuns of St. Blaise were all teachers, none of them nurses. Sophia was the only nurse in the convent, and Mother Paul was impressed by how smooth and efficient she was as she continued to assess the pilot and keep him warm. She asked for more blankets and one of the nuns brought them, with a hot-water bottle she had thought to bring.

"Thank you," Sophia said, and tucked it in next to the patient, as she continued to examine him inch by inch. So far, the worst injury she had found was the ankle, the rest of him seemed uninjured. She was still checking him as he gave a groan and opened his eyes. He saw Sophia and looked around, surprised.

"Where am I? Do you speak English?"

"Yes, I do," she said, looking at his eyes to see if he had a concussion. Her father had made her take English in school, and she had studied it as well in nursing school, to learn the medical terms. She had an accent, but she was fluent. "You're in Germany." She knew that wouldn't be good news, judging by his uniform. "But you're safe. We have you hidden. No one saw us cut you down from the tree your parachute was caught in. And a doctor is on the way."

"My name is Theodore Blake, Captain, Squadron Leader." He gave his serial number then and said nothing more, in case he was about to be taken prisoner in enemy territory. He was clearheaded enough to give the required information and stop there.

"Did you hit your head, Captain Blake, before or after you left the plane?" He didn't answer at first, saw that she was a nun, and his tone softened slightly.

"I don't think so."

"Do you know how long you were in the tree?"

"I must have been there all night," he said, slowly getting warmer from the hot-water bottle and the blankets. He could see that she had unzipped his flight suit and removed his helmet, and he looked worried.

"My name is Sister Anne, and I'm a nurse. You're in a convent, and the doctor who is coming is trustworthy. You should be in a hospital, but we'll take care of you here. You're in an underground safe room." He gave her a half smile at the details.

"Thank you, Sister," he said, and closed his eyes for a minute, and then opened them again and looked at her. "How did you find me?"

"I heard you moan when I was walking near the woods, and I looked up, and there you were, a rather large bird stuck in a tree," she said, and he laughed at her description.

"Thank you for finding me and getting me down. I don't suppose the welcome would have been quite so friendly if the German army found me."

"Probably not," she said, as Dr. Strauss came down the stairs with Mother Paul. "Here's the doctor to see you, Captain." She was formal and respectful, and the airman raised his head to look at the doctor, and then at Sophia again.

"Does he speak English?" Captain Blake asked her.

"I don't think so. I'll translate." She explained the condition they'd found him in, and told the doctor about the ankle. He glanced at it, winced, and told her it was a good thing she called. The patient could lose a foot if it got infected or if gangrene set in. She didn't translate the last of the message to Blake. "He said it's good that we called him." The captain nodded and lay flat again while the doctor examined him more thoroughly than Sophia had. She could see he was in pain and trying not to show it. Together, Sophia and the doctor managed to remove the flight suit. There were some bruises and a few scratches on the captain's face from the tree branches. The doctor checked his full body for broken bones, and the only major problem he could see was the ankle, which was a serious injury, as Sophia had seen immediately. They were going to have to ease the bone back in, which would be painful, sew him up, and cast it, no small feat in a cellar safe room with dim lighting. Anticipating the doctor, Sophia asked Mother Paul for more lamps. She came back with two more, as Dr. Strauss shared his plan with Sophia, and she translated it to Blake, while trying to make it sound less ominous and complicated than it was.

"With your permission, he'd like to give you a mild anesthetic to set the leg, in order to get the bone straight. It's liable to be painful, but it's important so you don't wind up with a limp," or lose the foot, she didn't add.

"As long as I don't lose the leg," he said.

"That's not going to happen. The procedure isn't easy, but my father was a surgeon and I've seen this done a number of times. I know you're among strangers in enemy territory, but I'd go for the anesthetic. This won't take too long, but

219

you need to lie very still." Based on her early assessment, the doctor had brought a bottle of ether and a mask, plaster to cast the ankle, an injection of morphine to make the patient sleepy, and enough local anesthetic to make the procedure bearable. It was one of the few drugs he could still get enough of on the black market, for farming injuries.

"Do whatever you have to," the airman said, turning his head away and closing his eyes while the doctor administered the morphine shot. He would have liked to give the airman a tetanus shot as well, but there was none available. It all went to the military. He then injected the local anesthetic, cleaned the wound thoroughly with kerosene, covered the wound with a pad soaked in alcohol, and washed the surrounding area with soap and water. Blake was already half asleep and mumbling as the doctor proceeded through each step meticulously and Sophia assisted him ably. He painted the surrounding skin with iodine to keep it sterile, and flushed the wound with ether, and then iodine. He then instructed Sophia to administer the ether with the mask, while he carefully replaced the bone, and closed the skin with loose sutures to allow for swelling and drainage. And he finally applied a sterile dressing, and Sophia removed the mask of ether. The patient was still sound asleep, while the doctor encased the ankle in a plaster cast, with a window he cut into it for dressing changes. He did the best he could in the circumstances, and Sophia was impressed by what a neat and thorough job he had done. He told Sophia in German that he would have liked to put a couple of pins in the ankle, but he didn't have the necessary material to do it, so it would be crucial for the patient to keep it immobilized for six to eight weeks, with no weight on it whatsoever. And they would have to watch the wound carefully for the next three days, to check for signs of infection, which could be very dangerous. He promised to bring the airman crutches, but he didn't want him out of bed for the next five days, so there was no rush for the crutches, and he would check him daily. Sophia was to call him with any sign of infection or unusual pain, and particularly a fever. The doctor had been impressed by her efficient assistance, and hadn't known she was a nurse.

"I'm a surgical nurse by training," she explained. "My father was a surgeon."

"You did a good job." He smiled at her before he left.

"So did you," she complimented him, as Blake stirred and started to wake up, and looked groggy and disoriented, which was normal from the morphine and the trauma.

"How do you feel?" she asked him in a gentle voice.

"Drunk. Like I drank a bottle of whiskey."

"I'm afraid we don't have any of that." She smiled at him. "The doctor did a very good job. He said you have to keep the leg still, without weight bearing for six to eight weeks. So, welcome to Germany, Captain. It looks like you'll be here for a while." But at least he wasn't dead, which could easily have happened. If no one had found him for another day or two, or even several hours, he wouldn't have survived. The doctor had saved the ankle and his foot, and Sophia saved his life when she found him.

"I need to get back to my squadron," he said with a groan.

"I'm sure you do. But you're lucky this wasn't worse. We'll take good care of you. I promise."

"You already have," he said weakly, feeling woozy. He had been through a lot, when his plane was hit by artillery, and since. He was lucky to be alive. He looked at her again then and smiled. "You look like an angel," he said, and she smiled too.

"I think you're a little drunk from the sedation."

"You do. Just like an angel. With a halo."

"Only because you don't know me. Now you need to get some sleep. And when you wake up, we'll get you something to eat. But first, sleep. And that's an order."

"Are you the boss here?" he asked, still a little giddy. She knew he probably wouldn't remember anything he had said to her when the drugs wore off.

"No, Mother Paul is. She's the Mother Superior. I'm just a lowly foot soldier."

"And I'm the captain," he slurred. "Theodore Blake, Squadron Leader. You can call me Ted." And with that, he drifted off to sleep, she covered him with another blanket, and turned off two of the lamps.

The doctor had left by then, and Mother Paul came to check on them shortly after. "How is he?" she whispered. Sophia was sitting in a straight-backed chair, quietly watching him. He was in a deep sleep still from the morphine the doctor had given him. He had left some pills for the pain for Sophia to give him when he woke up.

"Pretty out of it, but at least he's not in pain, and he didn't die. He could have, hanging up there." Or been shot if a patrol had seen him. But they didn't come by often here. It was a quiet community, with peaceful farms, and the nuns who ran the orphanage were above suspicion and seemed harmless, and all of the orphans had papers that said they were Aryan.

"Dr. Strauss says you're an excellent nurse," Mother Paul told her.

"Thank you." Sophia smiled at her. "He did a beautiful job. I'm going to sit with the captain all day today to make sure he doesn't have any complications or run a fever or try to get out of bed." With the morphine and the local anesthetic, he wouldn't feel the pain of the wound for a while, and could injure himself.

"I can sit with him tonight after the children go to sleep. We can take it in shifts," Mother Paul offered.

"Dr. Strauss says he's here for six to eight weeks, if he

heals well, if there are no complications." It was a long time to conceal an enemy airman.

"We'll just have to manage," Mother Paul said with a tired smile. She had handled it well too, and getting him out of the tree had been a smooth operation with the two young men helping. "Thank you, Sister," she said to Sophia in a whisper, and left the room, as Sophia sat on the room's only chair, and said her prayers as she watched him. It would be a long six or eight weeks nursing him, but it was what she was trained for, and it felt good to be nursing again.

It had been so long since she'd done it. And he seemed like a decent man so far. He was so tall that his feet hung off the end of the bed, and she had propped them up with a little table that was next to the bed, with a spare pillow on it. She had a feeling that as young and strong as he looked, he would be a handful when he started to feel better. She turned off the second lamp then so there was only a dim light in the room, and she sat quietly in her chair as Captain Theodore Blake, Squadron Leader, slept. For now, she was his nurse and he was her patient. It had been an exciting morning. She closed her eyes, and dozed for a minute too. It had been a long time since she'd used her skills as a nurse, since her arrest, and it was rewarding to feel useful again. Captain Blake had her full attention. She only slept for a few minutes, and then observed him quietly, as she said her prayers.

Chapter 13

When the sedation wore off, Captain Theodore Blake, U.S. Army, woke up with a groan. He glanced around the dim room, no longer remembering where he was, and saw the young nun sitting in a chair a short distance from him. Then it all came back to him. She was on her feet and at his side in seconds, gently reached for his wrist and took his pulse.

"How are you feeling, Captain?" she asked him in her slightly British English, which was how they learned English in Europe.

"All right, I guess. Better than the alternative." He lifted his head and looked around the room, and then back at her. "I remember the tree and then seeing you. How did I get here and where am I?"

"We brought you here in a truck. A boy from one of the farms cut you out of the tree. He won't talk. You're in a convent in Ahnsbeck in Lower Saxony. The doctor gave you something to sleep to set your ankle." He nodded, remembering a little more of it now. "How does it feel?"

"Like someone ran over it with a truck."

"I'm not surprised. You have a compound fracture. You were lucky. It could have been a lot worse." He knew it too, and was grateful to her and the people who had saved him. She had provided what he needed to relieve himself, handed it to him, and turned around. "I'm a nurse," she said with her back turned, and then took it from him. She was efficient and professional even in the cellar safe room. She helped him take a sip of water then from a pitcher Mother Paul had left for them, and then covered him with another blanket.

"You look too young to be a nun," he commented, as she supported him while he took another sip of water. His lips were parched, and he was grateful for the drink and her gentle ministering to him.

"I'm not too young," she assured him, "I'm a trained nurse. My order is in Berlin, but I'm staying here now. The nuns here are very kind. It's a teaching order normally. They have a house full of orphans." She smiled at him. "The war has turned the convent into an orphanage."

"And you're a very efficient nurse," he complimented her.

He was taking in every detail of his surroundings, as he'd been trained to do. She was young and pretty despite her simple nun's habit. Her eyes were green, and he wondered what color her hair was. Every inch of her was covered, except her hands and face. She had gentle, graceful hands, which cared for him efficiently, and her eyes were wise and kind for someone so young. "I'm sorry if I'm putting your convent in danger by being here," he apologized. "You were all brave to take me in." And he'd been bombing the hell out of their country.

"You do what you can in a war. It's the people who suffer, and the children. The rest doesn't matter."

"It matters to us," he said firmly. "You can't let a man like Hitler take over the world." Hitler already controlled most of Europe and wanted the rest, especially England. That was the prize he wanted now, and the English were determined not to let that happen, and the Americans, and so were Germans like Sophia and the nuns at St. Blaise.

"My country is starving," Sophia said, as she smoothed his blankets, put a pillow under his head, and tried to make him as comfortable as she could. He didn't appear to be in great pain, despite the severity of the wound, now that the bone was back in place. "Thousands are dying, not just soldiers. The country is broken, and Hitler has to be stopped. Thank you for helping us," she said sincerely as he watched her. He was surprised that she viewed bombing their cities as help.

"It'll get worse before it gets better," he warned her. "We want to stop him too. You hear terrible things about what he's doing in every country he takes over, and what he's doing to the Jews." She nodded. She had seen it firsthand.

"You should rest. Don't think about all that now."

"At least it must be easier here, if you're in the country, away from the air strikes."

"It's not easy anywhere. People are suffering here, and in the cities, and in the camps."

"Is that why you're here, and not in Berlin?" he asked, curious about her. She shook her head and didn't explain. But her eyes told him she had suffered.

Mother Paul arrived a few minutes later with food from the children's lunch for Sophia and the captain. There was chicken from a neighboring farm, barley soup that had a rich flavor, and a slice of bread. There would be vegetables for dinner, soup, and eggs. They tried to give the children nourishing meals. Sophia was still getting used to eating normally again. She had been at the convent for seven months and was shocked every day by how delicious everything tasted.

"Do you have rationing in the States now that you're at war too?" Sophia asked him, curious about it, and he nodded.

"It's not as severe as in Europe. It's meat, cheese, sugar, and canned goods. We came into the war late." Europe had been at war for three and a half years by then, America only for a year, since Pearl Harbor. "Do a lot of people feel the way you do?" he asked her. It was interesting talking to her. He had expected Germans to feel very differently than she did, and the nuns who had taken him in. They were risking themselves for the enemy.

"Many do. Most people are afraid. We're helpless to stop him. Everyone is terrified. It will take a country like America to end it. The punishments here are severe. He doesn't care how many of his own people he kills. It's a kind of madness." She said it very seriously.

"It seems like it when you hear what he's doing to the Jews." She nodded, and reached across him to pull his blanket up higher, and as she did, her sleeve slid slightly further up her arm and he was startled to see the scars of several vicious beatings, which shocked him. Her sleeve covered them again, when she moved, but he could imagine what she had endured to get them. He had heard of people who had escaped the concentration camps, but very few. He didn't mention it, but wondered if she was Jewish and had converted to seek safety in a convent and escape the camps, although he had been told that that didn't always work either, and that the Germans were putting converts in the camps now. But he didn't want to ask her about it. He didn't know her well enough, but seeing the scars on her arm had moved him. It explained why she felt as she did about Hitler.

She helped him sit up to eat his lunch after Mother Paul left it for him, and he said it was delicious. He was ravenous. After he ate, he slept again. It was evening when he woke, and one of the other nuns had replaced Sophia so she could go to Vespers.

"Where's Sister Anne?" he asked, like a child looking for its mother.

"She's at prayers with the other sisters. She'll be back soon with your dinner. We're lucky we have a nurse here to take care of you." The older nun smiled at him. "The rest of us are teachers."

"Has she been here since war was declared?" he asked, fishing for information about Sophia. The scars he had glimpsed intrigued him, and pained him for her at the same time.

"No. She's only been here for six or seven months, since last summer. She came to us from . . ." she hesitated and caught herself quickly, "from Berlin. We're lucky she decided to stay here, and not go back to the city. It's more peaceful here, and she's wonderful with the children. Her order is different from ours. They're Catholic. Our order is Protestant, but we all do the same work and serve our Lord as best we can. It really doesn't make any difference."

"Where do the orphans come from?" he asked. The nun was very chatty, and happy to answer his questions, although careful with her answers. They didn't often get adult visitors, and never Americans, obviously. The whole convent was whispering about him. "Do the children come from the cities?"

"They come from all over Germany, and even some from France and Holland," she said. "People concerned about them bring them to us. Most of them have lost their whole families." He found that interesting too, wondering how a single child could survive and lose all their relatives, and why there were so many of them. The simple answer were the air strikes that were happening all over Europe and in England too, but he wondered if there was another reason for the orphans coming from all over to them. In spite of the acute pain in his ankle, his mind was sharp, and he was astute.

Sophia traded places with the other nun an hour later. She had eaten with the nuns and the children, and brought the captain his food, a tasty omelet with herbs, and a small piece of pork sausage, some of the leftover soup from lunch, and another slice of bread. Considering that they were rationed, it was a hearty meal. And as it had been at lunch, it was delicious.

"Your fellow nuns must be good cooks," he said as he ate. "I hope I'm not depriving anyone with what I'm eating." He looked worried for a minute.

"The sisters are very good at stretching what we have so there's enough for everyone. The children don't eat a lot, and the farmers are generous with us. Some things are impossible to get, but what they have on the farms fills in for us. You'll be seeing a lot of chicken," she said with an easy laugh. He liked talking to her and wanted to know more about her. He sensed a story there.

After he ate, she dealt with his bathroom needs again, smoothed his blankets, and watched him as he fell asleep. He had slept for most of the day. He felt comfortable now, knowing that she was in the room. Every time he opened his eyes, she was there, watching him. And whatever need he had, she took care of it. She really was like his own personal angel, sent to earth to minister to him.

He said that to her the next day, and she laughed at the idea. She was getting comfortable with him too, spending every hour with him, while he slept or they chatted. He said the pain was a little less on the second day, and they were already getting into a routine of care and sleep. She had given him a sponge bath that morning and he felt almost human. The doctor came to check on him and was pleased at the wound. Sophia had changed the dressing and there was no sign of infection.

It surprised the captain, but there was something about her nun's habit and the professional way she nursed him that kept him from feeling embarrassed with her, and she seemed at ease with him, although she was less so than he thought. She told herself that he was just another patient, and this was her job. But he was still a young, very handsome man, no matter what she said to herself. He had short blond hair, moss green eyes, and strong features. They were existing in isolation from everyone, just the two of them in the small airless cellar room. It was always a breath of fresh air for an instant when one of the nuns opened the trapdoor, and came down the stairs to bring them something, or to relieve Sophia when she went to eat a meal with the other nuns.

"Tell me why you wanted to be a nun," he asked as he ate his lunch. She ate a hard-boiled egg one of the nuns had prepared for her, which was easier to eat sitting on a chair than his meals, which needed to be more substantial while he recovered, and he was a man, and ate more. His lunch was pork sausage from one of the farms.

"I always knew it was what I wanted, ever since I was a young girl. It was kind of a dream. But I became sure of it when my mother was sick. My mother had tuberculosis and was in a sanatorium for a year before she died. I tried to visit her every day. The hospital was outside Berlin. I learned to drive so I could see her on my own."

"How old were you?"

"Sixteen when she got sick, and seventeen when she went to the sanatorium. I was eighteen when she died," she said seriously.

"So, you're telling me that you decided at sixteen or seventeen to be a nun? Isn't that too early to make a lifetime decision?"

"Not really, if you have a calling. I wasn't completely sure until after she died. But then I knew."

"Maybe you just thought you had a calling, and felt guilty because you couldn't save her, and you wanted to atone for it by becoming a nun and punishing yourself." It was a more complicated way of looking at it, but possible. Sophia insisted that wasn't the case.

"I didn't feel guilty, I felt sad. And that's when I decided to be a nurse too, to help other sick people, like my father with his patients."

"Two very big decisions for a young girl to make at a very emotional time. I can understand your wanting to be a nurse and help others. But depriving oneself of a normal life to be a nun has never made sense to me."

"It's a wonderful way of life and I love it," she said firmly.

"What did your father say?" He liked hearing about her life, and it distracted him from the pain he was in.

"My father was very upset. He didn't believe in God, and he thought it would be a terrible life for me. But it isn't. It's exactly what I wanted. I went in after nursing school. It's been almost three years."

"And you've taken all your vows?" he asked her.

"I took my vows for the novitiate two years ago. I should have taken my final vows a year ago, but I couldn't because of where I was then, and I can't do that now until I get back to my order, maybe at the end of the war. It's all a bit different at a Protestant convent, and I want to take my vows with my order. The war has disrupted everything," she explained to him.

"Do you have siblings?" he inquired as he finished the sausage, which was delicious.

"I have a sister. We're entirely different, and always have been. She wouldn't last five minutes in a convent. And she's married now, with two children."

"Where is she? Here in Germany?"

He was so open and easy about the way he asked her questions, but she hesitated to tell him such personal information. She had a feeling that it was just very American and the way they viewed things, so she answered him after all. There was no malice to it, nor criticism, just genuine interest, and compassion, she could tell. "No, she's in Switzerland. After war was declared, they discovered that her husband had a Jewish grandparent they didn't know about, which made him a quarter Jewish, so they had to leave. It was very distressing. But now she and her family are safe in Zurich."

"And you don't want to be with them instead of Germany, where there are heavy risks?" Not only from the Nazis, but the Allies who bombed Germany almost every day.

Sophia shook her head. "I'd rather be useful here than playing bridge with my sister and her friends in Zurich. I would feel much too guilty."

"Does she feel guilty?" he asked her.

"Not for a minute." They both laughed then. "Theresa leads a very comfortable, pampered life and she loves it."

"While you take a vow of poverty and chastity and live simply as a nun. It's amazing how different siblings can be. I'm very different from my brother and sister too."

"You have brothers and sisters?"

"One of each. My older sister is a country doctor in Vermont, and she loves it. She's a general practitioner, and treats everyone in the county. My younger brother is a banker in New York, married to an Irish Catholic woman, and they have six children. She was a nurse like you. They have two sets of twins. They're adorable, but six kids would drive me crazy. They're all a year apart. They have six kids under five and he loves it. They're great parents. Thank God he makes a decent living. My sister hasn't married yet. She says she doesn't have time and her patients are her children. And any time you call her, she's visiting one of her patients."

"And you?" She was curious about him too.

"I went to law school, I'm a lawyer. I thought I wanted to go into criminal law, but I didn't like it. I don't want to defend a bunch of people you know committed some heinous crime. I love to fly planes, I've been flying since college, so I enlisted right after Pearl Harbor. And ever since I've heard what's been going on in Europe, I've been thinking about defending human rights when I go back to New York. I'm passionate about it. My brother says I'll be poor for the rest of my life. He thinks I should do business law or tax law or divorce law, all of which would bore me to death. We'll see what happens when I get out. I think the world will be a different place after this war," he said, and she agreed. "Mr. Hitler is going to leave a lot of damage and crimes against humanity in his wake. And what about you after the war? Still a nun and still a nurse?" He made it sound like it wasn't enough and she didn't think so either.

"I'll go back to my order in Berlin. There will be a lot of homeless displaced people who have lost everything, not just in Germany but all over Europe. Everyone will be poor here. Women who've lost their husbands and their children, men who've lost everything. Thousands, maybe millions of orphans. I want to help take care of them, and get them on their feet again, if I can. I want to ask my order to take in as many people as we can, and maybe run a center for orphans and adults while they try to find what's left of their families and build their lives again. Germany will be in chaos for years," she predicted, accurately, he thought. And what she wanted to do was similar to what he wanted, but on a smaller, more personal scale, which suited her. He had broader ideas, dealing with the crimes against humans and human rights that were at the root of the war, and would have to be dealt with so it didn't happen again.

"If there are war crimes trials after the war, I want to be in on them. That would really be interesting and worthwhile. I'm not sure if I'd have to stay in the army to do it, or if I could do it as a civilian. I'll have to find out, if I can get out from behind enemy lines, back to my base in England. I may spend the rest of the war in a German prisoner-of-war camp, and that wouldn't be pleasant, from everything I hear. Hitler and his men are not respecters of persons, especially the enemy." Three months ago, Hitler had ordered the execution of all British commandos the Germans were holding captive, which had shocked the world. "I've been trying to figure out how to get out of Germany, ever since I was hanging from that tree. I have a contact to reach out to, but it's not going to be easy getting out of here. No one is going to send a plane to fly me out."

She had thought of it too, and she wondered if any of their contacts would help him, if Max could. "You don't need to worry about that now. You'll be here for at least another six or eight weeks until your ankle is healed. Hopefully your army will help you. And there's a strong underground here of people who don't agree with what the Nazis are doing. You'll figure out a way. Now you have to rest and get strong again in the meantime." She sounded like a nurse as she said it, and he smiled. He wondered if these would be his last days of freedom, hidden in a convent, and he'd end up in a German prisoner-of-war camp after that. It seemed almost inevitable as he lay there. He wondered how the other pilots had fared and how many there were on the ground, like him, either injured or not, who had to find a way out of Germany from behind enemy lines, or end up prisoners, or dead. It made him even more grateful for the refuge and care provided by the convent, and this very unusual young woman, who was so bright, compassionate, and kind. He had never met anyone like her.

Their conversations were lengthy and candid. They talked about important things, and he thoroughly enjoyed every moment he spent with her.

Sophia was intelligent and they had similar ideas about many things. Her points of view were often colored by religion, but she was also practical and open to new ideas. Mother Paul and the other nuns took turns taking care of Ted, to give Sophia time to spend with the children and do her chores. And he was always happy to see her get back so they could pick up the thread of their last conversation. Sometimes she brought cards to play with him, to distract him. The days in the cellar safe room were long and boring, and he had cabin fever as he started to feel better. His ankle was healing well, and the doctor was pleased that with Sophia's diligent care, infection had not set in. But Ted was very hampered by his ankle and couldn't put weight on it, so he had no choice but to stay until he could.

Every few days, once he could use the crutches and keep the weight off his bad foot, Mother Paul would approve a brief walk late at night, just to get some air and a change of scene. She would agree to let him walk around once the children were asleep, so they didn't see him, and slip and tell someone about him. Only the other nuns and the doctor knew he was there, and the two farm boys.

Everything looked beautiful even in the dark, once he got out to take a walk. He missed his freedom and being able to fly and fight the Germans, but talking to Sophia was enormous compensation. She went on his nightly walks with him. They talked about everything from German literature to religion. The only thing that frustrated him was how determined she was to remain a nun and take her final vows when she returned to her order. She firmly believed, without a single doubt, that it was the right path for her, and nothing he said could dissuade her. It also meant that he couldn't express his growing feelings for her, which she remained unaware of. But expressing them to her seemed inappropriate and disrespectful to him, if she truly wanted to remain a nun, and she said she did.

"Do you believe in God?" she asked him bluntly one day, and he was surprised by the question.

"I do, very definitely. I grew up Catholic, but I don't practice my religion anymore. I believe in God, I'm just not so crazy about the people who represent him. I had a lot of mean teachers who were nuns when I was a kid. And priests who weren't nice to us either. Every now and then you'd get a jolly one who bought everyone ice cream or gave them candy, but a lot of the time I thought they were hypocritical and didn't believe what they were preaching. I never liked the idea that Catholics thought they were the only ones who got it right. Who said? And a lot of the Catholics I grew up with seemed smug to me. They think they're better than everyone else. Maybe I should have become a Protestant instead of giving up on religion completely. I think you're the closest I've ever come to someone who actually lives their religion and doesn't preach about it. You're genuinely humble and I think your faith is real. But I've never met anyone else like you. And the way things stand now, going to church on Sundays bores me, and I'd rather go to a football game.

But you'd better believe that when I was hanging in that tree when I landed here, I was praying like crazy. I think you were the answer to my prayers, and you've actually got me believing in religion again, in living it, not talking it. But in spite of that, you still haven't convinced me that you should be a nun. You're too young and too pretty, and I think it will be a terrible waste if you take your final vows one day. You should have a husband who's crazy about you, and some kids—not as many as my brother, but one or two or three. Don't cheat yourself of that for a lonely life as a nun, giving all of you to everyone else, while no one gives anything to you."

"God gives me all I need," she said, and smiled at him. Nothing he said shook her faith in the path she had chosen, and he was beginning to believe that he couldn't either, so he never told her he was falling in love with her. Mother Paul had seen it, and one or two of the other nuns suspected it, but Sophia remained oblivious to it as she nursed him back to health and tried not to think about the fact that once she accomplished that, he would leave. She liked talking to him and their exchange of ideas. And she liked the ease with which they could say anything to each other. He reminded her a little of Claus, except that she knew Ted even better, because they spent so much time together. She'd never been as close to any man as she was to him.

Chapter 14

For Ted Blake—Sophia called him Ted now at his insistence, and no longer "Captain," and he had finally convinced her to tell him her given name, although he never said it when someone else was present—the room lit up whenever she was in it. They were comfortable with each other and spoke about every subject. Sophia loved their conversations and she knew she would miss him when he left, but it didn't sway her from her decision to stay in the religious life now or when the war was over. There was so much she wanted to do to help people then.

Mother Paul was concerned about her too. She believed that much of Sophia's determination was sincerely based in faith, but she wondered if she was afraid of what the outside world would be like if she didn't have a habit to protect her, and the convent to hide behind. Both of her parents were gone, and she hadn't seen her sister in three years. She had survived a concentration camp and lost her father to one. The world had been a dangerous place for her, and to Sophia the love of a mere man, and not the Almighty, seemed like a dangerous place to her. What if a man or a husband stopped loving her one day, or died, or abandoned her? She knew that she could rely on God forever. The people she loved most had disappeared all too quickly. Mother Paul was well aware of that, and she also saw how much the American captain had come to love his nurse, and she was sad thinking that Sophia might miss an opportunity that would never come again, in order to lead a life of deprivation and self-sacrifice. She was still so young, at twenty-four, and could have a full life with a good man one day, and Mother Paul saw nothing wrong with that. There were many ways to serve God, not just as a nun. And she was certain that Sophia would always find ways to serve Him.

She said as much to Sophia one afternoon while they were driving to a neighboring farm to pick up eggs for the convent. The local patrols almost never stopped them. The nuns were a familiar sight in the area, and they never caused any trouble. The young soldiers let them pass with a wave without bothering with their papers, although Sophia's heart nearly stopped every time she saw them. Mother Paul wanted her to be a familiar sight as well, so her presence didn't arouse curiosity among the patrols, so she took Sophia on errands with her whenever she could.

"You know, our religious path is not for everyone," she said gently, and Sophia wondered where she was going with it, and if Mother Paul was questioning her faith. "There are many ways to serve God, even as a mother and wife. Not everyone is cut out for a life of celibacy, and a union between a man and a woman can be a sacred thing and a great blessing to both of them," she said.

"Have I done something wrong, Mother?" Sophia asked, worried. "Do you think I'm unsuited to the religious life?"

"No, my dear. I think you're very much suited to it, maybe even too much so. I just don't want you to deprive yourself of the love of a good man, or having a family, and regret it in later years, when you don't have a husband and children."

"Do you regret it, Mother?"

"No. But I never met a man I loved, or the right one who loved me."

"And you think I have?" Sophia asked her, beginning to suspect the Mother Superior's reason for her comments. Mother Paul glanced at her and nodded.

"I do. I don't know if he has expressed it to you, but I think Captain Blake is very much in love with you. I think he's a good man, and a good person, and you might be very happy with him." She thought Sophia should examine all her options and be open to what life offered her, before making a final choice when she took her vows.

"I like being a nun," Sophia said, sounding petulant for a moment, which was unlike her. She was good-natured about everything, which Ted Blake had noticed too.

"It's a long life, Sister. You enjoy his company, and he values yours. You might miss him one day. I think you will when he leaves, more than you think. And these are strange times. If you do love him, I don't think you should let your vows in the novitiate hold you back. You've done a lot as a nun. And I think you could still do a lot for the world as someone's wife."

"That's what he says, not about him with me, but generally. He doesn't think I should stay in the convent. But I'm happy there. I feel safe."

"He could make you feel safe too, after the war is over. For now, none of us is safe. I pray about our safety every day."

"So do I," Sophia said, momentarily confused about what Mother Paul had said. "I've never had any doubts about joining the order." At Ravensbrück Hans had loved her too, and she had never been tempted for a single moment to violate her vows, but he was a Nazi, and that was different.

She and Ted had very like-minded ideas, but she didn't want to give up being a nun. "I'm sure about my vocation, Mother. I promise you, I am," she said fervently, and the Mother Superior nodded.

"I wanted to be sure. Remember, there are many, many ways to serve God, not just one. And some of them in the world, not behind convent walls." Sophia nodded and they drove on in silence while she thought about it, but she was sure she was already on the right path, no matter how good a man Ted Blake was. She was certain that, like Edith Stein, her destiny was to be a nun.

Despite their many conversations on a multitude of subjects, the one subject Ted had never dared broach with her, even after a month, when they called each other by first names and nothing seemed taboo, were the scars he had glimpsed on her arms. She had none on her face and hands. It was all he could see of her. But he had glimpsed the angry-looking, vicious scars on her arms several times while she nursed him. He knew there had to be a frightening story to the scars, but he was afraid to ask. And she never mentioned them or how she got them.

They were playing cards one afternoon after lunch, and the sleeve of her habit fell back as she held her cards. They were laughing about something, and his expression grew serious as his eye caught her badly scarred arms again.

He spoke to her softly when she noticed what he was looking at.

"Would it be too intrusive if I ask you about that?" He was a gentle person, and he didn't want to hurt her or revive ugly memories, but he knew it had to be an important chapter in her life. He wanted to know everything, in case she ever softened her position on remaining in the religious life. She had been adamant so far, as he skirted around the subject as carefully as he could. He had always hoped she would explain the injuries herself, after he'd seen them on the first day.

"No," she said quietly, and folded her cards, and put them facedown on the table. She couldn't tell him about it and play cards. "I try to put it all behind me, but there are reminders of it that come up."

"Do you have Jewish blood?" he asked her. It was the simplest explanation for it, but she shook her head.

"No, I don't. My father was an extremely successful doctor, with his own private hospital. He was a surgeon. People came from everywhere to be operated on by him. Some of his patients were among the High Command of the SS.

"I never knew what happened and he never told me, but a year after the war started, he was arrested for treason against the Führer and the Reich. There was a medical program they had instituted right after the war started, called

Aktion T4. It was a program to 'euthanize' anyone the Reich deemed undesirable, people with handicaps, old people, babies, children with minor defects.

"I treated children like that myself as a nurse, a little boy once who was very intelligent but partially deaf. As nurses, we had to report any anomalies or chronically sick or damaged or disabled people to the Health Ministry. I never did. The Health Ministry had a board of 'experts' who decided which patients to kill. They euthanized them by lethal injection. I've always wondered what happened to the little deaf boy. I think they killed him. There were killing centers for Aktion T4 apparently, to speed up the process, and private doctors were asked to participate. It was called euthanasia, but it was apparently wholesale murder of anyone the Reich wanted to get rid of. Some physicians were 'invited' to join the program, by invitation of the Führer. A Nazi officer told me about it, so I believe it's true. My father would never have participated in something like that. *Never.* He profoundly believed the oath he had taken as a doctor to preserve and improve life, to heal and not to harm. He even taught me that as a nurse. I think that may be why he was accused of treason against the Führer personally and the Reich. It's only a guess. It's the *only* reason I can imagine them accusing him of treason. He hated Hitler but was discreet about it, and he treated all of his patients equally, rich or poor. But I can't think of any other reason they'd have to accuse him of being a traitor, although it doesn't take much these days. I was already in the convent then—my sister had already left, which made a bad impression. She and my brother-in-law escaped to Switzerland and were safe, and still are, but her husband's parents were arrested like common criminals and everything they had taken from them. They were sent to a concentration camp, and no one knows what happened to them. They're probably dead by now.

"The day my father was arrested, his whole hospital was destroyed, vandalized and burned to the ground while the firefighters stood by and watched. The fire had clearly been ordered by the SS. They burned our home too, with everything in it, after they took the art. They sent my father to Dachau, and I didn't find out till last year that he died seven months after he got there. I didn't find out for nearly a year, and then only because I met someone in the records office. My father died in a concentration camp as a traitor, which I can promise you he never was. I was more of a traitor than he was, which they never knew.

"I belonged to a small, quiet group of dissidents and went to meetings twice a week even before the war, and after it started. When they started deporting the Jews in earnest and taking whole families away, one of my friends from the meetings was saving children, and I escorted them sometimes from one safe place to another. I was an intermediary, a chaperone, sometimes with great frequency, at other times less often. And I did it even from the convent. The Mother Superior knew. I continued doing it after my father went to Dachau. I thought that every life we saved was a life stolen from the Nazis, and a victory. I was never caught. I was careful. But I was stopped by a patrol one night on my way back from dropping off a child. They let me go. But they came to see me several times. They had no evidence, but they were suspicious of me. My father was a traitor, my sister and her husband had escaped. They assumed the worst of me, and they were right, although they couldn't prove it. I was arrested as a criminal and sent to Ravensbrück. It's a concentration camp for women, and a hellhole of the worst kind. People were beaten, whipped, killed, and starved. I won't tell you all the things they did there. Sometimes they had the prisoners torn apart by dogs.

"We were four to a bunk, and five hundred women assigned to three toilets. The barracks were at double and quadruple occupancy. Babies, women, and children were killed. I made four friends in my barracks—three were my bunkmates, and one had the bunk below us with three other women. I was sure I wouldn't survive if I stayed there, nor would the others. I came up with a plan for the five of us to escape. It took three months to get ready. I was in Ravensbrück for eight months, the closest to hell I will ever get on this earth. By sheer miracle, the plan worked. It took us two days to get here last June, eight months ago. One of the women died in the woods the night before we got here. She was sick and her body just gave up. She was older than we were. I was the youngest. The other three have gone on, with false papers and new identities. One is in Portugal now, another one in Munich, one went back to France, to the free zone, and I'm here, safe at St. Blaise. The Nazis have better things to do than track me down. They probably figured we got killed along the way by a patrol. You don't get far in Germany without papers. But they're not as smart as they think. People find ways to get out if they want to badly enough. My sister walked over the mountains into Switzerland nearly seven months pregnant. People run to save their lives, or their children.

"So that is how I got the marks on my arm. In Ravensbrück. I have them on my legs and back too. I've been free for eight months, and I don't believe it yet," she said solemnly, and she saw that there were tears sliding down his cheeks as he listened, and he was holding tightly to her hand. He couldn't imagine what she'd been through, but he had never admired anyone so much in his life. He loved her more than ever and wished he could protect her now, but he was in danger himself, and indirectly putting her and all the nuns at risk too. He realized that even more acutely now.

"Why don't you go to Switzerland now, to be with your sister and be safe there?" he asked her.

"Because I'm not like her, and I don't have a husband, and children to protect. I can't walk away from those who may need me here. I can't leave children in danger and suffering, hidden away like you are now, some of them for years. Some of them have been in hiding for seven or eight years, even before the war, and it won't be over for them until the war is over and the Nazis are gone. I can't walk away now, Ted. I can't. If even one of them needs me, I want to be here, not in Switzerland having lunch with my sister's friends." He nodded. He knew now that that was who she was, and had guessed it for a while.

"And if they call on you again for help, to transport a child or children to safety, would you still risk that now?" He needed to know, for his own peace of mind, to know if she would be safe when he left her, or even alive if he came back.

"Yes, I would," she said simply. "That's why I'm here, and who I am, why God sent me here, and why he saved me from Ravensbrück, so I could be useful again. It's what they do at St. Blaise. The orphans they have are all Jewish, their families deported and probably killed. They all have new identities and papers, but that's how they came here, and if more need to come, we'll take them, and I'll bring them

253

myself if I need to. We can't let a single one of those children die because this country is being run by madmen."

"For God's sake, Sophia, will you at least be careful?" He looked desperate as he asked her. It was the answer he had expected but not the one he wanted to hear.

"I always am. I was never caught. Only suspected. I'll be more careful next time."

"And if they catch you again?"

"Then I'll either die for my sins, whatever they are, or I'll escape again, or die trying."

"That's not reassuring," he said, profoundly upset. He loved her and didn't want to lose her. And she wasn't even his.

"Will you stop flying bombing missions when you go back?" she asked him, and he smiled and shook his head.

"No, I won't. I guess we're freedom fighters, both of us, fighting for what's right and the lives we can save, but when this bloody war is over, then what? When do we get our turn to have a life?" He wanted a life with her.

"I don't need a life. I gave mine to God to use as He wishes. And when this is over, I want to help put the broken back together, to find a home for the children, better than an orphanage. I want to comfort the men and women who lost all their children, and the children who lost their parents and brothers and sisters. There is a lifetime of work to be done, and I want to be here to do it. I need to be, Ted. It's who I am."

"There are other ways to do that," he said to her.

"How? Where? Unless I'm here where it started, how can I help finish it? When this is over, you'll go back to New York. I'll be here, with lots of work to do in Germany. I'll go back to Berlin when the war ends. It's where I'm meant to be."

"Maybe not. And maybe I'll be here working at the war trials, and there will be war trials after the atrocities that have been committed here, and we don't know the half of them yet," he said, and she nodded in agreement with him. "When this is over, I'm coming back to see you, Sophia. I want to see you again, and you can tell me then what you want to do. None of us knows how long this will take, or how much damage there will be when it's over." There was a good chance that neither of them would be alive when it was, but he didn't say it. "I just want you to know that if I'm alive and breathing, I'm coming back." She smiled, wanting to believe that it would happen, even just as friends. She still missed Claus, her friend from the meetings, who had gotten her started transporting children, saved Theresa and Heinrich, and died trying to blow up a train. It was a savage war, which caused savage casualties. She hoped she and Ted wouldn't be among them, as two more. But for now, nothing was sure. And both of them were still in danger.

* * *

Ted spent another month at St. Blaise after that. He looked at her differently after he knew her story, with even more respect and admiration than before. But he still didn't believe that her destiny was to be a nun, and that she couldn't serve those in need in some other form. But he knew he couldn't convince her of that now. She wasn't ready to hear it yet.

It agonized him to imagine the horrors she had seen and experienced at Ravensbrück, and how lucky she had been to escape. She didn't tell him about Hans, but there wasn't much to tell, except that they had been friends to the limited degree they could be, as enemies in a war. But she was grateful that Hans didn't seem to have reported them that night, or they probably would have been caught. So he had had a hand in their successful escape. Whatever she had said to him that night had hit its mark.

There was a strong feeling of peace between her and Ted. They knew everything that there was to know about each other. He knew the tragedies that trailed behind her. And she knew his goals and what tormented him. He felt guilty every time he dropped a bomb while on a mission, wondering who he had killed. But his guilt and her scars were the price of war, which they were willing to accept. What Sophia would not accept was to do nothing. He understood that now.

*   *   *

It took a full two months for Dr. Strauss to be satisfied with the healing of Ted's ankle, and sure that the bones had knitted properly. Ted was still using one crutch to support himself, although he needed it much less. He stayed another two weeks, until mid-April, when he was steady on his feet and could make a safe escape. He was grateful for every minute he could spend with Sophia, and she didn't admit it to him, but it was getting harder and harder to resist the logic and emotion of his arguments, and she was beginning to question her own path in light of the love she felt for him as well. She thought that in the long run, she would be glad she remained true to her vows, and she would always know he had loved her, and she loved him. She told herself that knowing that would be enough, and she would remain faithful to her vows. She knew they wouldn't be able to communicate with each other after he left, until the war was over. And she hoped he would still be alive then. The coming months or years were going to be far more dangerous for him than for her, flying bombing missions. Every time he flew, he risked being shot down again.

In the middle of April he made radio contact with the intermediary who could help him. One of the farmers Mother Paul knew had a radio, which they used from time to time for subversive purposes. A code message came back two days later, and Ted knew where he had to go. It was a few hours' walk from where they were, and he was able to cover the distance now.

They said goodbye in the cellar room where he had spent two and a half months and they had talked for so many hours. And even knowing he shouldn't, he kissed her, and she didn't stop him. It was the one kiss she allowed herself before closing that door forever.

"I love you, Sophia," he whispered to her with all the emotion he felt for her. He was taking the memory of her with him.

"I love you too," she whispered back. She felt like two people now, one of them in his arms. She was both Sophia Alexander and Sister Anne. Sister Anne would remain to do her work, and whatever was asked of her, no matter how much risk was involved. Ted knew that she was too brave for her own good.

Ted thanked Mother Paul and the other nuns, got a glimpse of the children he had never met, and set off across fields and behind farms and across small streams, in the direction he'd been told to go. He looked tall and strong, with his blond hair shining in the sun as he turned back and waved. A slim figure in a nun's habit, Sophia stood and watched him, and he knew he'd always remember that final image of her, and then he disappeared in the trees. They were going to pick him up at six o'clock in a daring move on an old, deserted airstrip. They'd have to be fast and lucky, and he was hoping to be both, when they landed and took off again within minutes shortly after sunset, and headed toward England and his base.

Sophia was just shepherding the children in for dinner, coming back from the field where they'd been playing, when she heard a humming sound above them, looked up into the sky and saw a small plane in the distance roll and dip its wings and then head straight up into the sky and disappear into the clouds. It was his final goodbye, as they both prayed they would meet again.

Chapter 15

After Ted left Germany in mid-April of 1943, the tides began to turn slowly in the Allies' favor in May. Ted sent a message to the farmer with the radio in a code easy for Sophia to decipher. The farmer delivered the message to her. Ted was back at his base, safely arrived. That was all it said.

In May, the Allies took Tunisia, German and Italian troops surrendered in North Africa, after bitter battles there. German U-boats stopped cruising the North Atlantic and the eastern coast of the United States.

In July, the Allies landed in Sicily, and bombed Rome. The British bombed Hamburg. In August, the Americans bombed Regensburg and Schweinfurt in Germany in broad daylight. Three weeks later, in September, the Italians surrendered to the Allies. And in November, the British effected a massive air raid on Berlin. As the year came to an end, people were beginning to hope that the end of the war was coming near, with an Allied victory. It wasn't certain yet, but it was a growing possibility.

Soviet troops were fighting hard battles as well and began the new year advancing into Poland.

In March of 1944, there was a massive Allied daylight bombing of Berlin, and two weeks later, the British dropped three thousand tons of bombs on Hamburg. It was a savage war with endless casualties, and both sides were relentless in the pursuit of victory. But the Allies were coming closer. In June of 1944, fourteen months after Ted Blake had last seen Sophia, the Allies entered Rome, and the D-Day landings began on the beaches of the northern coast of France in Normandy, with the ultimate goal of reaching Paris and reclaiming France. The Germans were shipping trainloads of art treasures and plundered goods from France to Germany in case they were forced to take flight by the advancing Allies. They were taking all the spoils of war they could, although members of the French Resistance had hidden many of the national treasures in underground caves.

The nuns at St. Blaise occasionally got news from their friend with the radio. There were no messages from Ted, and Sophia had no idea if he was still alive. There had been so many American air strikes and combined missions with the British that she had no way of knowing if he was safe or not. She hoped he was. Her world remained small, confined to the convent, listening to the news on German radio. She was encouraged every time she heard of another Allied air strike on Berlin. The Allies were decimating the city and steadily weakening the German power base. She worried about the Sisters of Mercy in her convent there, but she knew that they were all willing to give their lives to see Germany defeated.

Only a few more children had joined the nuns that year when the families who had been hiding them couldn't keep them any longer. One of them had been hidden nearby and Sophia went to get her, the other two were brought to them by couriers from other cities, and within days, they blended in with the others. Their papers appeared to be in order, although all were convincing forgeries, and the local authorities suspected nothing. They left the nuns alone and had never suspected them of subversive activity, and believed them innocent.

Sophia had had a postcard from Hedi in Portugal, and one from Brigitte in Munich. She'd had a letter from Jo at Christmas, under another name. They were all leading their lives as best they could, given the war and air raids everywhere, except in Portugal. But it was good to know that they were alive and as safe as the times allowed. They wrote to her as Sister Anne. Sophia hadn't heard from her sister Theresa since she'd been sent to Ravensbrück. She was intending to contact her when the war was over. They had had no communication for three years, due to circumstances Sophia could do nothing about, and her sister didn't know where she was.

In July the newspapers were full of an account of an assassination attempt on the Führer, mounted by a group of German army officers, which had failed.

And in August, when Sophia was playing with the children with a garden hose and spraying them to their squealing delight—she was as wet as they were and the other nuns were laughing—the farmer who had brought Sophia Ted's message before arrived in his truck with a message he had written out for her, from Ted. "Paris has been liberated. Drinking champagne at the Ritz. Berlin is next. Keep the faith, T." It was the first message she'd had from him since his safe arrival back at his base in England sixteen months before. He was alive. And Paris was free. It was a long message for the farmer to have written down, not speaking English. She reported it to Mother Paul immediately.

"The Americans have liberated Paris. I had a message from Ted. He says Berlin is next."

"That won't happen overnight. It will be a hard fight for the Allies. The Führer won't give up easily," Mother Paul said.

Sophia nodded and knew it was true, but the end was in sight, however long it took. "Did he say anything else?"

"He's drinking champagne at the Ritz." The two nuns exchanged a smile. Mother Paul didn't ask her any questions about her feelings for him. Sophia hadn't even known if he was alive for the past year and a half. He was a tender memory now, but no longer seemed real. And like when her father was at Dachau, she didn't want to harbor feelings for him, and assume he was still alive when he might have been dead for more than a year. They were ghosts in each other's lives now. He risked his life every day on his bombing missions. Her life had been quieter for the past year, with only one child she had transported. Children had long since been settled into hiding places or been given up to the Nazis and killed in the camps. It was the reality of children who were at risk during the war, usually because they were Jewish and their families were deported, with or without them. The Germans had even rounded up children in France without their parents and sent them to camps in Germany to be exterminated, "for the purification of the master race." Sophia thought of it every time she looked at the twenty-five children the nuns were harboring who could easily have met the same fate. It seemed so few children to save, but every life counted. The nuns had cheated death as many times as they could.

Sophia was eager to take her final vows. She had been due to take them in 1942, and was two years late, due to her arrest and being separated from her convent. She couldn't take her final vows with the Protestant nuns at St. Blaise. She had to wait until she was back with her own order in Berlin, whenever the war ended. Until then she remained a novice, but her conviction hadn't changed and she was still anxious to take her vows. She had had no contact with Mother Regina or anyone at her order since her arrest. She missed them, but she got along well with her Protestant sisters at St. Blaise, and one day she would go home to the Sisters of Mercy in Berlin and pick up the threads of her religious life with them again. She wasn't a practicing nurse here either. It would have exposed her forged papers, so the only nursing she did was for the children with runny noses, stomachaches, and flu, except for her two months nursing Ted with his severely fractured ankle. She missed nursing at times, but it had to wait for the war to end too. Everything did. Their lives were on hold until they could breathe again, and the Nazis released their chokehold on them—unless Germany won the war, which would be disastrous.

There was less and less food to be had these days, and the children were better off near the farms than in the cities. The soldiers took all they could from the farms, but the farmers the nuns knew always kept something in reserve for them and the children at the convent, and the local soldiers turned a blind eye to it. Many of them had children too. And although the Führer was not fond of religious zeal, the nuns had always been treated with respect locally. The fact that the nuns of St. Blaise were Protestant helped too. There was no question in any of their minds that they were better off here than in Berlin, which seemed to become more chaotic every day, with countless displaced people roaming the streets. At Saint Blaise, they were all safe and had a home.

There were no further messages from Ted in Paris, but at least they knew he was alive. And according to the farmer's radio, there was celebrating in the streets of Paris after the Germans left. The Americans were king there now.

From the liberation of Paris until the end of the year, the Russians were having steady victories.

Christmas was even thinner at the end of 1944. Food had grown even more scarce, rationing was more severe. The nuns' gifts to the children were smaller, and everyone was waiting for news of the war. Many of the children were old enough to be aware of it now. Some of them had the illusion that when the war ended, they would find their families again, but it was less than likely in most cases. Their families had most likely all died in the gas chambers.

As 1945 began, the Allies hammered German cities merci-lessly. They took Cologne in March, and Soviet troops took Danzig. The Americans entered Nuremberg, as the Soviets began their final attack on Berlin. They reached the city in April. Adolf Hitler committed suicide at the end of April. And all German forces surrendered unconditionally to the Allies on May eighth. The nuns' farmer friend came speeding down the road and jumped out of his truck to tell them. All troops had vanished from the area. The war in Europe was over. The Führer was dead, and the Germans had lost to the Allies. The farmer hugged all the nuns and kissed the children. The nuns hugged each other. The terror and the agony, six years of hell and the shameful murder of innocents was over. Sophia thought of Hans Mahler in Ravensbrück and wondered if he had survived. In January, Auschwitz had been liberated by Soviet troops who told of unspeakable horrors, and the Allies had freed Buchenwald and Bergen-Belsen in April, and the Americans Dachau two weeks later. The troops relayed horrors that the world could not believe, of the millions of murdered people. Sophia knew she could have been one of them at Ravensbrück if she and her friends had not escaped.

There was considerable chatter among the nuns at dinner. Germany had surrendered and Berlin was free. Mother Paul saw the look in Sophia's eyes and spoke to her after dinner.

She knew what Sophia had been waiting for, for years now, but the city would still be dangerous for a while, in the hysteria of the Liberation. It wasn't as docile as Paris, and competing armies had freed it, which was going to create chaos and fresh risks for citizens in Berlin. Russian, American, and British troops had freed the city, with the French on their way, which caused confusion and disorder in the streets, looting and pillaging, and even rape by soldiers out of control. Their commanding officers were doing their best to subdue them, with little success so far.

"Sophia, you need to give it a little time, before you try to go back," Mother Paul warned her. She could see how impatient Sophia was to return to Berlin.

"They're not going to attack me in a habit," Sophia tried to argue with her, to no avail.

"They're going to attack anything and everyone. They're going to be drunk and crazy, plundering and looting. There are three armies running loose there, the Russians, the British, and the Americans, and even their own officers won't be able to control them at first. You need to give it a few weeks, a month, even two, before you go back. I won't allow you to risk your life again. You've been away from your order for three and a half years, you can wait a little longer to go back. I know how excited you are to start the work that is crying out for you there, but you won't get anything done

269

anyway in these early days. Give the armies time to regulate themselves, and then go back."

"My sisters there need me," Sophia pleaded urgently with Mother Paul. Technically, she wasn't part of the order and she didn't have to obey her, but she respected her, and wanted to leave with her blessing.

"They can manage without you for a few more weeks." Mother Paul smiled at Sophia. Even at twenty-six, she looked like a child, or a teenager, desperate to go out.

"They'll think I died if I don't go back now."

"They'll see that you're very much alive when you go back and walk through the door in one piece, ready to help."

It was an ongoing discussion between Mother Paul and Sophia for the next three weeks, as news of the chaos in Berlin was reported on the radio. Hundreds of thousands of refugees had poured into the city. Having liberated the city, the Russians took over at first, and then the Allies divided it into sectors, with each of the four liberating countries running part of the city, the British, the French, and the American, as well as the Russian. The French weren't onsite yet, but the others were. And Russian soldiers were being accused of savage treatment to the Germans, women were being raped, men were being murdered. The city had been reduced to barely more than rubble, with six hundred thousand apartments destroyed and a million people homeless and living in the streets. Food was only available on the black market, and there was mass starvation in the city, worse than during the war. The various armies who were running the city jointly were having trouble controlling their troops. Half the people who had lived there were still living there now, along with all the refugees who were pouring in.

What remained of the German High Command was also in disarray. After Hitler's suicide, one of his generals, Hermann Göring, was captured by the Americans. Reichsführer Himmler also committed suicide, like Hitler. And the remainder of the High Command had been imprisoned by the Provisional Government of the city.

By the first week of June, a month after VE Day and the German surrender, the four Allied governments were struggling to calm things down. Sophia couldn't contain herself any longer. She packed a small bag with her few belongings and told Mother Paul she was going.

"God be with you, child," Mother Paul said, knowing that she couldn't stop her any longer. She had begged her to stay, and convinced her for a month, but Sophia wanted to go home now and see what she could do to help the lost souls of her home city.

She had tried to reach the nuns at the convent in Berlin but phone lines had been destroyed in the bombings and she couldn't get through. She also wanted to call Theresa to tell her she was alive and well, but the circuits out of Germany were constantly busy so she hadn't reached her yet.

There was a single bus to Berlin the next day, and Mother Paul and one of the other nuns drove her to it. Sophia kissed all the nuns and the children before she left. It was like leaving home again.

"Where are you going?" one of the children asked her as Sophia hugged her.

"I'm going home to the convent where I lived before, to see my other sisters and help people."

"Why can you go home, if we can't go home?" the little girl asked with a sad face. The real answer was because they didn't have homes anymore, or anyone to go home to. Neither did Sophia, but she had the Sisters of Mercy and the convent, and people in the streets who needed comfort and her nursing abilities. She couldn't wait another day longer, which was why Mother Paul had stopped arguing with her.

"It's still dangerous in Berlin, but I have God's work to do there," was Sophia's answer to the child.

"Let us hear from you," Mother Paul reminded her. "And be careful!"

"I promise I will, and thank you for everything." There weren't words enough to thank them for all they'd done for her, and she was deeply grateful for it, but now she had work to do. She had waited almost six years for this moment.

And there were so many who hadn't lived to see it, like Claus and her father. But at least the monsters who had destroyed Germany and killed so many people were either dead or in prison.

She hugged the nuns one last time and boarded the bus to Berlin. It was old and dirty and half full as they headed toward the city. She had borrowed a small amount of money from Mother Paul, knowing she wouldn't need any once she got back to the convent and would return what she'd borrowed to Mother Paul quickly.

She waved as the bus pulled away. And as they drove to Berlin, she was shocked to see how many people were going there on foot, with no other means to get there, but desperate to get to Berlin. Probably Berliners who had taken refuge in the country. It would normally have been a four-hour drive, but it took them six because of the people walking, crowding the road. It reminded Sophia of when she and the others had escaped Ravensbrück and arrived in Windberge on foot themselves, through a tortuous route in the woods.

They reached Berlin at the end of the day, and the bus left them at the Stuttgarter Platz, near the Charlottenburg train station. The bus driver warned them that the bus and train stations were a hotbed of black-market activity now, with everything imaginable for sale at astronomical prices, and told them all to be careful. It was a long walk to the convent and her old neighborhood, and Sophia was impatient to get there.

She set out on foot carrying her small valise and hadn't eaten since breakfast. But she didn't see a single restaurant or café open and there was nowhere to buy food. All the shops were closed, there were throngs of people in the streets, some making deals, selling or trading food or blankets, others wandering aimlessly, many lying on blankets on the streets with nowhere else to sleep. She saw hordes of soldiers in many different uniforms. She had her forged travel papers, which would be useless to her now, but she had no other documentation, and what she had was false. The convent would vouch for her when she got there. She could hardly wait to see it. It shone in her mind like a beacon she was heading for.

She threaded her way through the crowds, past the familiar landmarks of Berlin, many of them damaged or destroyed. But it still felt like home, even in its current state of disarray. She walked past whole blocks of bombed-out buildings, and the hem of her habit was filthy. She was tired and hungry, but she didn't care.

It took her an hour to get to the convent on foot. She walked past the barren site of her old house and her father's hospital, and saw that many parts of the neighborhood had been bombed and lay in rubble. The site of her father's hospital was part of a much bigger bombed-out area now. It was unrecognizable, and brought into much sharper focus the extent of destruction in the city. But it was worth it if it had driven the Nazis out. It hadn't even occurred to her that the convent might be damaged, or worse, be in rubble too. She hadn't had news from them in years and didn't want to expose her location for their safety and her own.

She reached the convent a few minutes later. It was intact but the entire building was dark. There were no lights on, and she wondered if the sisters had turned the lights off not to attract attention, in case there were bands of soldiers roaming the streets. Much of the neighborhood had been destroyed by Allied bombs, and there were few houses with lights on. And some were abandoned. She wondered if the convent was too.

Many people had fled the city during the final bombings. She realized that the convent had a deserted look to it. The plants in front were old and dead. The paint was chipped on the front door. She rang the bell and no one answered, and she walked around to the back. She rang the back door, and no one answered that either. She peered in through a window, and it was hard to see anything. The house was dark, and it looked like some of the furniture was gone. But she had nowhere else to go, and she didn't want to roam the streets with the crowds of homeless people. She tried all the windows and found a broken one. She reached in and unlocked it, careful not to get cut by the broken glass, and slid it open. She hadn't thought to bring a flashlight with her. It hadn't occurred to her that she'd need one. As she looked in, she saw that what remained of the furniture was covered with sheets.

She tucked her habit around her and climbed in through the window. She was standing in the big cozy kitchen she had so often worked in. She flipped a switch and there was no electricity, and as she walked from room to room on the ground floor, she realized that the house was deserted. She had just come from Mother Regina's office when she heard someone running up the basement stairs, and she shrank into the shadows. She had no idea what she'd be facing. A man's voice called out asking who was there, and she was afraid he might have a gun. Shaking from head to foot, she took a step forward. He shined a flashlight on her face so she couldn't see him.

"Who are you?" he shouted at her, and then saw that she was wearing a nun's habit.

"I'm Sister Anne of the Sisters of Mercy. I live here." He shined the light away from her then and she could see him too. It was the handyman who had done repairs for the nuns when she lived there. He looked old and worn now and not quite so young, and he looked shocked when he recognized her.

"Little Sister Anne. What are you doing here? Where have you been?"

"I've been away for four years." It seemed incredible, even to her. "Where are the sisters?"

"They left two years ago when the Allies started bombing the city. They went to the Mother house in Cologne, and it was bombed, and then they moved to a house in Dresden, and it burned to the ground in a bombing raid. They're in Hamburg now. I haven't heard from them since the surrender. I'm sure they'll come back, but I don't know when. The phone isn't working, and I turned off the electricity. I've been staying in the basement since they left to keep an eye on the house, so no one breaks in and steals anything. It's been crazy here for the last month, and dangerous. You were brave to come."

"I tried to call, but I couldn't get through. I just assumed they'd be here," Sophia said, still shaking.

"They've been gone for a long time. So have you." She nodded, trying to think of what to do. "The neighborhood was badly hit a few times. A lot of people left, or were killed."

"Can I stay here?" She remembered that his name was Charlie.

"You're still a nun?" He smiled at her, happy to see her.

"Of course. I've been living with an order in the country." She remembered how dangerous Mother Paul had said it would be in the city, and she was right. But if she stayed here, she would have Charlie to protect her. And she had a right to be there, as a novice of the order, but she would have to tell them.

"Of course you can stay. You belong here. It's your home. They thought they'd be back sooner, and it would all be over. They left linens in the cupboards, and some other things. I locked up anything that looked valuable to me. I'll show you tomorrow." She knew what she wanted to do now, as she looked around in the dim glow of his flashlight. They had a lot of work to do, this was why she had come back to Berlin. She just didn't know she'd be doing it alone. But now she had Charlie to help her. She realized how lucky she was that he was still there. "Here, take my flashlight." He handed it to her. "I'll turn the electricity back on tomorrow," and then he thought of something. "Have you eaten?" She shook her head. "You can't buy anything, except on the black market. None of the stores are open. I'll be back in a minute." He ran back down the basement stairs and came back holding a heel of bread and an apple. "I don't have much else. I was going to try to find some food tomorrow. People here are starving, and willing to kill each other for a piece of bread."

"Thank you, Charlie," she said gratefully, and took the heel of bread and the apple. The bread was stale and hard and she didn't care. She hadn't eaten since breakfast at St. Blaise, which seemed a million miles away now.

"I'll fix the window tomorrow," he said, pointing to the broken one. "I thought you were a burglar."

"I thought you were too." She laughed.

"Welcome home, Sister. Welcome to Berlin, without the Nazis. It's a mess, but it will be beautiful again one day. Thank God, they're gone."

"Yes, thank God," she echoed his words, and he waved and headed back to the stairs.

"Sleep wherever you want. They won't mind."

"I'll go back to my old room," she said, and groped her way up the familiar stairs in the dark to the third floor where her cell had been. Most of the cells had been full when she moved in, and it was one of the last free ones. There was still a mattress, and she didn't know where the sheets were and didn't care. She sat down on the bed and looked out the window. There was a bomb site behind the convent, and the streetlamp was broken. It was pitch-black outside, as she sat on her old mattress and ate the stale bread and the apple. And when she thought of Ravensbrück, it was pure luxury, a meal she would have been willing to die for, and a bed without three bunkmates. After she ate, she went to the bathroom and found the water was still on. She drank some water and went back to her cell, lay down on the mattress in her habit, and smiled. She was home again. That was all that mattered. She was home, in Berlin. And then she fell asleep.

Chapter 16

S ophia was back in the kitchen the next morning, looking around. All the cooking utensils were there. They were dusty, but everything was serviceable. In the dining room, the three long refectory tables that the nuns ate at were there. They were covered with sheets. The nuns' sitting room was intact too. She went from room to room, and all was as it had been when she left, arrested by the SS. Everything was covered with a thick layer of dust from the bombings. There was plaster dust from the ceiling, when the house was shaken by the bombs falling.

She went from room to room after that and saw that the nuns had what they needed. It was all there, but the house required a thorough cleaning. She went back to the kitchen just as Charlie came up from the basement. His clothes looked rumpled but clean.

"I'm going to start scrubbing the house today," she told him.

"Do you think they're coming back this soon? I think they'll wait a while until things calm down here. It's been pretty rough. You came back early."

"At least we can get it ready for Mother Regina when she comes back, and the sisters." He gave her an odd look then.

"She's not coming back," he said, and Sophia looked stricken.

"Did they kill her?"

"No, she died of liver cancer two years ago, before they left. It was very quick. I think that's part of why they moved the sisters to Cologne then—they didn't have anyone to replace her. I don't know who will take her place now."

"Well, we need to clean the house anyway," Sophia said firmly, sad to hear the news of the Superior she had loved so much and who had been a comfort to her.

Sophia cleaned all the cells on the top two floors that day. There were twelve cells on each floor, and a bathroom. The next day, she cleaned the next two floors, and beat the mattresses and the curtains. Charlie turned the electricity on, and the lamps worked in every room. The rooms were spartan, each with a single mattress, a narrow bed, and a small chest of drawers, and in a few of them there was a desk and a straight-backed chair. There were forty-eight cells in all, for an equal number of nuns, which gave them beds for forty-seven women in the meantime, since Charlie didn't think the nuns would be rushing back any time soon. Sophia needed someone's permission to do what she wanted to do, but she didn't know who to call, and Charlie didn't have the phone number of the house the sisters were in now in Hamburg. He said they were only there temporarily, as both their other convents had been bombed in Dresden and Cologne. She wondered too how many nuns there still were, or had left the order or died in the bombings.

It took Sophia and Charlie four days to get the house clean, working constantly. Charlie had managed to buy some meager food supplies, enough to feed them both for a few days if they ate sparingly, and he said it had cost him a fortune. She gave him the money she had and told him to use it for food, the next time he ventured out to the black-market vendors on the streets. They were selling food for extortionate prices. And then she asked him to come with her to the Red Cross, and to the headquarters of each of the supervising armies. It took them almost all day to find the right offices, but by nightfall Sophia's mission was accomplished. In each case she told them that there were single cells for women who had nowhere to sleep at the Sisters of Mercy Convent, and she left the address with them. The officials asked how much she was charging, because scams to exploit homeless women had already crossed their desks.

"Nothing, it's free. We have no food, but we have beds, and if they buy their own food they can cook it in our kitchen," she said simply, and in each case the person she was speaking to looked at her like she was crazy. She had put her spare habit on to make the rounds, because the one she'd cleaned the house in was filthy. She washed it that night, and the next day the women started coming. The British sent four young women who had no parents, no family, and no home. They were between eighteen and twenty and could fend for themselves. The Americans sent three older women, and the Red Cross sent four women who had been released from Auschwitz in January and had no place to live and no money for an apartment or a hotel. Eleven of the rooms were occupied by that night. They each brought very little food with them, which they were afraid to leave in the kitchen for fear someone would steal it.

Sophia tried to call Theresa in Switzerland again but the lines were still overloaded and she couldn't get through.

Sophia wrote a letter to the convent in Hamburg to tell them what she was doing, until further instructions from them. Two nuns from the order arrived three days later. She didn't know either of them, but they were impressed and couldn't believe what she'd done. The house looked clean and orderly, and the women staying there were polite and grateful. One or two new ones showed up every day. The nuns went back to Hamburg and promised to come back in a few days and bring two more sisters with them to help her. It was exactly what she had wanted to do, provide housing for women who were homeless and had no money for a safe place to stay until they got on their feet. Most of them were looking for their families and had asked the Red Cross to help them. There were so many people coming out of the concentration camps, and they didn't have full access to the records yet. The Red Cross was trying to help people locate their families and lost loved ones.

Sophia was in the kitchen, making a short list of things they needed, when one of the young women the British had sent came to find her.

"There's someone asking for you, Sister," she said. She lowered her voice then, "She looks very fancy. I don't think she wants a room." She smiled and Sophia went out to the front hall to see who it was.

The woman standing there had on a red silk coat over a white dress. She wore fashionable high heels, which Sophia knew wouldn't get her far in the rubble and debris still on the streets from the bombings. She was wearing a beautiful straw hat, and diamonds glistened in her ears.

Sophia couldn't imagine what she was doing there. There was something familiar about her, and as she turned and Sophia saw her face, she gasped. She was still as beautiful, and all grown-up now. Sophia hadn't seen her in five years. It was Theresa. Theresa burst into tears the minute she saw Sophia, and they flew into each other's arms, and then Sophia backed away.

"Oh, don't hug me, I'll get you dirty. I've been cleaning in the kitchen." Neither of them could stop crying, and Sophia led her into Mother Regina's office so they could be alone. "What are you doing here?" Sophia asked her.

"I came to find you. I didn't have an address for you, or a phone number, but I knew you'd come back here eventually. I wanted to see if one of the nuns knew where you were."

"I was living at a convent in the country for the last three years, with false papers. I escaped from Ravensbrück, and I was afraid that if I wrote to you someone would find me." They sat on chairs next to each other, holding hands and hugging. And then Sophia told her sister the bad news about their father. "Papa died in Dachau four years ago," she told her, and Theresa nodded, dabbing at her eyes.

"I know. The Red Cross told us. The city is such a mess. You can't be safe here." Theresa looked worried, and Sophia could see that she was more beautiful than ever.

She had grown into her beauty. She was only twenty-four, and Sophia felt decades older as she looked at her. Theresa had been comfortable, safe, and pampered throughout the war, compared to the hardships her older sister had endured.

"I'm safe enough. Our old handyman is living here. And the Mother House is sending four nuns to help me. I'm running a hostel for homeless women who have no place to stay. We'll have about forty free beds once some of the nuns come back. It's not much but at least it's forty fewer women in danger on the streets."

Theresa looked at her like an angel fallen from Heaven. "Do you have food? Everyone says it costs a fortune. Do you need money?" Sophia looked at her sister and decided to be honest with her.

"Actually, I do. No one can afford to eat—they're living on stale bread crusts and rotting fruit. I can't afford to feed the women here, and Charlie, our handyman, and I are sharing whatever we can get." She'd been living on apples for the past week, and some of them had worms in them. Charlie had come back with carrots one day, and a rotten banana, which they cut in half and ate.

"Heinrich thought that would be the case. He brought money with him. He's outside in the car, he didn't know if he should come in."

"Of course he can come in. I haven't seen you two in five years. How many children do you have now?"

"Four," Theresa answered proudly. She took pictures out of her bag, handed them to Sophia, and went back to the car to get Heinrich. He looked the same as ever, a little fatter and more prosperous. He was wearing a handsome dark suit. They looked like they had walked off a magazine cover. The whole city was either in uniform or looked like vagabonds, and they looked exquisite and immaculately clean. "We have two girls and two boys," Theresa told her when they got back, and Heinrich had hugged his sister-in-law and looked at her seriously.

"You saved our lives. I'll never forget it. You have to visit us, for as long as you like, or live with us. We're going to stay in Zurich. Berlin will be a mess for years." Sophia couldn't imagine visiting them in her ragged, dusty habit, or even in a new one. The difference between them had become even more extreme after the last five years. Theresa was what she had always dreamed of being, an elegant baroness, with beautiful clothes and jewels and a wealthy husband. And Sophia was who she knew she was meant to be, reaching out to save whatever lost souls she could, housing them and nursing them and comforting them, with no care about how she looked or how shabby her habit was. As she thought about it, Heinrich handed her a fat envelope filled with bills.

She was too embarrassed to count it, but needed it too much
to refuse. She had no shame since it was to help others.

"Thank you, Heinrich. I promise you I'll put it to good use."

"I know you will, but spend some of it on yourself too. We
were afraid you had a rough time." They had been afraid too
that she'd died, as they had had no news for years.

"She was in Ravensbrück," Theresa said, lowering her
voice, and he looked shocked.

"Thank God you survived."

"She escaped," Theresa filled him in.

"You have to come to Zurich and we'll talk about all of
it," he said, and glanced at his gold watch.

"Where are you staying?" Sophia asked them. She didn't
think any of the good hotels were open yet. "You can stay
here if you like," she offered.

"We're going back to Zurich tonight, now that we've found
you. Heinrich thinks it's too dangerous to stay here."

"He's right," Sophia confirmed. "Come back when it's a
decent city again, and not a bomb site. Or I'll come to you.
I want to see your children, before you have ten of them and
I can't remember their names," she said, and they laughed.

"We named our oldest daughter after Mama," Theresa
said. Their firstborn son had been named after her father,
their second after Heinrich's father, and their two daughters
after their mothers.

They spent another hour together, and then Theresa and Heinrich left. All three of them cried when they said goodbye, but they were tears of joy this time to have found each other. Heinrich had shared that he knew his parents had died in Sachsenhausen. They had been killed days after they got there, too old and too unsuited to hard labor. But he had his brother, and Theresa and Sophia had each other. It seemed like a lot now, compared to people who had lost everyone and everything, their children, their spouses, their parents, their homes. Sophia stood outside and waved as they drove away, and then went back inside to see how her residents were doing. There were sixteen women there now. As she walked back into the convent, she noticed that the hem of her habit was torn, from the rubble on the ground, and didn't care. She would sew it when she had time.

When she went back to her cell, feeling greedy and mercenary, she counted the money Heinrich had left her. It was the equivalent of twenty thousand dollars in Swiss francs and it would take care of everything she needed for the house, and even feed the women she was helping, and she could pay back the small sum she had borrowed from Mother Paul to come to Berlin. Heinrich had given her Swiss francs because German marks were useless now. She locked it in a drawer in Mother Regina's office and would put it in the convent account when the banks were open again. Some of them already were, but not many. Heinrich had been very generous with her, and she suspected that he also felt guilty that they had spent the war so comfortably, and she had suffered so many losses. Theresa would never have survived what she had, but she didn't have to. She had Heinrich to protect her. And Sophia had God and herself. And so far, in her opinion, He hadn't let her down yet. She was still standing and had survived everything that had happened to her. And St. Blaise had been a safe refuge for her after Ravensbrück.

The nuns who had promised to come back and help her arrived five days later, and were stunned at how efficiently Sophia had organized everything. The new Mother Superior who had taken Mother Regina's place had approved everything Sophia was doing from the temporary house in Hamburg. Eventually they would want to fill the convent with working nuns again, but they weren't ready to move back from Hamburg yet, and didn't think they would for a year, until it was truly safe. In the meantime, using the building to help displaced women suited the mission of the order and they thought it was a wonderful use for their convent in Berlin. They were perfectly satisfied to let Sister Anne run it, since she had set it up so well. All through the war, it had been her dream to come back and do this, and now it was happening.

The four sisters who came from Hamburg cooked and

cleaned and helped the women staying there get organized. Most of them had nothing to wear, and they opened their old closet of clothing donations for the poor that they had kept. The clothes weren't beautiful by any means, and some were quite ugly, but they were clean and practical and allowed the residents to look respectable again. For an instant, it reminded Sophia of the closet of confiscated gowns and furs the SS had run through Ravensbrück for her to check before they distributed them to the wives of the High Command. The clothes that the Sisters of Mercy gave away had been given, not stolen, and served a worthy cause, giving back devastated women some sense of self-esteem. Some of them had nothing but the filthy, ragged clothes they wore when they arrived.

Sophia used Heinrich's money carefully, but it allowed them to run the house smoothly and do a few repairs. They needed some new towels and sheets, and most of all, they needed food, which was in short supply and being sold for extortionate prices all over the city, particularly on the black market. Thanks to Heinrich, they were able to feed the women who stayed there at least one meal a day. For many, it was the only meal they had.

A month later, in July, Sophia was going through the clothes closet to look for some summer dresses for new arrivals. She found a few. They weren't fashionable but the women would look nice in them. She even found a new straw hat for one of them. She was coming out of the closet with an armload of the clothes to offer them, when Sister Mary, one of the Hamburg nuns, came to find her.

"There's an officer to see you, Sister," she said. A few of the military had come to check out the convent to make sure it was everything she said, and they'd been pleased at the clean, good conditions and safety the convent offered.

"Which army?" Sophia said, laughing.

"I'm not sure," Sister Mary looked embarrassed, "British or American, I think. He speaks English, and mine isn't so good."

"Where is he?" Sophia asked her, and handed her the pile of clothes and told her who they were for.

"In the Superior's office. I didn't know where else to put him."

"That's fine." She hurried into the familiar office and saw a man standing at the window with his back to her. He was tall and slim, and she recognized the uniform. He was American, and she gasped when he turned to face her with the long slow smile she knew so well. It was Ted Blake. He stood there, admiring her for a minute, and then walked toward her. "How did you find me?" she asked, breathless as she looked at him. She didn't expect to see him. She hadn't seen him in just over two years.

"I went to St. Blaise, and Mother Paul told me you left a month ago. I should have guessed. I thought you'd let the dust settle here for a few months, but I should have known better. Hello, Sophia," he said softly, and she could feel everything in her tremble, as she invited him to sit down in the straight-backed chairs. "How are you?" He didn't reach out to her or touch her. He was afraid to.

"I'm fine. Are you still based in Paris?" She hadn't heard from him in eleven months, since the liberation of Paris. With the war still on in Germany, he knew he couldn't visit her, or even contact her.

"I am. Billeted at the Ritz, that's hard to beat. They were going to send me home in August. But they just extended me to December. I'll be home for Christmas. I'm trying to get assigned to the war crimes trials here in Germany. They haven't organized them yet. It's still pretty fresh. I may have to ask you to give me German lessons to convince them. I want to be in on the trials. What are you doing here?" His eyes were drinking her in while they caught up, and he wanted to reach out and put his arms around her, but he didn't dare.

"I'm running a residence for displaced women. Most of them are still looking for their families. Everything is still a mess here, but the convent is a perfect place for them and it's safe. Some of them were sleeping in the streets, or in the camps set up in the bomb sites. It was exactly what I wanted to do, and it's working. When I got back here the convent was empty and the nuns were gone. They had moved to Dresden and Cologne and got bombed out there. The order is in Hamburg now. But there are five of us here."

"So you opened it all by yourself?" She nodded. It didn't surprise him. It was so like her.

"How's your ankle?"

"Fine. You and Dr. Strauss did a very good job. It's working great."

"What are you doing here, Ted?" she asked him gently.

"I came to see you. I told you I would. Have you taken those final vows yet?" he asked, his stomach fluttering as he asked her, afraid of what the answer would be, now that she was back in her home convent again, with her own order.

"No, there's no Mother Superior here right now. The one I knew died. And the new one is in Hamburg, and they won't do it just for me. It'll be a ceremony with a number of nuns doing it. I don't know when the next one will be."

"Are you planning to enlist, whenever it is?" She nodded in answer, which was the answer he had feared. She looked busy and happy and was following her plans. "Are you sure?"

"I am. This is the life that I was meant for. I need to help people. It's the only thing that's meaningful to me."

"There are other ways you can do that. You're a nurse.

295

You've helped run an orphanage. You transported kids out of danger at great risk to yourself. You saved four other women by planning an escape from a concentration camp. There has to be some way to channel all that knowledge and courage and energy into something other than giving up everything else to be a nun."

She smiled at him. "You sound like Mother Paul. She said something like that to me before I left. It's different in wartime. You do heroic things without thinking about it, because you have to, and if you don't, you or someone else might die. I don't know what I'll do in peacetime. Go back to nursing, I guess. The nuns here will want their convent back eventually, but right now I have forty-three beds to give homeless women until they find their feet again."

"And what about you? When does someone get to take care of you?"

"I don't need to be taken care of. I take care of others, that's the whole point of being a nun."

"What if you had both? Someone to care about you, and the people you take care of. There are lots of poor, needy people in the world. You can't take care of all of them, but you can help some." It was what she was doing now. "It doesn't have to be in a convent, and you don't have to be a nun." She didn't answer him. He was echoing Mother Paul's words to her.

"My sister came to see me. She's more beautiful than ever, her husband adores her, she looked like the cover of *Vogue*. They have four children and she wants more. She goes to lunch with her friends, and to parties with her husband. She's adorable and I love her, but I would die of boredom with a life like hers, and feel guilt for the people I wasn't helping."

"So would I," he said, laughing at the description. He could envision her perfectly. "And with all due respect, I'd go nuts married to a woman like her. What do they talk about? Their next vacation or the next dinner party? I want the same things you do, Sophia. To help people. I want to nail every single one of those bastards who tortured you and everyone in Germany, and killed millions of Jewish men, women, and children. That's how I want to contribute. You can run shelters for poor women if you want, or kids, or orphans, or abused women. There are lots of ways for you to give without giving up yourself."

"I can't, Ted," she said sadly. "This is who I am. I think I was born to be a nun. I'm happy here." It nearly broke his heart when she said it.

"Okay, if that's it, I respect it. I just had to ask one more time. I told you I'd come back to see you." He took one of her hands and held it to his lips. "I love you, Sophia. This might be the last chance I ever have to say it to you, so I am. Even if it's not appropriate to say to a nun. If you ever need me, call, and I'll be there, no matter what else is going on. I'll be in Paris at the Ritz till Christmas, and I'll give you my address in New York before I leave." He stood up then. There was nothing more to say. He had her answer. The one he had dreaded and feared most.

"Thank you. I know this sounds crazy and confusing, but I love you too. The convent just got there first, and I want to honor what I started. Even though I haven't taken my final vows, I should have by now, and then it wouldn't be a question at all." He looked at her for a minute and thought of something.

"Did it ever occur to you that 'He' didn't want you to take your final vows? If He had wanted you to, you would have. And you wouldn't have met me. I think we met for a reason two years ago. Maybe He has something else planned for you." She thought of that for a minute herself. The possibility had never occurred to her and then she smiled.

"I think it was just a wartime delay in taking my vows, like a late train."

"Don't be so sure. There are no accidents in life. He had to drop me into a tree in Germany so I could break my ankle and meet you and spend two months being nursed by you. Sounds like a hell of a plan to me, and I'm not complaining." He smiled the familiar smile she loved, and he gave her a hug. And then she walked him to the front door, and a minute later he walked away and was gone. He had said he was taking the morning train back to Paris. His dreams were dead.

She felt sad after he left, and bereft, as though she had lost something precious that she would never find again. And what if he was right, and she wasn't meant to take her final vows, and she had been meant to meet him instead? But there was no way to know. And she wanted to finish what she started, make her final vows, and be a nun. She knew she had made the right decision, but it hurt so much. She told herself that he was a sacrifice she had to make for the religious life, and the commitment, that meant even more to her than Ted. She was willing to give him up for the life she had now. This was her destiny. She was sure it was why she had survived Ravensbrück, to serve others as she was doing, not for him. There was some comfort in knowing that now. She was sure.

Chapter 17

S ophia tossed and turned all night after she saw Ted. She thought about their conversation, and every word they both had said. She wondered if he was right about the delay of her final vows or, more likely, if he was just a temptation Life had put on her path to test her strength, to see how she responded to temptation, and if she kept her word. Her word was her bond, and she was going to take her final vows. And then she lay in bed and thought about him again, and she remembered Mother Paul reminding her that she could serve God in different ways. She had served Him well so far, in Ravensbrück and with the children at St. Blaise, and those she had saved. She turned it all around in her mind a hundred different ways, lying on her narrow bed in the dark in her cell. And then she stood up and looked out the window, and saw a small red bird sitting on the bomb site behind the convent, even though it wasn't daylight yet. She wondered if the red bird was a sign. She gazed at the bird and he looked happy, and then as she watched him, he flew away, and she felt sad knowing she would never see that same red bird again. And suddenly she knew what she had to do and where she had to go.

She ran to the bathroom and took a shower, and then hurried down the stairs to the closet. She picked a pink summer dress with a white collar and a silly little pink hat that looked like something Theresa would wear. She chose a pair of simple white shoes, took it all back to her cell, and put it on. She didn't have a mirror to look in, because nuns weren't allowed to have them. As the sun came up, she brushed her hair, put on the hat, and grabbed a purse she'd been planning to give one of the young women. She went down to the kitchen then and looked at the clock. It was seven A.M., and Ted had said he was taking the nine o'clock train back to Paris. She went to find Charlie and asked him how to get to the train station quickly. He looked startled at how she was dressed, but didn't comment. She looked pretty and young. He told her he'd call her a cab. There were some in Berlin now. The taxi came in half an hour, and took another half hour to get to the train station, avoiding bombed-out streets. At the train station, she looked at what platform the train to Paris was leaving from, but it was easy to spot with all the men in uniforms standing next to the train.

The station was crowded. It looked like thousands of soldiers, in different uniforms. She didn't see Ted as she approached, and he had never seen her out of her habit, so he wouldn't recognize her. She hurried from one cluster of men to the next, and then she saw him far down the platform and flew like the wind to catch him before he got on the train. When he first saw her, he didn't know who she was. She was just a woman running toward him, and then he knew, and he smiled.

She waved frantically, and he laughed and took long strides toward her and caught her in his arms.

"What are you doing here?" he asked her. "And what are you wearing?"

"I saw a red bird this morning and I knew . . . it was a sign . . . and then the bird flew away and I knew I had to see you before you left." He was smiling down at her. She was breathless. She'd been so afraid she wouldn't find him. And if she didn't, she would know what it meant.

"I love your dress and your hat."

Finding him was the sign she needed. "I think you're right. I was meant to meet you and not take my vows, and you were meant to wind up in the tree," she said, and he kissed her before he had to leave. "Just give me one more month to organize everything, and the others can take over what I started. And I'll teach you German and you can do the war crimes trials." She was talking in a rush before he left. He

303

kissed her again and kept kissing her until the train whistle sounded.

"I love you, Sophia. I'll come back in a couple of weeks and we can talk about all of it then. Or you can come to Paris. I'll get you a room at the Ritz. We have a whole lifetime ahead of us to figure it all out." He was beaming at her, and the train started to move slowly out of the station. "And if you ever see that red bird again, thank him for me!"

"I love you too," she said, following him to the steps, as he kissed her one last time and hopped on. He stood on the steps until the train picked up speed and he kept waving to her as she stood there beaming, and this time she knew she really had done the right thing. He was the life she wanted, and the gift and opportunity that had been given to both of them, and they had been brave enough to reach out and grab it. She had almost missed her chance. And all they had to do now was be brave together from now on. It wouldn't be hard compared to everything else they'd been through. They had each other now. The war was over. She was certain that this was why she had survived, for the life they would share, and the good they would do, together. A little red bird had been the sign and given her the answer just in time. Ted was right. There were no accidents in life. They had been meant for each other. They had been brave enough to come this far, and were brave enough to face the future together. The future they would share shone like a bright light ahead of them.

Danielle Steel

Have you liked Danielle Steel on Facebook?

Be the first to know about Danielle's latest books,
access exclusive competitions and stay in touch
with news about Danielle.

www.facebook.com/DanielleSteelOfficial

RESURRECTION

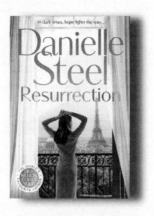

In dark times, hope lights the way . . .

Darcy Gray leads a charmed life. A wildly successful influencer, she has spent twenty happy years with her husband, raising their twin daughters in New York.

But when a shocking betrayal leaves Darcy reeling, she flees to Paris, nursing a broken heart. As she struggles to rebuild her sense of self, rumours of a dangerous new virus begin to circulate, forcing Darcy to take refuge at the home of eccentric retired actress, Sybille Carton, along with a fellow lodger, the handsome and enigmatic Bill Thompson.

As the world enters a terrifying period of global lockdown, the Gray family must find ways to cope, letting go of old dreams and working towards new, unexpected futures . . .

Coming soon
PURE STEEL. PURE HEART.

ABOUT THE AUTHOR

DANIELLE STEEL has been hailed as one of the world's most popular authors, with a billion copies of her novels sold. Her many international bestsellers include *Never Too Late, Upside Down* and *The Ball at Versailles*. She is also the author of *His Bright Light,* the story of her son Nick Traina's life and death; *A Gift of Hope,* a memoir of her work with the homeless; and the children's books *Pretty Minnie in Paris* and *Pretty Minnie in Hollywood*. Danielle divides her time between Paris and her home in northern California.

daniellesteel.com
Facebook.com/DanielleSteelOfficial
X: @daniellesteel
Instagram: @officialdaniellesteel